Fix It For Us

A Novel

Emme Burton

Fix It For Us
Emme Burton
Copyright 2014

Disclaimer: This book is a work of fiction and any resemblance to any person, living or dead, any place, events or occurrences, is purely coincidental. The characters and story lines are created from the author's imagination or are used fictitiously.

Editor: Sharon Korn
Cover Design: Sarah Hansen, Okay Creations.
Author Photo: Dana Colcleasure
Formatting: Polgarus Studio

DEDICATION

To all my friends-Long time, New, College, High School, Facebook, Twitter, People I talk to in the grocery store line. You have been my inspiration and so supportive.

And of course, to my family-BC, Thing One, Thing Two and J-Dog. I love you all so much. Thanks for accepting me just the way I am.

Fix It For Us Playlist

I'm Yours-Jason Mraz

Everything Has Changed-Taylor Swift (featuring Ed Sheeran)

Wicked Game-Chris Isaak

Cherry Pie-Warrant

Just Give Me A Reason-Pink (featuring Nate Ruess)

Here Without You-3 Doors Down

The One That Got Away-The Civil Wars

Dance With The Devil-Breaking Benjamin

The Unforgiven-Metallica

It's Been Awhile-Staind

Roar-Katy Perry

Fix You-Coldplay

Green Eyes-Coldplay

Winter, Second Movement, The Four Seasons-Vivaldi

The Prince of Denmark's March (Trumpet Voluntary)-Jeremiah Clark

Trumpet Tune-Purcell

I Knew I Loved You Before I Met You-Savage Garden

All I Want For Christmas is You-Vince Vance and the Valiants

All I Want For Christmas is You-Mariah Carey

Chapter 1-JANUARY

Before I even flutter open an eyelid, in those floaty, fuzzy seconds, no, moments before you quite realize you are waking, I already have the sense that I am safe. With my eyes still closed as my brain warms up like an old-school transistor radio, I analyze why. The smell, it's familiar and pleasant. It's him and me and clean(ish), smile, sheets. There is something warm, heavy and a little scratchy in the palm of my hand. I rub my fingers of that hand together, as they are not pinned down by the heaviness. Mmmmmm, silky. When I make an attempt to adjust a bit, I feel held down and realize there is something holding me at my hip. I am lying on my side and, though a little bit sad to do so, I enter into full consciousness by finally lifting my lids. It all floods back in a soft warm wave, like I felt bobbing in the ocean on vacation in Florida as a kid. Wow. What an amazing view to wake up to. The scratchy is the stubble on his beautiful face and the silky is my fingers in his hair. The thing on my hip is a strong firm hand grasping my hipbone. There he is...Mavis. My brand spanking new, dare I think it...boyfriend. Whoa. That's the first time I've even said that in my head and now it's going to be...fiancée? His name is not really Mavis. His name is Davis Brandon and he is, not to overstate in any way, freaking wonderful – green eyes with lashes so thick I used to think it was guyliner, an amazing sexy smirk, body beyond belief, and best of all, the biggest sweetheart ever. I sigh softly and murmur, "I can do this. I can SO do this." What I've just

1

whispered is my mantra. The words I use to pull myself together when I am anxious and unsure. I AM a little anxious and unsure. Who wouldn't be after the last whirlwind 24 hours? But I don't feel in the least panicked. I feel, for the first time in a long time, content.

"Why are you chanting that?" Davis' sleepy voice questions, his eyes still closed, his face nuzzling my hand.

"Oh, I thought you were still asleep."

"Why are you saying your mantra? Is everything okay?" His eyes open and meet mine. Little worry lines appear between Davis' brows.

"I'm fine. I'm more than fine. I'm with you."

***

"Not a word. Not a word to anyone, okay?" I giggle. "I'm serious." More giggling.

Davis? Well, he's kissing my shoulder and agreeing half-heartedly. "Ummm, okay."

"Seriously, we cannot tell anyone we are getting....Oh My God.... married. It sounds crazy. More crazy than I actually am. We have never even been on a date. We have never really been in public together as a couple yet." I am earnestly trying to get his attention with my words, my trademark chatter, but it's not working at all. He is too interested in sucking on my earlobe and kissing down my neck. Davis is totally stomping all over my attempts to concentrate.

"Sssshhhh, Lizard, Relax....you said you were fine," Davis says with soothing tones.

"I HAVE been doing fine, but I swear you are going to trigger a panic attack if you don't stop that. I mean I like it, but Mavis, baby, I am overwhelmed by information right now."

In the past few days, I have broken up with the guy I thought was my boyfriend, confessed my love to my friend (and now boyfriend and, did I say, fiancée? Yes, fiancée), learned of the devastating family tragedy he has endured, made love.... *several* times, been holed up in a snowstorm and, yesterday, proposed to. In general, most of that was pretty positive, but any one of those things in isolation could easily produce a panic attack in me, so all of them at once is, well, yeah, overwhelming.

"I am TRYING to overwhelm you," Davis tells me as he pulls the straps of my tank top down, while licking and kissing my shoulders.

"Mmmm." It feels amazing to have his lips on me. "We are not going to get breakfast yet, are we?"

"No, not for at least fifteen minutes."

"Fifteen minutes?"

"Okay, I lied….14 minutes, especially if you keep doing your chatter talking. I'll be done before you even have that top off." Davis giggles. Actually giggles.

He's wrong. He already has my top off. Davis has pushed the straps of my tank top off my arms and pushed it down around my waist. He is behind me on his knees, kissing from my ear down my neck to my shoulders. His hands have moved to my now naked breasts. I have finally stopped talking and am just giving into the feeling. He cups and fondles my breasts, tugging on my already hardening nipples. I reach up to put my arms back and around his neck. I achieve two wonderful sensations this way. I get to play with and tug at his smooth dark silky hair with my fingers, and I can push my breasts further into his strong capable hands. The movement causes me to rock slightly forward on my knees and then back, feeling his hardness directly on my lower back.

I stutter, "I think, I…I can wait a while to eat."

"Mmmm, Good."

I have tilted my head around to kiss Davis over my shoulder. I can't get at him the way I'd like, but the combination of our kissing, his hands on my breasts and the friction of his cock against my lower back and buttocks is fueling a wild sensation in my core. One of Davis' hands moves down between my breasts, sliding down my stomach. His fingers dance over the top of my black panties, sliding back and forth across the smooth top, teasing, but not going further.

Tugging them down my hips with one hand, the other never leaving my breast, he somehow steathily manages to divest me of my panties, while never losing contact. Still behind me and torturing me with his hands and lips, he moves his hand down to find my now oh-so-sensitive core. His middle finger pushes onto my clit firmly and slowly, so slowly, he circles and circles. He slides his finger back, pushing it into me, rotating, gathering wetness and then dragging it back up to again to rotate around my most sensitive place. The build up is upon me, I am burning with need. I wish I could touch him more. I remove one of my hands from his hair and reach behind me to stroke him. He is long, hard and ready. I feel it twitch in my hand as I stroke. We are both so close, moaning together with want. I want him inside me. He seems to know because in the next moment he growls in my ear, "Lizard, just let me move you, don't think, just let me."

"Okay." I'm not sure what he is going to do, but I trust him. I go with it.

He moves his hands to my hips, moving me upward and tilting my pelvis slightly backward. I feel him under me. One of his hands directs his firmness into me and I slide down, taking as much of him as I can. We are kneeling; my back to his front and it feels different, deeper like this. Still grasping my hips with one hand, with the other he continues his circular assault on my clit. I can barely keep myself upright. I want to lurch forward onto my palms the sensation is becoming so strong.

"Davis, I'm going to fall… Davis… uh… I… I… Oh MY GOD!"

"You feel so fucking good. Let go, Biz….Let go, Lizard Baby…I've got you," And he does have me. He keeps me upright and fused to him, even as I shatter into a million pieces around him. Calming down all I want to do is see him, kiss him. It was sensational and I am still experiencing residual vibrations, but I want to look into his eyes. I can feel that Davis is still hard inside me.

"I need to see you, I need to turn around, baby." I pant at him.

"Okay" Davis husks. Swiftly, in a smooth movement he pulls out of me, causing me to wince, spins me around to face him and is in me once again. Sitting upright as we are, I can look him in the eyes. I can get lost in him. I look at every part of his face and watch as he gazes back intensely. How did this happen? How did I get so lucky? Were all of our individual and mutual heartbreaks just the road to get us here? I sure hope so. I rock into him, never breaking eye contact. I want to see him fall apart for me. And then, I can't help myself, I have to kiss him, be as close to him as possible. I push him back on the pillow and attack his lips, licking and biting until he opens his mouth to lick and suck my tongue. The kiss goes on and on, as I buck furiously, trying to elongate and grasp his hardness with every stroke, pull his pleasure out of him. He breaks the kiss, stills and fixes on me with the most intensity I've ever seen from him. His mouth opens slightly and he groans out, "Lizzzard, Oh Baby." I smile down at him. And he smiles back. I love watching him.

Then I inform him, "Mavis, babe…that was *way* more than fifteen minutes." I knew it would be.

***

The snow is melting slowly. Plows have been coming through frequently overnight and our time being snowed in is going to be over soon. I finally got Davis to agree to leave the condo and get some breakfast. I think my stomach, rumbling louder than a monster truck, convinced him we had to get up and get dressed. We walk down to The American Bistro, a restaurant about four blocks from his condo. I've never been there before, but have heard good things. The theme of the restaurant is French bistro, but it serves classic American food in a contemporary way. When we enter, I get the concept completely. Four mirrored pillars form a square dining area in the middle of the restaurant, with the menus written in cursive on them. It's got bentwood chairs and warm, dark wooden wainscoting. It's open, so you can see everyone in the place upon entering, but once you are seated, it's comfortable and intimate. I am STARVING. As we walk to our table, I check out everyone else's food. It all smells SO delicious. Reviewing the creative and expansive menu, I decide on ricotta cheese pancakes. Evidently, I can have them with any number of toppings, not just the usual butter and syrup. I select lemon curd and blueberries. And a side of bacon. Davis is smiling as I order.

"I have never seen you order that much food before. Are you sure you can eat it all?"

"Baby, I'm starving. You see, I have been on this new exercise program, the Total Brandon Horizontal Bop, and it makes me SO hungry," I keep my face as serious as possible and bite my lip. Davis is smiling ear to ear.

"You better watch it or those pancakes are going in a To-Go box," Davis says in his sexy not-so-subtle growl.

Part of me is hoping he's serious; the other part is still really hungry...for food. "Oh my God, you are insatiable aren't you? I have got to eat something soon or I'll pass out, Mav."

Davis shakes his head and chuckles, "So now it's Mav?"

Davis orders his own breakfast. In the end, he eats all of his and the little bit of the pancakes I can't finish. It's fun to do something so normal with Davis. Breakfast. A breakfast date. Our first date. I have to tell Davis something right now.

"You know when you said last night that you are going to marry me?"

Davis frowns a bit. "Yes, and I meant it. I love you. I want to marry you."

"And I want to reassure you that I am completely on board with that idea, BUT we cannot tell people about it yet."

"Why not? I was planning on telling everyone I run into. As a matter of fact, I am going to tell everyone in this restaurant, right now," he moves to stand up. I grab his elbow and pull him back down in to his seat. Davis laughs.

"Seriously, Davis, like I said, we've never even been seen out in public together as a couple. We appeared briefly in the cafeteria at brunch. This is our first real date. Here. Now." I appeal to his rational side.

"I don't know. We've been talking a pretty serious game, Lizard. I think we should be honest."

"And we will be, but I think we need to give everyone else in our lives a little time to catch up – our friends... my parents... oh my God... YOUR parents. Perceptions are other people's reality. I don't want anyone to think you are some rebound hook-up after Jake. Or that I "stole" you away from

Kathleen. I think we need to date." I add in a princess voice, "I need to be courted."

"You want to be courted?"

"You know what I mean."

"Yes, Lizard baby, I do. We're going to do this right. I wasn't lying. I want everyone, I mean everyone in the entire world, to know I love you, that you are *the* one, *my* one… and when the time is right, we will tell everyone we are going to be together…forever. No more secrets."

No more secrets. Except I think I am harboring a big one, maybe even from myself. I can't confirm my suspicions about the night before my dad came to rescue me last year. The night before I snuck out of Randall's house, the place where my ex-boyfriend, Neil, dumped me with his creepy friend, the end of Junior year. I have no real memory of that night – other than passing out, I guess, waking up naked, and running away from Randall to hide in a coffee shop for six hours until my dad arrived. I worked all last summer with my counselor, Dr. Matt, trying to recall that night. All I feel is something creeping in along the fringes of my mind. The feeling leaves me unsettled.

Davis' voice pulls me out of my fog of recollection, "Lizard, is that okay? Say something."

"Um…yeah." I shake my head slightly, and come back to the conversation. "We'll date. And then we'll tell people – slowly. But no one at school yet. No one. Not until we talk to our parents." I can't wait to see how that goes.

My parents are rather conservative. Not like Tea Party conservative, but right of center for sure. I am pretty sure Davis' parents are Democrats. His father, the Former Lieutenant Governor of Illinois, James Brandon. ran as a Democrat. The whole family is way into gun control and the promotion of mental health awareness, for obvious and personal reasons. Davis' brother Cole accidentally shot his father with a handgun and then took his own life, in front of his whole family and his (and later Davis') girlfriend, Kathleen, after suffering from untreated bi-polar disorder. The incident left Davis' father with a spinal cord injury and wheelchair dependent. It devastated them all for a long time. I just learned of it. I have been wondering how much of it is still unresolved in their hearts.

My cell phone whistles a text alert at me. I pick it up to look.

"It's Jules."

"Who else would it be?"

"Smarty pants. She says classes at Weldon are cancelled again today, because the commuter lots aren't cleared and some of the roads out there are still a mess, but they anticipate class tomorrow." I frown a bit and add. "Much as I hate it, I think we have to go back today. I'm sure I have exhausted all the favors I can call in for RA coverage over the 'extended weekend.' I'm going to owe the other RAs big time."

Davis agrees. We have to go back to reality. That is why he was so determined to keep me in his condo, naked in his bed, all morning, he confesses. I like that. He is as sad to see our time alone end as I am.

We walk hand in hand back to the condo. There is no need to talk. We just want to enjoy the rest of our time together. I realize when we get back to the condo, I don't really have anything to collect. I am wearing the clothes I arrived in four days ago and I already have my purse. During our dreamy alone time, I was either wearing my underwear, a pair of his boxers, his sweats or nothing. I check my phone. No more messages from Jules. I guess we really have to go back. Davis asks me if I'm ready and I tell him, a bit forlornly, "Yes."

Still silent, we get in Davis' big black Escalade and make our way back to Weldon University and my last semester of college.

***

I haven't been in my dorm room since Sunday morning. It's Wednesday. Opening the door and walking in with Davis, it feels small and unfamiliar. With Davis in the room, it feels even smaller, not that I mind at all having him so close to me.

"This feels so weird." I blurt out.

"What do you mean?"

"Well, we've been tucked away at your place for so long and I got so comfortable there in such a short amount of time. It feels strange to be back in my dorm room. Does that make sense?"

"Sure." Davis turns me toward him and picks my chin up to look at me. His hands are sliding up and down on my upper arms in the most comforting way. "We escaped and were in a fantasy for four days."

I explain to Davis that now that the storm is over and classes are going to be back in session, I won't be able to spend four days in a row at his place anymore. I have to be responsible. He isn't pleased with the update. I have to be available at the dorm for my RA duties on the nights and weekends I am scheduled. "I'm not happy about it either, Davis. I'd much rather go to class, go to rehearsal and go home with you, honestly."

Davis kisses me quickly on the lips and says, "You could always quit."

I step back a bit. I probably have my mouth hanging open. "Quit?" I gasp. "I can't quit. I can't pay to live somewhere else. This RA job is the only thing that pays for my room and board."

"You could move in with me." He has a huge, hopeful grin on his face and has raised his eyebrows in question.

I just stand there and blink and gawk at Davis like a fish out of water. "Me moving in with you is hardly along the lines of the 'dating' and then slowly telling people plan we talked about."

"That's more your idea than mine. I would move you in tonight, if you'd let me." Davis is dead serious.

"I can't... we can't... I can't just quit. I don't do that. I made an agreement to finish this RA position. I really can't quit after finally winning Little Jan's trust back." My junior year ended in a series of minor dorm disasters that had me on the verge of losing my position and threatening my completion of school. I got another chance, and so far this year has been going very well. Little Jan, the Residence Director, is happy with my performance. "We're just going to have to spend time here on the nights I'm on duty. I really only have one or two nights off a week. I know it's not perfect, but that's the way it is."

"I can't say I am happy about it." I believe Davis is actually pouting. "I'm going to keep trying to change your mind, too."

I recall another bit of information Davis needs. "Oh… and we are going to have to have Charlie check you in as his guest when you stay over." This evokes a huge eye roll from Davis and a giggle from me. "Hey, I have been checking Jules in as my guest for a better part of the year. They totally owe me."

"You know what's going to happen?"

"What?"

"People are going to start thinking I'm dating Charlie."

"I can assure you, they won't."

"Oh, yeah….Promise?"

I shake my head 'Yes' and launch myself onto him, thrusting my hands in his hair and kissing him hard.

There is a loud, insistent knock on the door. "Biz, are you in? It's Roger. Hey, are you back from wherever it is you've been, 'cause I am locked out and I don't want to have to go search for another RA."

I stop kissing Davis, sigh and rest my head on his shoulder in frustration, "It begins…see? I'm needed. Duty calls."

Davis waves for me to go open the door. I open it and there is one of my residents, Roger, waiting hopefully. He smiles at me, up-nods to Davis and says sheepishly, "Uh… Hi, man. Sorry to interrupt…Biz, can you let me in my room?"

"Sure." I turn to Davis. "I'll be right back." He thrusts his hands in his front pockets, smiles and nods.

I leave and go down the hall to let Roger back in his room.

I want to get back to my conversation with Davis. I want to make sure he understands my reasoning and is not too disappointed by having to spend time in my tiny dorm room instead of his luxurious condo. It is only minutes, but when I get back to my room, the door is closed and locked. I look up to see a note hanging on the bulletin board on my door.

I'll be back.
-Mavis

I'll be back? In a few minutes? An hour? Tomorrow? He didn't seem happy with our conversation before he left. I go into my room and look around the small space. Really how could Davis possibly be thrilled about spending nights here? It isn't very roomy. Are we on the verge of our first squabble? Great. After less than a week together.

I decide to change into something comfortable, check my class schedule for tomorrow, and then if I haven't heard from Davis, give him a call. I feel a little more relaxed after taking off the clothes I've worn (off and on) for four days and putting on clean lounge pants and a soft hoodie.

My schedule for spring semester is lying on my desk, right where I left it. Only four classes this semester: Acting, Private Voice, Jazz Dance, and the class I am looking forward to the most, Production. It's a class that will give us insight into producing in different medias and venues; theatre, TV, radio, film and special events. I enjoyed associate producing last semester. Seeing something come together, watching all the components merge to achieve the final product, is exhilarating. Even the small contribution I made to producing so far was very rewarding.

After an hour and a half, I am surprised Davis hasn't returned or called yet. I look for my phone to send him a text. I can't find it. It's not in my purse… or my jacket pockets… Hmm… no wonder I haven't heard from him… or Jules for that matter. I have a landline in my room. All the RAs do. The problem is, I don't know Davis' phone number. I generally just use the contact list in my cell phone to call everyone. Where could my phone be? I recall checking it right before I left Davis' condo. Maybe it's there. I catch myself feeling on edge, wondering where Davis is. I try to shake it off as silly. He's fine, I'm sure. I have become surprisingly attached to his presence at all times in only a few days. Now, only after a couple of hours I feel a bit empty. I miss him. This could be problematic. We can't be together all the time. We have school and jobs and if we are going to make this work we have to be independent people. I look at the clock again. I have been pondering and well, yes, moping, for about three hours. Time to do something constructive. I get up from my desk and look in my mini fridge for a snack. The pancakes were filling, but I am starting to feel hungry, since the pancakes were brunch and it's getting late in the afternoon. Grabbing some yogurt and a spoon, I return to my desk. Since I don't know where my phone is, I decide to call it. Perhaps if it is at Davis', he's picked it up.

I hear my own ringtone with each dial tone on my landline. There's a ringing in the hallway and it sounds like my phone. I get up and open my door. My cell is lying on the floor, ringing. There is a neon green post-it on it that reads, "MISSING SOMETHING?" I pick up the phone with the note attached, look both ways down the hallway, and seeing nobody around, step backward into my room. I hang up the landline and my cell phone stops ringing. Almost immediately my phone chirps a text alert. It's from Davis.

You should be careful where you leave your cell phone.

I am just about to text back asking where he is, when another text comes through.

I'm downstairs. Leave your door open.

He's back. I am more gleeful than is probably necessary. I don't think we're having a squabble after all. I actually sort of spin around in my tiny room in anticipation of his return. So excited, I can't make myself settle. I don't know where to be when he gets here. I decide to act calm, so I sit back at my desk and check whatever messages I've missed on my cell phone, while I wait for him. If I act calm, maybe I'll appear calm.

Checking the missed messages, I see I have several texts from Davis from this afternoon asking me to text him back or call him. They are from a little after the time he left, so I guess when he found my cell phone at his place he stopped calling. There are a couple of calls from my landline from when I called myself and one text from Jules asking if I was back at the dorms yet.

Hearing the door to my room swing open, I look up from my seat at the desk. I see Davis and my friend and Jules' guy, Charlie, grinning back at me over the threshold.

"Well, Hello, Charlie Boxwood." I love calling him by his full name.

"Hey, Biz...Look what I found in the lobby." Charlie teases and indicates Davis. "He was all alone and he doesn't have a collar, so I brought him home....Can we keep him???" Oh, okay the stray puppy bit. I get it. Davis gives me big, sad begging eyes.

"Wellllll, I don't know."

"Please, Biz." The begging commences. Davis whimpers. I am about to crack up laughing at this routine.

"Okay...He is sorta cute, but I think he'll need a bath and a warm comfy bed." Davis now has his tongue out and is shaking his head up and down. This is ridiculous.

Charlie nudges him on the shoulder and tells him smarmily, "Lucky Dog."

Needing to stop the goofiness, I say, "Oh my God, guys, knock it off...come on in."

Shifting gears, Charlie tells me, "I just gotta help Davis with one thing and then I gotta go, Biz. Rehearsal. Boxwood has another big gig. I'll tell you about it later." Charlie's band's name is Boxwood, his last name. I am proud to say I came up with it.

Charlie and Davis move out of my doorway and around the corner. I get out of my desk chair to see what they are up to. I peek out of my door and see them coming toward me with a rather large, flat rectangular box. Davis is also carrying a paper bag with handles.

I ask, "What's all this?" Neither one of them answer. They are talking to each other and ignoring me. On purpose, I think.

"On the wall across from the bed, I think"

"You think so?" Davis questions.

"Yeah, then you can either lie down and watch or sit up against the wall."

"And it's already set up?"

"Uh huh, all the rooms are. Biz has just never used hers before." I don't know what they are talking about and I would like to know what it is I've never used that Charlie knows I've never used.

I loudly question them both, "What are you talking about? And Charlie, what have I never used?"

Charlie is smirking, about to laugh, "Biz...your cable. What did you think we were talking about...a vibrator or something?"

I know I am blushing. "So what if I have never used my cable..." Then I add more quietly. "Or a vibrator, not that it is any of your business."

Davis is getting a big laugh out of our exchange. "Lizard...Baby, I did not bring you a vibrator. They don't come in boxes this big, or flat." Now, he is really tickled and can't stop laughing. "It's a television. This way we can hang out in your room the nights you can't come to my place." He winks at me and after he and Charlie put the box down, he moves to me and puts his arms around my neck and whispers in my ear. "It's in case we run out of other things to do." I'm glad Charlie wasn't able to hear, but he can probably guess, 'cause he is still laughing.

"I can't afford a TV." I say, mildly admonishing Davis.

"I already had it," Davis informs me. "It was supposed to be for the guest room in the condo. I think it will be put to better use here. My guests will just have to do without. Not that I ever have any guests."

Charlie and Davis disassemble the box that holds the new flat screen TV. It looks like it's too big for my little room. The boys assure me it's not. I swear it is over 40 inches. My room is only 12 feet wide. They discuss and argue and eventually get the TV situated on the wall, just as Charlie suggested, and hooked up to the cable. I have to admit, once I see the clarity of the picture and all the channels, I can see I have been missing out and could enjoy this unexpected luxury. The only television I have watched in the past three and a half years has been at my parent's house on breaks or in the student union between classes. I surf through the channels and come upon a Jane Austen movie. I have a few movies, that, if they are ever on while I am channel surfing, I'm likely to stop and watch. Pride and Prejudice is one of them. The Devil Wears Prada is another. Davis thanks Charlie for assisting with a bro hug and a slap on the back. Charlie comes over to me and gives me a hug and a kiss on the cheek.

"I'm glad you said he could stay," Charlie tells me, looking over his shoulder at Davis and pointing his thumb at him. "I think he's a keeper."

I smack him lightly on the chest and whisper, "Thanks, I think so too."

Charlie adds, "And I'll sign him in anytime. Just let me know."

"Thanks for that, too. Hey, is Jules sleeping over tonight?"

Charlie thinks a second, then replies, "I hope so. I'll know after rehearsal. I'll tell her to call you or find you, okay?"

"Sounds good."

While I've been talking to Charlie, Davis has come over and is standing behind me. He has wrapped his arms around my waist from behind and has buried his nose and lips in the hair on the top of my head. He is sniffing me. Claiming me. Telling me with his actions he wants Charlie to leave.

Charlie gets the clue. "I really gotta go now, I need to find a new guitarist for the band. Later."

Charlie's last statement makes me feel a bit guilty and I sense a frown forming on my face. I am the reason he has to find a new guitarist. Boxwood's last one, Jake Gianni, was my....what was he? Pseudo-boyfriend, I guess. He cheated on me with my fellow RA, Suzette, before we even really got started. I broke it off with him. I think I knew it wouldn't work. I was already in love with Davis, but I didn't think I'd ever have him. The end result was, I got Davis and Charlie kicked Jake out of Boxwood for being an asshole. I love how loyal Charlie is to me. The brother I never had. I sigh audibly as Charlie closes the door behind him.

Davis breathes warmly into my ear, "I thought he'd never leave."

"Mavis, he was helping."

"Yeah, yeah, I know, but I feel like I've been away from you all day. I just want you to myself."

"Okay, now you do."

Davis smirks and then kisses me below my ear, "I know… and we'll do something about that later, but now," he points, with his hand still holding me, to a bag on the desk, "…I've brought dinner."

"You did?"

"Yep, Chinese. So we can have a 'dorm date.' Dinner and a movie." He teasingly adds, "I am courting you."

"Mavis, you are so smart."

"Come on, hop up on the bed. I'll feed you and we'll watch whatever you want."

Davis grabs some paper plates from the basket on top of my mini-fridge and fishes the chopsticks out of the brown paper bag. He pulls out four Chinese food boxes. It all smells delicious. Davis scoops a little out of each box onto our plates. He brings mine over to me, returns to get his own and then hikes himself up to sit on the bed beside me. We talk about what he did for the few hours he was gone and he asks questions about what I was up to. He tells me he decided on a whim to go get the television from his place, along with some dinner. He figured if he needed to date me, he'd better start right away. That way we could tell people sooner. There was a method to his madness after all. He wasn't angry with me. He wanted to move things along. I tell him about how I worried he was upset, that maybe he wasn't coming back tonight and he shut that down immediately, telling me I no longer needed to expect the worst. I am growing to trust him. I wonder why my thoughts lead me to the worried and scared places. I told him I got a little panicked when I couldn't reach him.

"I was surprised when I saw your phone at my place. I stuffed it in my pocket when I got there. I figured you knew you left it," he tells me.

"I couldn't find it and then I couldn't remember where it was… I might be a little tired," I yawn. "I thought about calling you, but I don't have your number memorized yet. And you don't have my landline number in your phone yet, I'm sure." I pause for a beat and stare directly into his compelling green eyes. "It made me think about how new this is and how little we really know each other."

"I know. It was driving me crazy not being able to reach you and tell you what I was doing. Let's just remediate that situation right now." Davis places his empty plate on the bed, skootches off and goes over to the desk. He writes a phone number down on a post-it and sticks it over my desk phone. Then he turns and hands me his phone, "Put your landline number in there. At least this way, you'll have my number if you misplace your phone," he points to the post-it, "and," holding up his cell, "I can try to reach you here, if you don't answer your cell. And maybe we should try and memorize at least each other's cell numbers." He says the last part with a grin.

I collect the dishes and throw them away in the trash can in the hall, so my room won't smell like potstickers all night. I pack up the leftovers and store them in my fridge. Davis is sitting up on my bed with his back against the wall, flipping through TV channels. I climb up, grab a pillow, place it on his lap, lay my head on it and settle in for the remainder of our dorm date. Before we decide on a movie, we talk about our individual schedules for the day tomorrow. Davis has to be up early. Now that he is a master's student, he has to co-teach a beginning lighting class. He mentions that we still need to go to the student clinic. We arrange to meet at lunch in the cafeteria and then go afterward, since we are both free at 1:00. I look up into his green eyes, from my position on his lap, as we plan this together. "Thank you for dinner and the TV and for, well … taking care of me."

Davis replies, "I'm taking care of us, Lizard baby. US."

We watch Pride and Prejudice, as Davis strokes my hair and every now and then leans down to give me kisses. I am more tired than I realize because the next thing I am aware of is Davis picking me up and placing me on my feet by my bed, holding me firmly.

"Lizard… Lizard Breath, you're asleep, baby. We are going to go to bed now, okay?" I nod my consent and let him undress me to my tank top and underwear. While still steadying me, he throws back the duvet. He lifts me gently onto my bed and then slides in behind me to spoon me. I don't know when he took off his jeans and I don't care. I am so sleepy and it feels so good to fall asleep next to him.

"Goodnight, my little Lizard." He kisses my shoulder.

"'Night, Mav. Love you…" I wanted him to know. I have just enough energy to kiss the air in front of me.

I think I hear him chuckle.

***

There is something buzzing in my ear, it's sort of annoying and… tickly. Eyes still closed I reach up to brush it away, but I touch something soft instead. I move my finger around and deduce that it's lips. Davis' lips. The buzzing is him whispering in my ear.

"Biz? Lizard Baby? I wanted you to know I'm leaving for class. I left you coffee."

I turn my face and kiss him, eyes still closed, and slur out, "Thank you, it smells so good," I open my eyes and pull away from his face a bit and ask, "Hey, how do you know how I like my coffee?" I've been meaning to ask that for a while now.

"I've kept my ears and eyes open. I'm very observant."

"You know how I like my coffee, but there is still so much we don't know about each other."

"Time, baby, we will in time," he reassures me as he hands me my coffee, kisses me once again and leaves for the day with his usual sign off, "Have Fun" and a wink.

I want to know everything about Davis. I don't even know his middle name or his birthday. I could Google it (ha! Google, our secret word for sex), but looking up information about him sent me into a panic last time. I'll just wait until I can ask him or he tells me. I sip my coffee and roll over to check the time on the alarm clock. It's only 7:30. Davis *did* have an early class to teach. I don't have to get up quite yet. I'm actually feeling a bit sluggish. Perhaps fatigue from my extended weekend with Davis. No class until 11:00, so I can drink my coffee and generate the list of "things I want to know about Davis" in my mind.

***

I have just finished my first class of my last semester of college, one of many "first" lasts I'll face in the next few months. It was a private voice class. I signed up for it last semester, but now it's really fortuitous that I did. I've decided to take the advice Davis gave me a few months back. I am going to ask for what I want. Sort of. I am going to audition for a part I want, and the voice lessons should help me get it. I want a major part in the spring musical. I've had small parts in the past, chorus parts, but for my final semester I'd like a bigger challenge. I have a bit of an advantage being a senior.

The musical is Once Upon A Mattress. I talked to my mom about it over winter break. She told me about the original version and I did some research online. I also watched a new version on cable that starred that teacher, Mr. Schuster from Glee in it. The story is about a prince that needs to find a princess, but his mother rejects all the candidates. Then an unorthodox sort of princess comes along. The prince falls in love with her but his mother, the queen, doesn't approve. The prince's father, the king, is under a spell and can't speak, so he is dominated and controlled by the queen. The spell, that the king shall remain mute until "the mouse devours the hawk," is broken when the prince stands up to the queen. The king can then finally talk and the prince can marry the love of his life, the quirky princess. That all sounds rather dramatic, but it's actually a musical comedy.

There are three lead female roles in the show: The Queen, Princess Winifred (or Fred, as she is called through most of the show) and Lady Larkin, the pregnant lady-in-waiting. I would be happy to have the opportunity to play any of the three. There are other minor female parts and I'd be fine with that too, but I really think I could play Fred or Larkin. Auditions are at the beginning of February, so I have a couple of weeks to work on my song and monologue. My voice teacher, Dee, is excited to help me find the right song for the audition.

As I walk into the cafeteria, I see Davis at our table. For a while I only see Davis and the sparkle that comes to his gorgeous green eyes when he sees me. I allow myself briefly to acknowledge that Jake, my pseudo-ex, and Suzette, my fellow RA and Jake's skank, are nowhere to be seen. They have been made "unwelcome" at our table by my friends, due to their treatment of me. Davis stands when he sees me and pulls the chair out next to him. The buzz, the excited tension whenever I see him, is right there. I hope it's something I always feel. I walk right up to him and kiss him square on the lips. A huge melt-my-thighs grin comes across Davis' face as I pull away.

"Well, I guess you missed me, too, Lizard baby."

I nod my agreement and smile back.

Smitty pipes in, "Okay, so I guess we all officially know that Biz and Davis are together. I suppose it's not worth it to ask for the PDA to be controlled, is it?"

I ask him, "What's your problem?"

And Davis says at the same time, "We'll work on it, Smitty. It's difficult."

Smitty continues, "For those of us 'going without' it's a bleak reminder of our pathetic solo state."

"Poor Smitty," I say and walk over and give him a kiss on the forehead. He seems mildly placated.

After kissing Smitty, I grab some lunch and return to our table, sitting close enough to feel Davis' warmth. The group is gabbing about the new semester – who's taking what class, who the instructors are, when auditions for the semester's productions are.

Then Charlie asks for our attention. "First of all, I want to announce that we have found, at least, a temporary replacement for Jake." Hearing Jake's name makes me shudder and Davis' arm immediately wraps around my waist, his hand settling on my hip. "His name is Ian. He's a sophomore music major. Great guitarist. I'll be bringing him to meet all of you soon. BUT even bigger news is Boxwood has been hired to play HeartSmash!" Everyone at the table claps and cheers. HeartSmash is an annual Valentine's party held either at The Lum or off-campus. The theme always focus on the dark side of Valentine's Day: a gangsters, Bonnie and Clyde, St. Valentine's Day Massacre feel. All in fun, of course. It's great news for Boxwood. I am excited by how quickly they are gaining an on-campus reputation. I hope they can retain their current line-up, if Ian works out.

Lunch was a joyous, upbeat reunion of the gang, but now it's time for Davis and me to go to the Student Health Clinic. As we discussed, after being "together" a few times and admitting our feelings for one another, we are going to go get tested and figure out birth control. It's a bigger deal than I imagined, doing this together. Neil, the guy who devastated me junior year and left me … left me unsure and devoid of trust for another relationship… never even asked about my sexual history. We never discussed birth control. He just always used condoms. In reality, we never discussed much of anything meaningful or made any plans together. He didn't care enough to ask questions. Davis is the exact opposite. Davis has already called the clinic to make appointments for us, so when we get there after a quick walk across campus, they're ready for us. No waiting. We go in together and speak briefly with a nurse, but are then separated for exams and consultation.

The nurse takes my vitals, looks over my chart, and begins asking questions.

"I see here you saw your gynecologist about six months ago and had a full examination," she states. I did, the summer between junior and senior year. The summer after Neil and Randall and… She continues, "Has anything changed since then? At the time of your last exam, you reported you weren't sexually active, but had been in the past. Is that correct?" I tell her yes, that was correct, and that I haven't been sexually active again until a week ago. She also quizzes me about my last period. It all seems pretty routine, and then she asks, "You're here for birth control and to have HIV/STD tests, correct?" Again, I say yes. "May I ask, how come there was no testing when you saw your doctor last summer?" I inform her that I wasn't planning on being sexually active again for a long time and at the time was not thinking at all about needing to be tested. Now that I'm in a relationship, a real relationship, I think it's important. She praises me for being proactive about my health now. I'm waiting for a lecture about not being responsible previously, but it never comes. I'm being harder on myself than she is. After discussing various methods of birth control and kicking myself at bit more that I hadn't been wiser in the past, I decide to go on the pill. It seems less invasive than the other methods, so I decide to try it first. The nurse sets me up with two months of sample packs and a prescription. We talk about when to start and what to do if I miss a dose. It seems pretty simple. I wonder how Davis' appointment is going.

Finishing up with the nurse, I carry my little brown bag full of contraception and meet Davis in the waiting room. He appears to be finished with his appointment. We begin to discuss how our individual visits went and then, before giving up any details, both look around the waiting room to see we are not alone. We tend to do that, it seems – think we are the only ones present, even in a room full of people. Davis gives me a look and cocks his head toward the door to tell me we will continue this conversation elsewhere. He stands and takes my hand to pull me out of the chair and out of the clinic.

"Do you have any other classes? Anywhere you need to be?" Davis inquires, raising one eyebrow and shooting me a smirk.

"No"

"Then I need you to take me to your room, now." He seems a bit serious.

I ask, "Is everything okay?"

"It's fine. I want to talk with you. I just need to be with you. Google, maybe?" The seriousness fades and the spark reappears in his eyes as he smiles a naughty smile. "Google" is Davis' newly-coined euphemism for sex. He's quite amused with himself.

"I don't know, my connectivity is a little slow." I tease him.

"Your connectivity is fine," he growls in my ear, as he stops us and pulls me up tight against his chest. "Let's go."

We are across campus and at my door in minutes. I am considerably shorter than Davis and have on boots with heels. I feel like I just ran a 5K, I'm huffing and puffing so loudly. I drag in a few more breaths and look at Davis wide-eyed before I fish my key out of my bag.

"Well, I guess I won't need to work out today." I gasp.

Davis chuckles and leans against the door jamb to my room, "We haven't even started the work out, baby." His words make me stop looking for the key and look at him open mouthed. He takes his finger and lifts my chin to close my gaping lips. "Need help locating the key?"

Taking a moment to settle my pounding heart and wobbly legs and not quite sure if it's from the running or his words, I reply, "I got it. I got it."

I hand it to him to unlock the door. He unlocks it quickly. Just like he's done everything else since we left the clinic. There is a sense of urgency pouring off of him. Once the door is open, Davis pulls me through it and slams the door behind me. He grabs my bag and jacket and sends them flying – I don't know where. He spins me away from him and puts my hands flat up against the door. Am I being arrested? For a moment, I want to giggle. And then, that moment passes, because Davis comes up behind me, slowly. As fast as everything has been to get here, it now feels like slow motion. He's not grabbing me or pushing against me, Davis is just close enough that I can feel his chest on my back and his breath in my hair and on my ear. He says nothing. Just inhales and exhales with a slight hum, like he's smelling a flower or appreciating a just-opened bottle of wine. And I am… I am slowly burning up from the inside out. Staying close, he purposefully, runs both of his hands down both of my arms. He stops when he gets to my hands and laces his fingers through mine, pinning my hands a little more up against the door. A shiver runs up my arms, back down and then straight to my lower belly. I can't really move anything from the waist up, so I back my ass up into him a bit to try and feel more of him. He isn't letting me get too close yet and it's causing my desire to increase.

"We rushed over here because I couldn't stand not touching you for another moment, but now that we are here we are not rushing anything, okay, Lizard?" I don't answer because I think I just lost the ability to speak, that was so hot. He asks/demands again, "Baby?"

I nod in agreement and almost whine, "Hmm… Oh, Okay…"

He still is not close enough for me to feel him the way I want to. Still holding my hands against the door, he moves one of his thighs between my legs and I can finally feel his hardness against my back. I practically moan in relief. Davis' lips are on my shoulder and then they are slowly moving with soft, warm, extended kisses up my neck and behind my ear.

"Biz, keep your hands on the door." He orders.

"But, I…I want to touch you, see you."

"You will. Slowly, Biz … Slow-ly. I don't have to be anywhere else until tomorrow morning. You?"

Oh my God, this is killing me. I, squirrely-chatter girl, have gone to the place beyond excited and am now mute, "Nuh … No-where."

"Good." He unlaces his fingers from mine, but presses slightly down on the backs of my hands with his palms as a non-verbal reminder to not move. His large, capable hands slide back up to my shoulders, down my sides and around my waist. All of the movements are measured, methodical. The path of his hands leaves a vibrating trail of sensation, and I am still completely dressed! Finding the buttons of my sweater and shirt, he slips them free of their buttonholes one-at-a-time, all the while kissing and sucking my neck, ears, hair, the sides of my face and inhaling deeply. He removes my hands from the door to slide my sleeves off and slip my sweater and shirt off of my shoulders. Without looking, he gently lays my clothes over my nearby desk chair. I haven't even touched or kissed him yet and I am shaking within. Davis slides one of his warm hands over my now exposed stomach and up to my breasts. He thumbs one nipple through my bra. I am instantly aroused. My nipples tighten, I moan and let my head fall back, as he continues to worship me with his mouth and hands. I feel his other hand unzip my jeans and then, ever so gently and with leisurely movements, drag my jeans down over my thighs. He slides his face down my back, kissing my spine for the entire descent. He lifts one of my feet and then the other to slide the jeans off into history. I swear if he doesn't let me touch him or hold onto something soon I will collapse. Every drop of blood in my body has taken up residence at the apex of my thighs. Standing back up and sliding his hands up my legs as if intent on not leaving any part of my body untouched, he firmly grasps my waist and pulls my pelvis back toward him. Holding me close with one arm, I feel him bring his black thermal up and over his head with his other hand and then pull me back against his chest.

He practically pants into my back, "I have been waiting all day to feel you. To make you shiver for me."

"It's working." I pant in response, as he slides the straps of my bra down my shoulders. He unfastens my bra, lets it fall to the ground and cups both my breasts, pulling me even closer to him. His erection is throbbing at my lower back. I moan and push into it as he skates his palms over my breast, stopping to squeeze and extend my nipples. Part of me is screaming to move faster, to turn around and rip his pants off, the other part is thinking of Davis' words, "Slow-ly." I try to heed them and soak up all the sensation, burning through my core. As I move in response to his touch, I become aware that he has divested me of my panties. I am completely naked. Pinned to him – back to front. I gain control of my thoughts long enough to reach both my arms up and around his neck. He has not stopped his relentless kissing and sucking of any part of my body his lips can find. I spin around, Slow-ly... to face him. I lift my leg up and hitch it around his hip to gain some traction for my achy, needy clit against his jeans, the entire time staring into the green eyes that I adore. I want him to see my burning need. He evidently does, because "Slow-ly" begins to speed up at this point. My hands are immediately on his jeans. I pop them open with surprising deftness and thrust my hand into his boxers, stroking and sliding it over the velvety hardness. I actually hum. I have *got* to get these pants off. He takes my face in both his palms and pulls my lips up to his, kissing me hard, demanding that my lips open and take him. It doesn't take much convincing. I would surrender my mouth to much less eagerness. He groans into my mouth, as my hand is still in his pants, practically assaulting him. I release his firmness only to tear at his jeans, pushing them aggressively down his thighs. They drop further of their own accord and Davis steps out of them. Now, we are both naked, panting and grasping at one another.

"How many days?" Davis asks, his voice rough with desire.

"Til what?" I am confused.

"Until I can touch you, feel all of you ... without a stupid condom."

A low giggle comes from somewhere. Oh, that was me.

"Seven days."

Picking me up, lying me gently on the bed and then quickly hopping up himself, he declares to me, "Let the countdown begin." More giggling from me.

Davis' hand moves between my legs and finds my most sensitive spot, he circles and circles with his fingers while delivering kisses to my face and licks at my lips. I can feel the licking all the way down *there*.

"But while we countdown, can you be in me… soon?" I plead. Davis gives me a groan of agreement and an "Abso-fucking-lutely." He rolls on a condom. One of his magically appearing condoms. I am slick and ready and slow-ly … slow-ly he pushes into me. He rocks into me slow-ly. I respond and then can no longer comply with this languid pace. I begin to buck. Davis keeps right with me. So close, I am so very close. From the look on Davis' face and the unintelligible vocalizations coming from his mouth as we kiss, so is he. And not so slowly, we crash into a powerful orgasm together.

***

I can't move my body, it feels so heavy. My limbs are all rubbery and vibrating slightly.

The only movement I'm able to manage is to turn my head toward Davis. Lying next to me, shoulder to shoulder, he's staring at the ceiling, his hand on his forehead. He sighs deeply, "Whoa!"

"Yeah," I agree, "I am in no way complaining over here, but that was kind of … intense. What happened to spark that?"

Davis rolls up onto one elbow facing me, his head on his hand. "I was sitting there in the clinic, waiting for you to come out. I couldn't stop thinking about seeing you, holding you when you got out. Worrying a bit about your appointment. Wondering how you were. I remembered that it was about this time last year that Neil started pursuing you." He was thinking about me while *I* was wondering how his appointment was going. Funny.

"Mavis, that's so weird. *I* was sort of thinking about the same thing."

An instant frown changes his previously relaxed face. He pinches his eyebrows together and lines of concern form. I see uncertainty in his eyes. "And?" he asks.

"No need to frown," I run my fingers up to smooth away the lines between his brows, "I was thinking how much you must actually care ... love... me, to make that appointment for us. Us." I pause a moment to consider how to explain. "Neil, God I hate to even say his name, NEVER thought of anything but himself. Not me. Not US. Because to him there was no US." I am pleased to see the frown leave Davis' face. He reaches over to stroke a piece of my hair away from my face and trace his finger down my jaw to my lips.

"I used to be like Neil." There is audible sadness in his voice.

I shake my head in disagreement. "You are NOTHING like him. Neil never cared for me like you do. He didn't. Ever. He dumped me. Dumped me when Robyn turned up pregnant. Dumped me with Randall to fend for myself." The last thought causes me to shudder.

"You cold?" Davis asks and pulls the blanket up around me. He doesn't know what the shudder was about – that it wasn't from a chill. At least not an external one. Something nagging at the back of my brain has made me shiver.

I cover, "A little."

"We're good, right, Lizard?" Davis asks.

I reassure him, "Mavis, we are more... than... good." I kiss him in between words.

Inside, I still question how we are going to be. As a couple. As individuals. How are we going to be together and not become obsessive and consumed by each other. It's impossible to be together all the time. I don't know how Davis feels, but I want to be with him *all the time*.

When I voice my concerns, he is nothing but positive. He tells me he feels the same – he wants to be with me all the time, too. Good, so it's not just me that is swept up. Davis tells me it will work out. We'll hang out at the dorms when we need to and go to his place when I have nights off. We can't plan everything, he says. We have to let it happen. But I just want to know him better. Jeez, we've discussed birth control, but I don't know his favorite movie or color or ice cream. He again reassures me that we have time, and that the answers to those questions are, The Hangover, blue and chocolate. I store the information.

The remainder of January flies by, just as Davis said it would. He was most happy seven days after visiting the clinic. We ran away to his condo and he did finally get me naked – in every way.

Chapter 2-FEBRUARY

I went to my first audition for Once Upon A Mattress four days ago. It must have gone well because two days ago, they called me back to read for all the female leads, sing a bit more and dance. Of the three, dancing is probably my weakest area. I love to dance, I'm just not good. Not terrible, just not great, you know? I have danced in choruses of musicals. My saving grace may be is that this particular musical is a comedy – so if it's comedic dancing, I can probably handle it. I felt good about my readings. I enjoyed reading the part of Fred the princess the most, and I might not have the dancing chops for Larkin. And now… now, I am in limbo. It's the waiting period until the cast list comes up. In most cases, the list is posted within 24 to 48 hours. We are over 48 right now.

I'm heading back to my dorm room after my last class on Friday afternoon, fretting about casting and trying to remain calm. Whatever happens, happens, right? As I reach my floor, the text alert sounds on my phone. It's Davis.

Where are you?

I text back

About to walk into my room. Where are you?

He replies

I think you need to come over to the theatre right now. It's a bit of an emergency.

I think about the cast list being posted, but that's not an emergency. Something must really be wrong.

Me: Are you OK? What's wrong?
Davis: *I* am fine. Just get over here. It's really urgent.
Me: On my way

I open my door very quickly and throw my books onto my desk in a flurry of movement. An emergency? Is someone sick? Did someone get hurt? Who would be there now, on a Friday afternoon with no show in rehearsal? Everyone should be heading out to Happy Hour. PJ. PJ is always there. Something's wrong with PJ.

It isn't far to the theatre, only about two blocks. As I enter through one of the stage doors, I realize I have no idea where Davis and the emergency might be. Then I hear voices, lots of voices, loud ones. There is a good deal of cheer and joy in them. Doesn't sound like an emergency to me. I spy Davis, as he emerges from the center of the crowd.

"What is it?" I ask. "Is it a fight or something?"

Davis isn't smiling. He actually looks sort of serious. He approaches me and turns me around. I am doing my squirrel chatter, firing a million questions at him, "Is everything all right? You seem okay. Is it PJ? Where is he?" He answers none of my questions and proceeds to blindfold me.

I resist slightly, until he whispers in my ear. "Quiet, you are turning me on with all the questions. Just let me blindfold you. You won't be sorry." This is getting a little weird. There are a bunch of people in close proximity. I notice it's gotten quieter, with only the faintest of whispers. I can't make out what anyone is saying. Davis turns me back around and with a hand on each shoulder, guides me toward the whispers. When he stops me, I can feel people around me. Their warmth, their breath. I am feeling a little panicky and claustrophobic.

Annoyed, I bite out, "Davis, what was so damn urgent?"

He laughs and then everyone else joins in. I swear I hear PJ's guffaw. "Lizard, it was *urgent* that you see … THIS." He whips off the blindfold and as my vision comes into focus I see I am standing in front of the cast list. I read down quickly to where Davis is pointing.

PRINCESS WINIFRED...............Elizabeth Connelly

I swear I've only done it once before in my life, but I feel my eyes bug out and my hand go up to my opened mouth. "I… I got it. I got Fred." I am caught up in a sea of congratulatory kisses, hugs and well wishes. Reality sets in. "Oh my God, I got Fred!" I am going to have a lot of work to do. Carrying a show. Huge responsibility.

I am a bit confused about the emergency part. I have to ask. "Mavis, I understand the urgent part, but why was this an emergency?"

The crowd laughs.

PJ steps up and wraps his arm around my shoulder, "It was an emergency because Davis threatened anyone who called or texted you the news, with bad lighting for the rest of their college career. Actor's Emergency."

"Well, that *is* a pretty serious threat." I giggle. I turn to Davis, who hasn't said a word since the reveal. His smile is huge. His eyes damp, from crying or laughing or both, I guess. "Thank you for making sure I saw it myself first."

Scooping me up in his arms and leaning down to kiss me, he whispers into my mouth, "Congratulations, baby. You are going to be a terrific Princess Fred, Lizard."

At this particular moment, I can only think of one time I've been happier. That was with Davis, too – when he asked me to marry him after our extended weekend of making love.

Rehearsals start in a week. Davis and I go to pick up my script from the theatre department office. PJ follows us and explains that since I will now have rehearsals, I won't be responsible for the management of the costume shop this semester. My theatre job will be given to someone else. It saddens me a bit because I really like hanging out with PJ. The good news is that for

Once Upon A Mattress, PJ is doing costumes and Davis is designing lights. They have brought in an alum of the Weldon theatre program, Owen Fox, to direct. I met Owen at auditions. He is talented and charismatic. A terrific musical theatre performer, he's been on Broadway a number of times. Two years ago he was nominated for a Tony award. It's a huge deal for us theatre students to work with him. I have my work cut out for me. And what's really cool is that I am not feeling panic or the need to use my mantra right now. I believe I can do it. That's huge too.

I have one week to wrap my head around this big role before I jump into it. I plan to take the time to familiarize myself with the script in general, but also to figure out how I am going to balance my classwork, RA duties and not least of all…Davis, with this new challenge.

Davis and I celebrate semi-privately in my room in Lawrence Hall after seeing the cast list. It's Friday night and I am, unfortunately, on call. I would much rather escape to Davis' condo, but I have a job to do. It's not so bad. Tonight we'll stay in and talk about Mattress and eat dinner and…. And tomorrow we'll go to his place, have some time alone and then go to HeartSmash.

***

We are parked in the underground garage at Davis' condo. The ride over was nothing remarkable. We listened to music and talked about Boxwood and HeartSmash and our costumes, but since pulling into the parking space, Davis has become very quiet. Still.

Looking straight ahead at the wall in front of the car, he heaves a rather large sigh and finally speaks, "Lizard?"

His sudden quiet sets me a bit on edge. I notice him looking at the little silver Mercedes sports car in the spot next to him. I've never seen it before. "What? What's wrong, sweetie?" I ask.

Davis runs his hands back and forth across the steering wheel, still not looking at me. Then he scrubs his face with both hands and finally turns to me to say, "You may not feel like calling me sweetie in a minute. I think I may have done something stupid."

I try to stay positive by replying, "I highly doubt that."

"Um. Wait 'til I tell you before you decide … You see the little Mercedes in the parking spot right next to me. Um … It's Kathleen's," I freeze. Maybe he *isn't* a sweetie. "I invited her to come stay with us… this weekend."

Kathleen. Davis' ex-fiancée. I say nothing. On one hand, I absolutely hate the idea and want to scream at Davis. It's OUR weekend. Our only weekend for quite a while now that we are going into production. And why is he just telling me now? He had to have known for a while. On the other hand, Kathleen has been nothing but nice to me and she HAS helped Davis in the past. I have many thoughts, arguments and protestations swirling about in my head, but eventually settle on a rational response, "Well, why is she here?"

"She had an interview with Arch Scene magazine for a position in their fashion and society department," Davis replies, "I'm so sorry. I agreed a few weeks ago. I have extra room and it seemed silly for her to stay in a hotel. I guess, I forgot all about it at the time and this week you were auditioning and every time I thought to tell you, I just couldn't. I thought it might distract you."

I don't really know what to say, so I smile and say nothing and get out of the car. I move to the back of the Escalade to retrieve my bag and costume for the party tonight. Davis has jumped out of his side and meets me at the back. He clicks the lock open with the remote.

"Are you mad? Upset? Say something" he implores.

"I don't know what to say yet."

"She's only staying until tomorrow morning. She had her interview today." He pauses and says the next thing tentatively, "And… I invited her to go to HeartSmash… with us." He has a pained grin on his face, like he is waiting for me to let loose on him. I sort of want to. What is this, Sister Wives? I don't want to share him. "If it helps at all, I asked Smitty to come over and go with us. Be Kathleen's escort for the night."

Davis' words strike me as funny and pushing down the irritation and upset I say, "I hope you didn't use the word *Escort* when you asked Smitty this favor. He'll totally take it the wrong way. Get all American Gigolo on us." Humor – my defense mechanism.

"I don't think I did. Oh God, I hope I didn't." Davis laughs. "So you're not too angry?"

"It's going to be weird." I tell him, "You can't think it's not going to be weird, right?"

"Yeah, I wasn't thinking … it's going to be weird."

***

As we come through the front door to Davis' condo, he yells out, "Kath … Kathleen? You here?"

I hear something, a door or drawer or something, close. "Um, yeah, in the kitchen." Kathleen replies.

We walk together toward the kitchen. Davis moves quickly around the island toward Kathleen, giving her a hug and a kiss on the cheek. I stand on the other side and, seeing her face over his shoulder, I wave and with a strained voice that sounds like I am about to cry, say, "Hey, Kathleen." Then I turn and head for Davis' bedroom. Why did my voice sound like that? I am trying to not be upset. After all, they're not together. I'm with Davis now. But there is a lot of history there. And why did he forget to tell me she was coming?

Not yet to the door of Davis' bedroom I hear them talking.

Kathleen admonishes Davis, "Davis, you didn't tell her I was coming, did you?"

"I did. But … not until just now." I hear him sheepishly confess.

"*You*, my friend, are an asshole." Kathleen laughs. Hearing her say that makes me a little less upset.

"I know." Davis sounds resigned.

I don't listen to any more. I need some time to myself to process the change in what I was envisioning for my weekend. Unpacking my overnight bag, I put my toiletries in the en-suite bathroom, shove the bag with my clothes next to the dresser and hang up the garment bag with my costume for HeartSmash tonight. I sit down on the bed to think and decide to call Jules. She'll have perspective. I'm so relieved that I don't have to leave a message when she picks up on the first ring.

"Hey, Biz … what's going on? All ready for tonight?" Jules' voice is chipper and bright.

"Yeah, I've got my costume. I'm here at Davis'. Gonna get ready soon."

She clues in on my less than enthusiastic response, "What's wrong?"

I tell her about how I thought my weekend would go. I would get all dolled up in my Roaring 20's garb and so would Davis. We'd look dapper and dangerous and go out for a fun night with friends and then have the rest of the evening and weekend alone together. But then, Kathleen happened. And it's not her fault. It's Davis'. I don't want to drag the pouting out, but I also don't want him to think I think it's great. I tell her about Kathleen telling him off.

Jules is reassuring. "It sounds like Kathleen may be taking care of this for you if she's already called him an asshole. By the way, I totally agree with her. He is."

"Yeah."

"Go out there and greet Kathleen. Between the two of you Davis will learn his lesson."

"Thanks for listening. I'm not being a baby about this, am I? This is weird, right? Like an awkward position to be put in?" I quiz for approval.

"Yes. Now, go."

I hear Davis and Kathleen, still in the kitchen. Laughing and joking. I am just about to round the corner when I hear her say, "Davis – I almost forgot. Happy Birthday!"

When I see them both, standing close, Kathleen apparently having just playfully slugged him, I pin Davis with my eyes, cock my head and again with the unexpected hurt voice ask, "It's your birthday? How come you never told me?" It's one of those things I don't know about him yet, like his middle name. How did we miss sharing that information?

Davis leaves Kathleen and immediately comes to me. He wraps his arms around me tentatively, like he thinks I might stop him. He kisses me gently, brings one hand up to my face, and pushes my hair behind my ear to look at me more closely.

"Yeah ... today is my birthday. February 12th. I didn't want to make a big deal out of it. You know, it's been a busy week ... and I am not super excited about turning 25," he says by way of explanation.

"I, I didn't know. I didn't get you anything. How come I didn't know? I feel like a moron."

Davis whispers in my ear so Kathleen can't hear, "I don't want anything but you."

It's very sweet. I still feel stupid.

Kathleen chimes in, "Wow, Davis, I thought you were an asshole for not telling her I was coming. Now, you don't even tell her it's your birthday. Dog house, buddy, DOG. HOUSE."

I've got to admit, I love that Kathleen can give him shit. As I think more about the interactions I've witnessed, they seem more like brother and sister than former lovers. Their relationship looks a lot like mine with Charlie.

I let him off the hook and lean around him to talk to Kathleen. "That's okay, Kathleen. Now I know. We really haven't been together long – I guess there is a lot I need to learn about him. He probably doesn't know my birthday, either."

Davis is right on that one. "Sure I do. It's September 28th." He opens up the calendar on his phone to show me.

"How did you know? I've never told you."

"Like I said before about your coffee, I'm observant."

"I'm beginning to think you might be a stalker."

Davis pauses, smirks and then admits, "Jules told me."

Kathleen has begun to laugh, "You guys are perfect together. Perfect. Davis, you might get out of the dog house by tonight after all." She leaves the kitchen for the guest room with a smile. "I'm going to get dressed. I hear my Rent-a-Date will be here soon."

Davis is still holding me, kissing my hair apologetically and rubbing his nose along the side of my face.

I tell him, "Sorry if I was a bit moody about Kathleen. I just didn't want to share you this weekend. I was being paranoid and selfish. She really is okay, isn't she? With us?" I wave my hand back and forth between us. "All of this? You guys just being friends?"

"I really think she is." Davis says. "We should get ready." He takes my hand and encourages me to come with him to the bedroom.

***

It's taking me longer than usual to get ready. Davis is already showered, dressed and out of the bedroom. I'm moving a bit slowly. Dragging my feet on purpose? Still a bit pouty? I just don't feel quite right, but decide to pull it together and get going.

I have a great little dress for the party that PJ picked out for me from costume storage. It's a red flapper dress, but instead of the usual fringe, it has strips of fabric with jet beading. It swishes and sparkles. I also have amazing "underpinnings" as PJ calls them – red bra and panties with black polka dots and satin trim. Roll top stockings, too. Very authentic. I want to be fun and sexy from the inside out. I'm feeling pretty good about the outfit, and I've spent a long time on my makeup. Did my research online. Bright red structured lips with a perfect bow and smokey eyes. The only other time I wear this much make up is on stage. The final touch is a black bob wig. Chin length. Smooth, shiny and sassy. When I put it on I hardly recognize myself. I wonder what Davis will think. As I finish up, I hear the door bell ring. That will probably be Smitty.

***

Entering the living room through the French doors of Davis' bedroom, I am met with a pre-party party. Smitty is being introduced to Kathleen. Davis has pulled a bottle of champagne out of a bucket of ice and is just pouring the first glass. He looks up as I come through the doors and has to quickly pull the bottle back, as he was pouring and not looking and almost overfilling the glass.

37

"Oops, shit," he says, shaking some champagne off his hand and wiping it on the towel around the bottle. "Lizard? God, you look so different. I mean, good .. Great, like you, but different. And Jesus, HOT. Smokin' hot." He is effusive with his praise of my look, while at the same time not believing that it's really me. "Smitty, Kath ... doesn't Biz look ... Oh my God, HOT."

I tease him because I've never seen him act this way before and I am getting a big kick out of it. "You said that already."

"It bears repeating. HOT." He is finally making his way over to me with a glass of champagne. Attired in a tuxedo with his hair slicked back like a 1920s gangster, I could say the same about him. HOT. When he gets right in front of me, he doesn't touch me, just puts his forehead on mine and breathes out, "I am totally going to get to fuck a hot flapper tonight. The wait is going to be excruciating" – and then he bites his lip. He's barely touching me and he is arousing all my senses. Jesus, now my little polka dotted panties are in flames. And we still have a party to go to.

Smitty interrupts our private discussion by clearing his throat, "Ahem. Other people in the room. You two are not alone. I apologize for them, Kathleen. It's really embarrassing."

"I think it's great," Kathleen comments. "I'm glad that Davis is so happy with Biz." If it was hard to be mad at Kathleen before, it's impossible now. I am beginning to understand why Davis minimized her coming. He probably figured I'd come around quickly. He was right.

Because Davis' response to my outfit was so animated, I am only just now getting a look at Smitty and Kathleen. Standing next to each other they look almost like a couple. Smitty has round 20s-era tortoiseshell glasses on and his brown hair parted in the middle. He is wearing a tweed suit with contrasting vest and brown shoes with cream color spats. The only thing out of place, historically, is the expensive, modern digital camera hanging around his neck. Kathleen has on a green velvet dropped waist sleeveless dress with a long strand of black pearls tied in a knot near her waist. Her hair is in long sausage curls with a green velvet band across her forehead. Her make up is era appropriate and perfect.

"You both look so great." I tell them.

Smitty agrees, "Yeah, Kathleen, you look amazing. Thanks for going with me tonight."

I think I see Kathleen actually blush a little. "You're welcome. I have to apologize. I was calling you Rent-A-Date to Davis, but now I retract that. He's done a decent job finding me someone to go with tonight." Now, I think I see Smitty blush.

Davis hands us all champagne. We toast to having a fabulous evening, good company and Davis' birthday. I only take a few sips of my champagne. That stuff goes right to my head, so I know I can't drink an entire glass. Besides, I told Davis that I would be the designated driver tonight. He laughed, looked at my breasts and re-used his old joke with a little modification, saying, "You are always the DD."

"Wait, wait, Davis, I have something for you for your birthday," Kathleen says over her shoulder as she moves away to get something off the island of the kitchen. Coming back to the living room, she hands a flat rectangular box to Davis. He opens it, ripping at the paper like a five year old. Opening the box and looking as his expression changes – first a frown, then a smile, then a little bigger smile, but with wetness in his eyes. He looks at Kathleen, who is mirroring his expression and then holds the present up for Smitty and me to see. It is a framed picture of Davis, Kathleen and Davis' brother, Cole, laughing – young, like 14 or 15, before Cole was diagnosed with bi-polar disorder, I'm guessing. They all look so happy. "You remember, Davis? It wasn't a special day or anything. We were just hanging around in your family room on the couch; all three of us, laughing at something stupid like Cole burping the alphabet or something, and your dad took that picture. I think it's the best picture of all three of us. I didn't know if you had one."

Davis' eyes are wet with unspilled tears. He is visibly moved by the gift. He puts an arm around Kathleen and gives her a squeeze, still gazing at the picture. "It's the best, Kath. Really. I am such a sucker for pictures. It's like I can feel what's in them sometimes. Weird." Not weird at all I think, very sweet. After all, Davis decided he liked me after seeing a picture.

Smitty, ever the photographer, has to comment, "It's great that you get that Davis. Not everyone is as drawn in to photos as you seem to be. Kathleen, it really is a great moment Davis' dad captured." I completely agree and tell Smitty so.

Davis sits down on the couch to look at the photo some more. I sit next to him and put a hand on his knee. He looks over and smiles at me. A smile that is both happy and wistful. I can tell the picture means a lot to him.

I whisper to Davis, "I'm sorry I didn't get you anything, Mavis. Sweetie, if I had known it was your birthday... I would have made a cake, or something."

"And jumped out of it?" The sadness is over. Smart aleck Davis is back.

"Possibly."

"Baby... Lizard Breath... I already told you. All I want for my birthday is you." Davis pauses for a second and then with a raised eyebrow adds, "And maybe Flapper you ..." He points to my dress and then my hair, "with the wig still on."

I know in a flash *EXACTLY* what his present will be.

***

First cocktail of the night finished, we prepare to leave the condo for the party. I go back to the bedroom to collect my coat and clutch. As I head back into the main living space, I see Davis, Smitty and Kathleen looking out one of the bay windows and pointing down at the street.

"I thought they might be here," Kathleen says, irritation evident in her tone.

Davis is shaking his head and puts a hand on Kathleen's back. Consolingly, he says, "I didn't know it was still an issue. I mean, I am so used to being left alone now that I am out of Chicago. How much does this happen, Kath?"

"It slowed down considerably when you came down here to school and your dad got the press to agree to leave you alone. Lately, since Christmas, if I go out at night, to a party or anything, they are around. You know we never publicly announced we were no longer engaged."

Davis' tone darkens as he tells her, "I didn't think we had to. It's nobody's business but ours."

Joining them at the window I am at a loss. What are they talking about? When I get to the window to stand between Davis and Smitty, I get it. Photographers. Paparazzi? Davis *is* the son of a politician – former Illinois state politician – and Kathleen a wealthy society girl. This is really out of my league. I look up at Davis, questioning with my eyes.

"Those guys give all photographers a bad name, damn vultures. It pisses me off." Smitty is more worked up then I have ever seen him. He doesn't usually show much emotion. He's all about portraying the hipster – or maybe just introverted. But right now he is huffing mad.

We work out a plan to get to HeartSmash while giving them minimal photographic fodder to peddle. Getting out of the condo is no problem. We are parked in the underground garage and Davis' car has blacked out windows. The challenge will be walking into the venue and coming back out. The plan is pretty simple. We will all go in Davis' SUV. When we get there, I will walk in with Smitty and Davis and Kathleen will go in together. I don't like it. I'd like us to go in together as a couple, but in the eyes of the world Davis and Kathleen are still together. I am not even on the radar. We haven't told his parents or mine how serious we are. Davis' mom still harasses him about breaking up with Kathleen. It's something we just need to suck up and do. The photographers are on Davis' car the moment we leave the garage. I'm surprised by the brightness of the flashes as they attempt to take pictures through the blacked out glass. It saddens me that I don't even get to sit next to my date on the way to the party. I am in back with Smitty.

Kathleen looks back and apologizes to me on the way, "I am so sorry, Biz, I seem to be ruining your weekend in more ways than one. I promise I will do my best to stay out of the way for the rest of the night." She shoots Smitty a look after finishing her last thought. It causes me to grin with suspicion and wonder exactly how she is going to "stay out of the way."

HeartSmash is being held at a small local ballroom off campus. Music acts – local, regional and national – sometimes perform there when they are trying out new stuff. When it's not being used for concerts, it's open for dance parties or rental. The paparazzi don't hesitate to get in our faces after Davis parks the car and we all get out to walk into the venue. It's not a huge crush of photographers or anything, just something I've never experienced before. Davis and Kathleen are in front of us, bearing the brunt of the flashes. Smitty and I aren't garnering much attention, which is fine with me. I am pleased that every few moments, Davis looks over his shoulder to check on me and say sorry with his gorgeous green eyes. I mean, how could I be upset when he looks at me like that? Catching my attention at an angle nobody else can see, he mouths to me, "Sorry... Love You." It melts my heart. Once we are inside the building, we're safe. There are no cameras allowed inside, except for the people attending and Weldon University photographers, like Smitty.

***

The ballroom is gorgeous. The columns around the outside of the dance floor that hold up the surrounding balcony above are draped with long lengths of dark red velour fabric. The lights are dim and there are large round paper lanterns hanging from the ceiling in shades of dark red, black and cream. The tables are covered with red and black paisley. There are small lamps on the tables. Real lamps with black shades. The ballroom walls and columns are made of rich dark wood. The room itself is a throwback to the 20s or 30s, and with the addition of the decorations, I feel as if I have stepped into an illegal speakeasy – dark, dangerous, a little dirty. It makes me laugh to myself that my panties and bra actually match the décor tonight. I hope Davis thinks they're dark, dangerous and a little dirty.

Not ten steps into the ballroom I am greeted by a very enthusiastic hug from Jules. She's practically hopping up and down, blonde curls bobbing. "You're finally here. What took so long? Never mind. Come on guys ... Hi, Davis, Smitty ..."

Smitty pipes in, "Jules ... this is Kathleen, Davis', umm ..."

I finish his sentence, "really good friend," and give Kathleen a look of support.

"It's really nice to meet you, Jules. Biz and Davis have told me all about you and... Charlie, is it, your boyfriend? His band is playing tonight?" Kathleen points up toward the stage.

Jules shakes Kathleen's hand, but then decides to really welcome her by giving her a hug too, "Great to meet you Kathleen. Yeah, Charlie's my guy and YES, Boxwood is playing tonight and they are tearing it up."

We all turn to wave and smile at the guys in the band. The are dressed in black and white striped shirts, pants and hats, old school prison garb with big red hearts on their upper left chests embroidered with their "inmate numbers."

"Get it?" Jules asks, "They are Prisoners of Love."

"That is great!" Kathleen approves. I nod my head in agreement.

I look Jules up and down. Well, she is just adorable. She could be straight out of The Great Gatsby. Light blue sparkly dropped waist dress with a matching head scarf that covers her forehead and ties in back, her gorgeous blonde curls tumbling over the top of the scarf. She looks as sweet as can be, except for the fake Derringer tucked into her bustline and a purse shaped like a Tommy Gun over her shoulder. She sees me looking at her gun purse and, giggling, tells me, "I'm packing heat. I gotta protect myself since my guy is incarcerated." She jerks her thumb up toward the stage to indicate Charlie.

"You are an adorable gun moll. I hope he gets paroled for at least one song, so he can dance with you" I say.

Putting the back of her hand up to her forehead, she dramatically says, "Such is the life of a prison band widow." We giggle some more.

At some point during my silliness with Jules, Davis, Kathleen and Smitty have headed to the bar. It's fine. I wanted some time with Jules. Seems like we have less and less of it. Davis knows to get me a Diet Coke. He needs to celebrate. It is his birthday after all. And if he is a little drunk my birthday present for him might be a little less embarrassing (for me, not him.)

We all dance as a group for the majority of the fast songs. Boxwood has come up with a unique set list. All the songs are about love, but with a twist. They are also about injury, pain, bleeding. Songs like Bad Medicine, Bleeding Love, Cuts Like a Knife, Tear Us Apart – all done in Boxwood's aggressive rock style. Finally, I have the opportunity to slow dance with Davis when the guys start playing Heart-Shaped Box. Charlie sings it more articulately than Kurt Cobain did, but still with an edge. When there is a break in the lyrics, Charlie hops down from the stage, swoops Jules up in his arms and kisses her with abandon. We all witness it and whoop our approval. He really is a prisoner of love for Jules. When he dances with her, he never takes his eyes from hers until it's time for him to get back up and finish the song. When he *does* finish he leans down and kisses her again. All the "Boxwood Groupies" that the boys have recently been acquiring, sigh with jealousy. Lucky Jules.

I'm happy the songs have gotten slower because I'm more tired than I realized. Davis is a little buzzed, having had more than a few beers and birthday shots of Jack. I can tell because he is singing in my ear, and *he* actually does sound a bit like Kurt Cobain. When he is not singing to me, he is kissing my neck, ears, my temples. One of his hands is on my lower back, his pinkie creeping toward my bottom. The other hand is laced in mine, tucked between us, pushed up against his chest and my breast. He slowly moves his thumb back and forth, stroking the top of my breast. I can't help but sigh, the movement is arousing and torturous. I feel a small trickle of moisture slide between my breasts. I think it's time to get out of here. I pull back to gaze at Davis' slightly loopy grin and then his beautiful eyes. They are roaming all over my face, but then jerk downward toward my chest.

Shooting me a lopsided grin, he slurs, "DD?"

"Yes, Mavis?"

"I'm a little drunk."

I flex up on my tippy toes to whisper sexily into his ear, "I know. Let me do my job and get you back home, birthday boy. You still have *my* present to open."

Still embracing me, he leans back slightly to look at me, "I thought you said you didn't get me anything."

"I realized I had something after all. I wrapped it before we came to the dance. Come on." I give him a wink and then a peck on the lips.

Davis becomes quite motivated at the prospect of unwrapping another present or maybe for some alone time with me. He goes to gather up Kathleen and Smitty. From where I stand, I can see an animated conversation between the three of them. Lots of pointing back and forth between Kath and Smitty and then a big smile from Davis. I wonder what they could be discussing. Come to think of it, even though I have been wrapped up in Davis all night, I haven't seen those two out of each other's company for the entire evening. Hmmm.

Like we did when we arrived, we walk out with opposite dates. Me with Smitty. Kathleen with Davis. None of us are holding hands, or giving any signs of intimacy. When we get to the car, Davis roots around in his pockets, pulls out the keys and then pushes them into my palm, sliding his fingertips across, sending a shiver through me. There are a few flashes from photographers, but less than when we arrived.

Davis says loudly, "Smitty, I'm gonna sit in front. I might get car sick … K, man?" I know he's said this for the benefit of the photogs, just so he can sit up front with me. He's never complained of motion sickness before.

I am filled in on the plan on the way back to the condo. After we get into the garage, Smitty and Kath will take off in his car, so as not to attract attention. If they leave in her Mercedes they'll be tailed all night. Neither Davis nor I bother to ask where they are going. It's really none of our business *and* this change of plans means we will have the condo all to ourselves. The two of them practically sprint to Smitty's Honda Accord once we get there.

Kath shouts over her shoulder, "Bye, don't wait up. I'll see you in the morning or something."

I notice when they get into Smitty's car that Kathleen ducks her head down onto his lap before they head out of the garage. Davis and I both look at each other bug-eyed, eyebrows raised.

"Well, that developed quickly." he chuckles.

I join him in his amusement, "Yeah, so much for worrying or being jealous of Kathleen anymore."

Davis narrows his eyes, tells me, "Nothing to be jealous of, Lizard Baby, nothing at all," and kisses me on the forehead, nose and then the lips, lingering a bit longer there. "Now, come on let's go in and unwrap my present. I'm dying to see what you got for me." And with that he grabs my hand and tugs me into the elevator. I slam right into his body, wrap my arms around his waist and gaze up into his sparkly, slightly loopy green eyes.

"Is it bigger than a bread box?" He asks. I cock my head and squint at him. Who says bread box anymore? Who even owns one?

"Are we playing 20 questions?" I counter. He nods a wobbly yes. "Yes, it is considerably bigger than a bread box."

With a smirk, he asks another question, "Animal, vegetable or mineral?" Oh, so we really are going to play 20 questions.

"Animal, definitely animal."

Davis' hands are anything but still. I am holding him tightly and his hands are all over me, running across my arms, up and down my back, and then stroking my ass and pulling me up close. I can feel him harden. The elevator dings and we are at the second floor – the floor to his condo. Releasing my hands from behind his waist, I turn to walk out, but Davis isn't letting me get away. He encircles me and walks very closely behind me all the way to the front door. It's a bit awkward, but I don't mind. He is sniffing and kissing my hair. It's revving me up … and might help with the "present opening" I have in mind. Oh, I hope I can pull this off.

***

"No, no, no, no," I protest. Once we get in the condo, Davis lunges for me. As I turn in his arms, he continues to try and lean in to kiss me and I push him back. "Take off your coat and shoes and then go sit on the ottoman. It's time for your present."

He groans with frustration but he does as he's told and sits. "Lizzzerd … I am not a kid…" He stops mid-sentence, because I have switched on the iPod, already cued to Wicked Game by Chris Isaak, (It's an oldie, but so sexy), and am standing a few feet right in front of him in a wide stance, still wearing my belted coat, one finger in my mouth and staring at all his gorgeousness. It's taking all of my will power not to laugh at how silly I feel, but I'm trying to be sexy for him. I walk slowly toward him, dragging the toe of each of my sky-high black Christian Louboutin pumps with every step. When I am an arm's length from him and he is looking up at me, dazed with confusion, I rasp out, "Are you ready to open your present, Mavis?" and I point at the belt to my coat.

Davis' eyebrows raise in appreciative surprise, "Uh...yeah!" he says enthusiastically and shoots his hand out. I move away suddenly.

Jeez, I hope I can do this, because actually with that quick move I am feeling a bit lightheaded and floaty. I want to just jump him, but at the same time am feeling lethargic. It's odd. I shake off the contradictions and focus. Teasingly, I ask, "Are you a careful unwrapper or are you a ripper?

"I'm a ripper." Davis confesses with a faux frown and mock sadness, "but tonight I can take my time." He crosses his heart with his index finger and then motions for me to come toward him.

His act is killing me as much as mine. I am almost wishing he'd rip into me, but I want this to be special. I slowly advance back to him and allow him to carefully undo the belt of my coat. I slide it off my shoulders and grab it with one of my hands. Then I throw it over his head onto the chair behind the ottoman. Davis tries to reach for me, but I wag my finger in front of him and step back again. I pucker him a little air kiss and the turn my back to him. Reaching behind myself, I tug the zipper to the flapper dress down and slide my arms out. I hold it to my body, my back exposed, then in one move let it fall to the floor. As it hits, I hear Davis moan, "Sweet Jesus, baby … that is a great present." I assume he is talking about the little red with black polka dot bra and panties and thigh-high black stockings I am wearing. His response is great and I am feeling much less self-conscious now that I've heard his words of approval. As Chris Isaak croons in the background, with my backside still toward Davis, I bend over completely, running my hands all the way down my legs, rolling the stockings down with them. My ass at Davis' eye level, I can just see his lower body between my legs and can make out the growing bulge in his pants. He removes his tuxedo jacket, loosens his bowtie, takes it off and throws it on the coffee table. In the time he's taken to do that, I have removed my stilettos briefly, disposed of the hosiery, and in the sexiest way possible, put the stilettos back on. Davis is getting into the swing of this, as I hear him command, "Oh, yeah … put those back on … and the wig … don't lose the wig." Bossy. Well, it is his birthday after all.

As I come back up to stand I feel very dizzy and lurch a bit. What's wrong with me? I feel weird. Davis reaches up to grab my hips and steady me. "Whoa, Lizard… You okay?"

Okay, that wasn't so seductive, but I play it off with a laugh, "Hey, no touching the present without permission." I playfully slap his hand.

Davis' groans become almost painful, "You are wrecking me over here … please, baby."

"Well, since you are begging so nicely…" and then right on cue the music changes to Cherry Pie by Warrant and I go into my novice version of a lap dance, "you can play with your present now."

I really have no idea what I am doing. I've never been to a strip club and only seen it in the movies and music videos, but Davis doesn't seem to be bothered (or maybe he is…) by my inexperience. I straddle first one of his thighs and then the other, grinding with all my might. I have to say, it's not like I'm not getting anything out of this either. I have to force myself to stop and slide down his thigh to the floor and then spin around to pop up and grind my backside into his deliciously hardened cock. I can feeling his heavy exhalations on my back. His mere breath makes my nipples pucker. When he tries to pull me closer, I slap his hands away lightly again.

"Wait, you said I could play!" he protests.

"Sorry, I forgot I said that, I was getting into the part." I laugh so deeply, I barely recognize my voice.

Pulling my hair to the side and running the back of his index finger down my neck, Davis rasps up into my ear, "I can already tell you the reviews are going to be excellent." With that he grabs my hips and twists me violently to face him, his mouth on my stomach, sucking and licking. His tongue dives into my belly button. I am straddling his thighs now and rotating against the strain in his pants. It feels delicious, but I want more. As if he read my mind, Davis divests me of my cute little bra and with one hand on my back pulls my breast toward his mouth. I pull him closer, raking my fingers through his thick, silky hair. He nips and bites at my nipple, eventually taking the whole thing in and sucking ruthlessly. His other hand is on my hip, encouraging me to thrust and rotate into him. I want to feel more of him and bring my hands down to undo and remove his tuxedo shirt. I push it off his shoulders and then run my hands back up and then straight down his smooth, hard chest. I stop just above the button of his pants.

Panting, I ask, "Do you mind if I rip open this part?"

I hear a deep chuckle and feel him shake his head, his mouth still on my body. He stands slightly and somehow I manage to get rid of his tux pants and black boxers. My panties still on, I slide my aching core over his rigid erection. This is becoming unbearable. I need him NOW. Davis is already on it, tearing the panties down my legs, miraculously pulling them over my high-heeled shoes without dislodging them. Before I can push my nakedness down on him, he cups me and slides a finger across my hard, slick clit, stroking me leisurely. I shudder and push into his hand.

"Mmmm ... Best. Present. Ever. But better now that it's unwrapped," Davis scorches into my ear.

I am so pleased and turned on. I tease, "I'm so glad you like it. You're very HARD to shop for."

"It's perfect" Davis says, scanning my entire body, stopping at few places to touch and admire. As he pushes into me and looks down at where our bodies come together, he adds, "Just what I wanted." I moan with joy. He feels so good inside of me and I can feel the waves overtaking me as I ride him. I push up and then plunge back down. I am still wearing my black stilettos and my wig and I feel so naughty and sexy for him. Davis becomes almost frantic with his thrusting, directing my hips and pounding into me. I know he is about to come and I want to do it with him.

Shivering, I know I am close, I whisper with the little I have left, "Ha…Happy Birthday, baby. I'm gonna come for you." The words send us both over the edge – loudly.

***

I hear voices, not close, in the distance. A man's – okay that's Davis, and a woman's voice, oh, I think its Kathleen, and then another man's voice. That's right, Smitty. Smitty and Kathleen didn't come home last night. They must be here now. I really should get up and say "hi." Why am I so lethargic? I can generally bounce out of bed no problem. I did dance a lot last night, at HeartSmash *and* in the condo. I probably just overexerted myself. I can just make out Kathleen say, "Okay, well, tell Biz goodbye from us. I'll see you soon. I'll let you know what happens with the interview." Then I hear a door close.

"Lizard? Lizard Baby, wake up, you are sleeping the day away." Davis is whispering in my ear.

I didn't drink last night, but I feel completely fatigued and barely able to move. My throat feels dry. I have a bit of a headache. I ask, "Did I just hear Kathleen leave? I'm sorry I didn't say goodbye."

"Baby, she left two hours ago. You must have woken up briefly and then gone back to sleep." He informs me.

"Two hours, whoa, that felt like two minutes."

Davis sits next to me and strokes my face and and hair. He tells me I look tired. He's got that right. He lets me know he is running over to campus to check on the project his class is working on. He told them he'd be in briefly to answer any questions. Sunday is a big day for students to get assignments done in the theatre's tech lab. Davis encourages me to stay in bed and take it easy. I tell him I want to come with him.

Davis protests, "Biz, you look beat. Just rest."

"I'll make a compromise with you. I need to get my script and I left it in my room. While you are at the lab, I can go to my room and lie down for a bit and study my lines."

Relenting, he agrees, "But when we're through, we are coming back here for the night, okay?"

"Deal."

***

Davis drops me off in the front of Lawrence. I am more fried than I thought, so I take the disco elevator up to my room on the fifth floor. Standing alone inside of it, I recall events from only a few months ago – all of them involving Davis. "Drunk, but not really drunk – only faking to spend time with me Davis" and "coming to my rescue Davis." I push down the thoughts of Jake Gianni that creep in. When the door opens on the second floor, I am unhappily met with the face of Suzette. She is my fellow RA and the girl Jake cheated on me with.

She sniffs, walks in and says, "Jesus, Biz, you look like crap."

Bitch.

"Everything okay with Davis?" She does not ask this to inquire into my well-being or that of my relationship. She is being sarcastic. Oh, yeah and did I say a bitch?

I don't even want to acknowledge her, but I just can't help it. I force a smile and turning my head slightly look her right in the eyes, "We are great. Thank you so much for asking. It's so nice to be in a relationship that isn't based on lies." The door opens to the fifth floor and I walk out before she can say a word. I don't look at her, but hear a little "cheep" of protest before the doors close. That felt great. It also took all the energy I had and reminds me, Davis and I *are* keeping a secret about getting engaged. That's sort of lying. Then there is *my* lie – to everyone and my own brain – Randall.

Finally reaching my room, I let myself in, grab my script off the desk, drop my purse and jacket on the floor and kick off my shoes. I don't bother to undress further. It takes everything I have to pull myself up into my loft bed and climb under the covers. I open the script to the first page and try to focus, but the words dance on the page. Well, obviously, I am too tired to read. I decide to take a short nap. I curl up like a cocktail shrimp and sigh to myself – why am I so tired and sore? I begin to shiver and pull the covers up to my neck. So, not just a cocktail shrimp, more like a cocktail shrimp on a bed of ice.

***

Jesus, what is all that racket? What's with all the ringing and knocking and loud noises? My head is pounding. I am so tired and when I try to move it just hurts …

"BIZ, Wake up!"

Holy shit, who is here? Who is in my room? It sounds like … it sounds like … I am shaking all over. I think I am going to cry.

"Open your eyes, Biz. Wake up."

I turn my head toward the voice, but I am scared. Scared to open my eyes. Scared of who is there. It sounds like … Randall. I feel a hand on my shoulder as I start to turn over. I open my eyes…Oh My God! It is Randall. Right in front of me. He doesn't have his usual creepy grin. He is looking at me with concern. Over his shoulder I see Neil, too. He isn't saying anything, just looking at me like I'm crazy. What are they doing in my room? As much as it hurts to move – I am sore all over – I scramble back away from them as quickly as I can, slamming my back against the wall and pulling the covers with me. I close my eyes and slap at Randall's hands and toward his face. I will not let him touch me again. I am enfolded in terror. This is worse than a panic attack. I close my eyes and keep batting at them while counting to five silently.

Randall's voice gets louder, "BIZ … LIZARD … STOP! Lizard Baby, Stop! What's wrong?"

Eyes still closed, I scream as loudly as I can, "GET OUT, GET AWAY FROM ME!"

"Lizard? Jules, what's wrong?" Randall says. Randall? Why is he talking to Jules? Why is he calling me Lizard? Then I hear Jules answer him, but can't make out what she is saying. Jules! She should run away. Get away from them, Jules! Petrified of what I'll see, but worried for my friend, I stop hitting the air and very slowly open one eye and then the other. Everything is blurry and wobbly, but Randall is nowhere to be seen. Only Davis with a very confused look on his face and Jules behind him with her hand on his shoulder. They are both looking down at me as if I were some kind of organism under a microscope.

Very softly Davis whispers, "Lizard?" I shake my head to clear my thoughts. Neil and Randall were just here. I'm sure of it. But now, Davis is here? With Jules. Did they scare them away? I start crying and lunge forward throwing my arms around Davis' neck, the only thing I can manage to say is, "Mav…" Jules reaches forward and rubs my arm. I can't stop crying, heaving really. I am so shaky.

Jules tells Davis, "She has a fever. I think she must have been hallucinating something scary." I wish I could tell Jules, 'Yes, there *was* something scary, it was Randall and Neil. They were going to hurt me, but you scared them off,' but no more words will come, only more tears. I can't stop my body from shaking.

"She's sick. Really sick, Jules. What do I do?" Davis sounds concerned. Are they talking about me? I'm sick? I was just napping and then Randall and Neil came in, or did they? Maybe *that's* why I am so exhausted and shivering. I'm sick.

I hear Jules tell Davis that I need to go to the Health Clinic and that it has Sunday hours but only for about another 30 minutes. Then I hear and see Charlie in the room talking to Jules and Davis. He is smiling at me with a tight smile and lines between his eyebrows. I must really be sick. Davis hands Charlie something and then comes over to me and leans over my bed. My hair is all wet and so are my clothes. Soaked. I am so confused.

"Baby… you're really sick. I am going to take you to the clinic." Davis says soothingly.

"Thank you," I breathe out. "And thank you for getting rid of them. Neil and Randall."

Davis looks at me and shakes his head, "Randall? And Neil? Lizard baby, they weren't … aren't here. Only us." He indicates himself, Jules and Charlie. I just shake my head and cry. He doesn't say anything more to me, just scoops me out of bed and places my arms around his shoulders. I ache all over and can barely hold on. My head drops to his chest.

Davis barks at Charlie and Jules, "I'll meet you at the clinic. Grab her stuff and bring my car over there."

I am being transported in Davis' arms, but am a passive participant. Is he carrying me through campus to the clinic? I only have enough energy to open my eyes and see Davis' black waffley textured thermal shirt in front of me. It rubs against my cheek as he walks. Then I feel myself being lowered down onto something firm. Blankets are being lifted over me and then settle on me. It feels so warm. My shaking begins to slow. Davis is standing above me, looking down at me. He is stroking my hair. It must feel gross, it's so wet. I should tell him to stop – it's really gross, but his hand feels so good – and I start to cry again. Why am I crying so much?

"You are so hot." He says.

I work to smile. How can he think I'm hot? I'm so disgusting right now. Oh, he means like literally HOT. I don't know how I do it, but I manage to say, between forced smiles, "Yes, but not in a good way."

Davis' face bursts into a large grin and he lets out a sob/laugh. And then huge tears begin falling from his eyes. "I can't believe you are making a joke. You are so sick and you are making a joke. My brave little dragon." His hand is on the side of my face and I push my cheek into it, while holding his wet, reddened, beautiful green gaze with mine.

I'm completely exhausted, but manage to roughly whisper, "Dragon."

The clinic nurse practitioner comes in and examines me. She allows Davis to stay, because I am having a hard time focusing and answering her questions.

"How long ago did this start, Elizabeth? The fatigue, achiness, fever, chills." she asks gently.

Davis begins to answer for me, "This morning she was really tired, but didn't say anything about feeling bad."

I interject, "Last night."

Davis directs his attention off of the nurse and onto me, concern and questioning in his voice, "You felt bad last night? Why didn't you say something? Why did you agree to go out and…" I know he is wondering why I continued with my birthday present for him if I wasn't feeling well.

"I didn't know I was sick. I didn't have a fever or a headache. I just thought I was tired, dizzy and sore from overdoing it." My last words bring a small half smile and gleam to Davis' eyes. He begins shaking his head back and forth.

The nurse tells me my fever was very high when I came in. 103 degrees. And it might have been higher. She gives me medicine to bring down the fever, takes off the blankets and puts some ice packs on me. Davis asks her if the fever could have caused me to see things – delusions. She confirms that yes, it could. Standing next to the exam table, stroking my hair, holding my hand and rubbing my knuckles with his thumb, I begin to relax and calm. I've stopped crying and can focus on his face a bit more.

"Lizard … don't worry, they were never there. It was just the fever causing you to imagine them there. Randall and Neil are nowhere near you. It's okay."

I nod my head up and down and release a large, cleansing sigh.

The nurse tells us that I have the flu. She scolds me mildly for not getting my flu shot in the fall. If I recall, I was a little preoccupied with the whole Jake/Davis thing at the time. She questions Davis and he informs her that yes, he got his. I'm relieved he, hopefully, won't catch this. Since it has been less than 24 hours since the symptoms started the nurse prescribes an anti-viral medicine that she says should shorten the length of the symptoms. She also encourages me to stay in bed for a couple of days, take ibuprofen for the fever and headache, and drink plenty of fluids. I understand from her that I could develop more upper respiratory symptoms.

Davis turns to the nurse and pronounces, "That's not a problem, because I am taking her home and taking care of her."

The nurse smiles widely at Davis and seems pleased with his answer. She looks at me and lifts her brow, "Lucky girl." So, Davis' charm seems to work on all women – no matter what age. I just smile and shake my head in agreement. I *am* a lucky girl. A lucky girl that feels like a bag of dirty laundry right now.

I protest in part, "Davis, I'm on-call tomorrow and I have class and lines and rehearsal starts soon. I can't go hang out at your condo. I'll be fine in my room. It's fine. It's no big deal."

Leaning down so the nurse can't see or hear, Davis locks onto me with his emerald eyes. "Baby..." he huffs in frustration. "If you say another damn word about doing this on your own... I'm gonna... I don't know what I'm gonna do. Just let me take care of you. And another thing..." He almost growls. "No more of your squirrel chatter while you're sick. You know what it does to me."

I find that hard to believe. "Really? While I look this good?" I ask with snark. I know I look a hot mess.

He does growl. "It's not about how you look." Then he turns to the nurse and in a completely different, civil, smooth, calm tone inquires, "Can I take her home now, please?"

The nurse nods yes, smiles at both of us and hands him some papers. Exiting she laughs at bit and says, "Take care" over her shoulder.

***

Davis drives me back to his condo and puts me in bed. He puts a glass of water on the night stand, kisses me on the forehead, draws the drapes, turns out the light, shuts the door and leaves. We barely talked on the ride to his place. I settle into the cool, crisp sheets and think for a moment. Why were Randall and Neil in my hallucination? I don't think of them too often anymore. I actively work to put it out of my mind and roll over in the dark to let some restful sleep overtake me.

***

Moments later, I roll over onto my back and open my eyes. There is soft light around me. Staring up at the ceiling, I realize I am not in my dorm room, but Davis' bedroom in this condo. The events of the day trickle back into my data banks. I'm sick and Davis… turning my head to the left I see two wet green eyes looking down at me from behind the glow of a laptop.

"Hey." Is all Davis says. He reaches over and strokes my hair. My greasy, clammy disgusting fever hair. I attempt to pull away, but he stops me, cradling the side of my head and shaking his head no.

I'm a bit confused. I swear I just fell asleep, but the room is dark except for Davis' computer. He is naked from the waist up and wearing his pajama bottoms. "Uh, What time is it?" I ask, schooching up slowly in the bed, til I'm semi-upright.

"10 o'clock"

"Whoa, how long have I been asleep?"

"Almost five hours."

"Really? How long have you been babysitting me?" I ask with a little smile and a raised eyebrow.

"A while" Davis answers smiling slightly right back. He continues to stroke my hair and look deeply into my eyes "How are you feeling?"

I mentally assess myself before I answer. "Better I think. Still tired. Sort of wrung out. I'm not so hot anymore."

Davis' facial expression changes from concerned to amused. His closed lip smile travels all the way up to his eyes and they crinkle up. He lets out a brief chuckle.

"What's so funny?" I accuse.

"You. Do you remember what you said in the clinic? 'Hot, but not in a good way.' That's when I knew you were okay. Once you made a joke." His eyes become moist and he looks away from me and up at the ceiling. "Before that I was worried. Really worried, baby. You were out of it. And you wouldn't answer your landline or your cell. That damn cell. You left it at the condo again. I couldn't reach you. Jules couldn't …" He is breaking my heart.

Attempting to lighten the mood, I hoarsely tell him, "Right now, I am not hot in any way. I feel gross and dirty. I think I am going to take a shower." I stroke his hand and move it away from my hair, move weakly to get out of the bed, and almost instantly everything starts spinning and I have to recline again. Davis pushes his laptop down to the end of the bed, gets up and is around to my side of the bed at light speed.

Wordlessly taking both my hands and helping me sit upright, then wrapping an arm around my waist, he assists me in walking to the en-suite bathroom. "Maybe you should take a bath instead? Safer?"

I know a bath would be easier, but I don't want to wait for the tub to fill. I just want to get clean. Davis understands when I lay out all the reasons for a shower – faster, cleaner, need to stand up a bit – and agrees only if he is allowed to accompany me. When I give him a questioning look like, "Really? You want to get naked now," he assures me, with a knowing smirk, it's for safety reasons. No fooling around. I don't think I could fool around if I tried. It's hard enough standing up.

Davis strips me down and sits me on the closed toilet seat, demanding that I hold onto the counter nearby. Then he proceeds to undress himself. Even in my current state of exhaustion, his body does not escape my appreciation. He is beautiful. I start at his gorgeous, beautiful face. I always start there. My gaze moves to his wide muscular shoulders and then to his side. As he twists and bends slightly to remove his pants my eyes stroke over his lats and abdominals. I wish it was my hands, but they are busy gripping the counter, keeping me upright so I can stare. I stare at the deep V down to his pelvis, his long, lean legs, hell, even his feet. Then I jump my eyes back up to peruse his firm rounded ass and his ...

Davis brings me back from my visual reverie when he turns to me full and says, "You like the view?"

I sigh, "Very much." And then, I don't know where it comes from, I start crying. Big, fat tears. Naked and blubbering sitting on the toilet seat.

Davis is quickly crouched in front of me. "Hey. Hey..." he says gently. "It's okay, it's going to be fine."

I sob to him that I'm sorry I got sick. To which he shakes his head as if mystified by my words. I sob that I am scared to not be at the dorms. That I'm shirking my RA duties. I sob that rehearsal starts soon and I'm not ready. I sob ... "You take care of me, Davis. TVs and my health and watching out for me. And I do nothing for you. It's so one-sided."

"Do you have a fever again?" he says feeling my forehead, "because you are absolutely talking nonsense. You do everything for me. Nothing was any good before I met you. I was just *acting* happy. Playing a part. I was a good actor, wasn't I? Now, I *am* happy. And as far as taking care of you?" He becomes serious. "I wasn't paying attention to Cole when he needed me, Lizard. You understand? I let him get sick. I let him go away." Now he is crying as much as I am. We are a pretty mess, naked, holding each other in the bathroom.

Our shower together is silent and almost reverent. He never lets go of me, keeping me steady and vertical. He washes me – every bit of me. Davis holds me around the waist, his front to my back, and shampoos my hair with one strong hand. Scrubbing out all the dirtiness, scrubbing in relief. He is so careful. Rinses me. Wraps me in a big fluffy towel. Dries my hair. Puts me in one of his t-shirts and some boxers. Settles me on the couch. Brings me soup. He reassures me that I'll be ready for rehearsal *and* that he called Little Jan, the residence director, to explain my absence. Davis teases me that getting sick is "not the best way to get alone time with him." He makes me smile and laugh. I feel so much better. He needs to make sure I stay. I'm not going anywhere.

Chapter 3-MARCH

Thanks to the medicine and Davis' care, the flu was short-lived. Rehearsal for Once Upon A Mattress started the end of that week and has been going on for over a month now. It is consuming my life and I am having a great time. Owen Fox, the director, is, simply put, a genius. The concept is medieval times, but with clever anachronisms – Fred in full period dress, but wearing pink high top Converse, the Queen carrying a little dog in a Louis Vuitton bag – things like that. The show will be going along and then a character will come on stage with something very "off" for the period. The anachronisms make the show unpredictable and are just a little bit of fun for the audience. Owen also has the ability to make me feel like I am doing a phenomenal job at my part, even at the beginning when I was just exploring. He is so encouraging. I feel very confident about my performance and the production as a whole.

When I'm not at rehearsal, which goes every night until about 11 pm, or in class, I am in my dorm room, asleep or on-call. Davis is equally busy, going to class and teaching during the day and then working on lights for the show at night. We haven't been back to the condo together since I got over the flu. He has somehow managed to go home, get what he needs and be in my room every night in time to crash. As much as we are crazy about each other, this schedule is making for little time for intimacy.

The strain is becoming obvious. We are getting a little snappy with each other. And that, not the play or my classes, is making me anxious. It's my pattern – when things are going well and I feel confident, things go sideways.

I have put off thinking about what happens next. After I graduate. The summer. Getting a job. Oh, it is lingering in the recesses of my mind, but I'm purposefully ignoring the thoughts. Davis and I have agreed we are getting married, but still have yet to reveal it to anyone. We haven't even discussed it much more. I think since I put the smack-down on discussing it, he is not touching the subject.

It's the night before technical rehearsals start. Once we are into those, the nights (and days) will get even longer, sometimes with rehearsal going on for 10 hours. Now, before techs, before the end of the year is upon us, before our parents arrive to see the show (and everyone meets each other for the first time,) might be the time to start the conversation. So I do.

Davis and I are lying in my little loft dorm bed. He is facing the wall and I am snuggled up against his firm, warm back. I kiss across one of his shoulders up to his ear. Then I softly speak into his ear, "Mavis, what happens next?"

Davis turns his head slightly to have more contact with my still kissing lips. "What do you mean next?" he asks.

I launch into full prattle. "Well, we have technicals for Mattress, and then your parents and my parents are coming for opening, and then there is graduation and then … what's next? I'm just trying to think ahead a little. I have been stuck in the here and now. And don't get me wrong, the here and now is great. It's where I need to be right now, but I guess… I guess I was just starting to think about, you know, us and the future and…" Davis has flipped over to look at me. We are face to face, heads on the pillow. He is smiling a big smile, and it's growing wider the more I chatter on. He isn't even trying to stop me or answer my questions.

When I finally stop and take a breath, he says, "First, I am so glad to hear you doing that crazy talking-too-much thing again. I haven't heard it in a while and I was beginning to wonder where it had gone. Secondly, I am now completely horny and you are going to have to help me out with that." I eagerly nod in agreement and push my head forward to give him little kisses along the side of his mouth and then lock in fully on his lips. He wastes no time pulling me right against him and I can feel exactly the affect my chatter has had on him. I hum. "But," he continues, holding me back slightly to look in his eyes, but still keeping his hardness close, "I think we need to talk about this 'NEXT' you were wondering about." I frown. "Oh, don't you worry little Lizard, we are going to get to this." He points his finger back and forth in a circle between our bodies. "There hasn't been nearly enough of this, lately. But as for NEXT? Next, after all the things you said and graduation…next, we tell everyone that we are engaged, then you move into my condo and out of this dorm forever. And then, then I don't know, Lizard Baby. We'll figure it out together."

I smile. He had a plan all along, he was just trying to respect my wishes. "So I'm moving in with you?"

"Yes."

"Okay … but I am not telling my parents until after graduation, okay?"

"Okay" he answers. I'm starting to lose him in this conversation. His hand is rubbing my arm and moves up to pull one side of my tank top over my shoulder.

"Are you going to tell your parents?"

"Sure, when we tell yours that we are moving in and getting married. Lizard, I'm 25 years old. I don't have to ask permission." He is finished with the talk and has moved on to removing my top completely. My breasts are receiving the bulk of this attention.

I feel the need to sum up the conversation, even as he has abandoned it, "Okay, so… after graduation we'll tell them, our parents, that we are getting married. And then we can tell everyone…" I don't get to finish my verbal assessment of the situation. Davis' mouth is on mine, his hands in my hair. He parts my lips with determination and covers my tongue with slow, luxurious strokes which I can do nothing but return. Well, I guess that's settled. With a sigh, I give into the sensations. Davis flips me on my back and while purposefully kissing his way down my body he groans out,

"Good, I finally got you to stop. Now, let me show you what's NEXT." He doesn't stop until he's kissed me all the way down to my inner knees. With his fingers he lightly trails them back up my thighs, until his thumbs, his magic thumbs, find and work my clit into a frenzy. As he enthralls me, his eyes are locked with mine, he rotates and presses, rubs and rotates. He has me whimpering and then plunges his flattened tongue onto my excitement, pushing with delicious pressure. I audibly suck in air through my closed teeth to try and absorb the overwhelming sensation. This is followed by light, tensing flicks of his tongue that become too much to contain and I cry out, "Oh, Oh yes." I don't have a moment to speak before he has climbed up my body and he is planted inside me. He just holds it there as my insides clamp around him. He hardens further, feeling the end of my orgasm and with slow rhythmic rocking, pulls out of me and then, with force, back in. It has been too long and we are making up for it. His lips on my neck, his full body weight flattening me, I shudder slightly as release arrives again and brings on loud groans and a long, low growl from Davis as he finishes right after me.

Davis pants in my ear, "And that, a lot more of that, is NEXT!"

I giggle. Glad to have *that* settled.

Chapter 4-APRIL

"Nice Shirt," I think and then say aloud. "You might want to consider changing it before my parents arrive."

Davis questions me. "Why?"

The shirt says: LIGHTING DESIGNERS CAN ALWAYS FIND YOUR HOT SPOT

Giving him my reasoning, I explain. "No, no, no don't get me wrong. I personally love it and find it to be 'truer than true,' but my parents don't understand theatre and theatre lingo. They'll just think it's dirty."

Really, it is sort of dirty and well, hilarious. Actors are famous for being unable to find their "hot spot" – that perfect place in the light. Men, I am told… I have no personal experience, but am inclined to believe, are frequently unable to find the G-spot – that's why I love the shirt. Who doesn't love a good double entendre?

Davis can ALWAYS find the hot spot. And not just with his lighting.

He relents with a sigh and takes the t-shirt off. He pulls another one out of his overnight bag. I really should give him a drawer in my dorm room, but I haven't had time to clear one out. When he turns around he has on a black t-shirt with the GOOGLE logo on it.

"Is this better?" He asks with one eyebrow and the side of one lip raised. Smart Ass. The word Google equals Sex in Biz and Davis-land.

"Where did you get that?"

"Um. Duh. Google." He tells me in a goofy voice, with an added goofy eye roll. "It's the only other clean shirt I have here. So it's this or HOT SPOT."

I choose Google, because other than me, Davis and a few of our friends, most people aren't in on our euphemism. I am going to have to work hard not to laugh when I look at it tonight. We're getting ready to go to the theatre for opening night. I'm dressed in yoga pants and a big t-shirt. No need to dress up now, when I have to go to the theatre and get into costume and make-up anyway. I have my nice clothes for the after party in my bag. Davis is wearing jeans, his Google shirt and a black suit jacket. As lighting designer, he gets to sit in the audience and basically just fret as the show goes up.

Both Davis' parents and mine are in town for opening night of Once Upon A Mattress. We are meeting them in the lobby before the show and then Davis is taking them all to The Lum for a drink and some appetizers. I have to get ready, so he's on his own.

***

We get to the lobby of the theatre before either set of parents. Davis is holding my hand, but also pacing back and forth in a short line next to me.

"You're not nervous, are you?" I ask. I know *I'm* nervous. My hands are sweaty and I have been silently chanting my mantra to myself. I am anxious about Davis meeting my parents, me meeting his parents and our parents meeting each other. Oh, and did I mention it's opening night of the show I have the lead in? Yeah, that little thing, too.

My parents arrive first. When I spot them through the glass door of the theatre, I immediately drop Davis' hand and my bag and move briskly toward them. I am keeping myself from running. I run straight into my father's open arms. There are other people around. A few other student's families, but I don't even notice them.

"Hey, Bizzy Girl... I'm glad to see you, too!" my dad chuckles. He releases me into my mother's arms. I could see her beside him flapping her arms and wrists for him to give me up to her.

"Hi, Sweetheart. You look so good. So happy."

Davis has appeared at my side holding my bag up to me. He looks at me with a smile and then at the bag. I take it from him. He leans in slightly and says with a half smirk, "Gonna introduce me?"

"Yesssss…" I tell him. Turning to my parents, I motion to Davis. "Mom, Dad, this is Davis Brandon, my boyfriend. Davis, this is Diane and Cal Connelly, my parental units."

Mom laughs a bit and hugs me with one arm, "Parental units … Biz, I don't know where you get this stuff. Hello, Davis," she shakes his hand, "very nice to finally meet you." Dad and Davis shake hands too. Dad gives a him a slap on the back.

Dad points to Davis' shirt, "Google, huh…You've got a shirt. You a fan of Google?"

"Big fan of Google, sir. Huge fan." Davis looks sidewise at me and winks. I press my lips together and a little snort releases from my nose.

"Diane, Davis likes Google… I give Diane a lot of grief because she is sort of Google obsessed. On it all the time." This is too much. Now Davis has my parents drawn into a Google conversation, but they don't even know what it is coming across as to us. We are both trying to suppress laughs. Every time one of them says 'Google,' all I hear is 'sex.'

Mom looks a little hurt or confused, "What's so funny? There is nothing wrong with Google."

Davis jumps in, "Oh, no Mrs. Connelly…"

"Diane, please…"

"Diane, NOTHING wrong with liking Google." ARE YOU KIDDING ME? Davis is having WAY too much fun with this. "We were just laughing because Biz is sort of obsessed with Google, too." I am going to kill him. My eyes go wide and I elbow him in the ribs lightly. Davis is chuckling. And then suddenly stops, his eyes change and become serious as he stares at the entrance of the lobby. He turns to me, "My folks are here."

Davis walks over to the entrance. Kisses his mother stiffly on both cheeks, then smiles down at his father in his wheel chair, shakes the hand that his dad puts out slightly and leans down to hug and kiss him. Mrs.

Brandon is very chic. Her clothes are obviously designer, her hair and make-up perfect. Lt. Governor Brandon looks like an older, more sophisticated Davis, in a dark charcoal suit with a deep purple tie. Davis ushers them over to us.

More introductions. Davis introduces me to his parents last. I shake his dad's hand. It's not very firm, but I think he is trying. His eyes are warm and pleasant.

"It's so nice to finally meet you Biz... or is it Lizard?" and then he winks. Just like Davis.

Davis continues, "and this is my mother, Meredith Brandon."

Standing a bit away, Mrs. Brandon's gaze travels from the top of my head, all the way down to my ballet flats and back, eventually making eye contact with me. Her smile is forced, just a line, no teeth. She looks almost pained. She gives me only the tips of her fingers to shake. They are icy cold. She retracts them after one quick shake.

I smile my biggest smile to try and get a response, "I'm glad you came Mrs. Brandon." She doesn't ask me to call her by her first name like my mother did to Davis.

In elegant, measured words she replies, "Wouldn't miss it. Love to see Davis' work." Her eyes are cold and she gives no indication that she is really happy to be here or to meet me.

I give my regrets to everyone for leaving them, but I need to go backstage and get into costume and make-up. Davis tells them all the plan to go over to The Lum until the show starts. My mom and dad and Mr. Brandon sound enthused about the idea. Mrs. Brandon is stoic, eyes still on me. Davis gives me a kiss good-bye, then pulls back slightly to look at me, with eyebrows raised, non-verbally telling me, "Here we go! Yikes!"

Before I turn to leave, I can't resist and tell him, "Have Fun!" Ha!

Mrs. Brandon's gaze burns a hole in my back as I go. I can feel it on me until I am out of the lobby and on the way backstage.

***

Opening night of the show is a BLAST. Everyone is killing it! The orchestra sounds perfect – not too soft, not too loud. Everyone is hitting every cue dead on, like we are riding some kind of comedy timing wave. I feel so strong and confident, belting out my solos. I get enormous laughter during the song Shy, the tune Winifred sings declaring her shyness, while she is the ultimate extrovert. Davis has told me repeatedly it's my song. In real life, I act shy and quiet, but really I'm anything but, especially when I feel good about myself. I really am starting to believe in myself. I'm not sure if it's this role, being back in Little Jan's good graces, or Davis, but I have never felt better about myself.

***

I sprint into Davis' arms. He and our parents have been waiting for me outside the dressing room. I've changed from my costume, removed my stage make-up, taken a quick shower, re-dressed and done my regular hair and make-up in record time. I am dying to see his reaction.

His face is one big beautiful smile as he hugs me so tight I can barely breathe and he rains kisses all over my face. He's doing it right in front of our parents, too. Declaring himself. My father clears his throat and I pull away from Davis to look at him. He is standing, slightly away from the others, holding a big bouquet of roses and looks so proud. He holds his arms out for a hug. I go to him and let him wrap me up. He kisses the top of my head and tells me, "Oh, Bizzy girl, you were amazing! It reminded me of when you were little and would sing and dance on top of the coffee table. You used to do a mean, They Call The Wind Maria. You remember?" Then my dad whispers, just to me, "I see all that spunk I thought was gone forever last summer. It's back." Davis joins us. My dad says a little louder, so Davis and I can hear, but nobody else, "You're back, huh?"

I squeak out, trying not to cry, "Yeah, I guess I am." He is killing me. I didn't realize how much grief and concern I'd caused them.

"Do I have Davis to thank for that?" he asks earnestly.

"Mostly, yes …"

Davis cuts me off. "No sir, it's all her. She is a sassy little smart ass, if you will excuse my language, sir. All that confidence is in there." Davis puts an arm around me and looks down at me with so much love and pride swirling in his amazing shining eyes. "It was just hiding for a while."

There are more hugs and kisses from my mom. Accolades from the Lt. Governor, who said he hadn't had so much fun in a long time. Mrs. Brandon stands back from the rest of us. After everyone has greeted me, they all look at her, waiting for a reaction. Her husband finally asks, "How did you like the production, Meredith?"

Meredith Brandon visibly swallows a few times, sniffs and then pinning me in her sites says, "I thought Davis' lighting was very good … inspired. The show was cute. I am more of a classical theatre enthusiast, but it was cute."

Tension. Palpable tension. The horrible awkward conversational pause.

Davis, thankfully, breaks it by going over to his mother, hugging her fully and telling her, "Thank you, mom." It's a sweet moment. I think I see Mrs. Brandon finally melt a little.

"Oh my gosh, Mavis …yes, congratulations. The lighting was perfect. Thank you."

I give him an appreciative kiss.

He whispers in my ear, "You found the hot spot every time." He is incorrigible and I love him that way.

***

Davis and I escort our parents to The Lum for the opening night cast party. The entire cast is there. Jules and Charlie show up and flatter me until I blush. I introduce them to the Brandons. They already know my parents. PJ and his pink hair make an appearance. I introduce him to my parents. My mother is completely intrigued by PJ. She has him cornered for most of the evening, chatting his ear off about fashion and hair. He plys her with many girly cocktails and even gets her to dance! I need PJ around more often to chill my mom out. My dad and Mr. Brandon convene in one of the salons, after being introduced around, and surprisingly, given their very different political leanings, seem to be quite companionable. Davis walks his mother around the party to meet people, introducing her to Owen, our director and the rest of the production staff. She's not as taken with PJ as my mother. I am beginning to wonder if she ever smiles or laughs or lets go. Then I remember this is a woman that has lost a child. Seeing all these other young adults, about the age Cole would have been, must be hard. Celebrating Davis' success must be bittersweet.

Davis' parents decide to leave after only a couple of hours. Davis explains to me that his father becomes extremely fatigued. His health care aide was dismissed for the show and the party, but meets them at the door along with their driver to get them back to their hotel. There are no plans made to meet up the next day for breakfast or anything. This is goodbye. Davis gives both his parents long hugs, kisses his mother on the cheek and whispers something in his dad's ear. Mr. Brandon looks at me, gives a half-smirk that reminds me of Davis' and says, "thought so." Mr. Brandon indicates that I should come over and hug him. When I lean down, he brings his arm up as high as he can to pat my back and with emotion tells me, "Welcome to the family."

I stand up and smile down at him and mouth, "Thank you."

Davis is standing by his mother. She is practically glaring at me when I turn back to them. I tentatively approach them and am relieved when Davis puts his arm around me. He turns back to his mom and informs her we are engaged. She says nothing. She has no change in facial expression. If anything she might look subtly more displeased. Davis gives his mom one last hug and then moves back to his dad. Mrs. Brandon and I just stand and stare at each other, incredibly awkwardly. She looks up to catch Davis' attention and then weirdly pulls me in for a hug. It is stiff and strange. The worst part happens next, she burns the words into my ear with a dark menacing voice, "Well, he was engaged to Kathleen once, too, you know … and he is quite the … how should I say this, ladies man. I wish you the best of luck." What? What is she saying to me? Warning me off. Warning me to leave him? Trying to scare me? And that didn't really sound like a sincere, "I wish you the best of luck," either.

Mrs. Brandon releases me with a tight thin-lipped smile and a gleam – not a gleam of approval – in her eye, then goes to her husband and tells him it's time to go.

We wave good-bye from the porch of The Lum. The Brandons get into a very familiar-looking black Escalade. Still waving as they pull away, I twist my face slightly toward him, narrow my eyes, nod a few times and break the news to Davis, "It's official, your mother hates me."

"No, she doesn't."

"Yes, she does." I insist.

"Okay, she's a little hard to get to know, but she'll come around. And if she doesn't… well…" Davis can't finish the sentence. It's his mother.

"Yeah."

***

We stay at the cast party for a few more hours. My parents have a great time, probably better than I do. I am stinging from Mrs. Brandon's attitude toward me and her unpleasant good-bye. I think back to the last cast party, when I got in a huge fight with Davis. When I was supposedly with Jake. What's the deal with cast parties? Can't I have a good one? I feel like it's time to leave.

"Lizard baby, come here." Davis is standing by my father across the room and calls to me, waving me toward him. I wonder what's up? I barely make it to his side, when he puts his arm around my waist, cupping my hipbone seductively and kisses the side of my head. My dad says nothing – he's just smiling like an idiot. I think he may have had one too many drinks.

Davis clears his throat and then loudly says, "Can I have everyone's attention?" My dad whistles his taxi driver whistle. The entire room quiets and all head turn to look at the three of us.

Davis continues, "Hi, Everyone. I want make an announcement. First of all, congratulations to Owen and the cast and crew of Once Upon A Mattress. Opening night was great and I can only predict that the show will be a smash. More importantly, though …I wanted to do this in front of all our friends and family and people that mean so much to us." Davis pauses and looks down at me, giving me his most mischevious half-smirk, "I just asked Biz's dad and he was fine with it and I asked Lizard a little while ago and she said 'yes.'" There is an audible in-unison gasp of the crowd. Davis pauses again. "I am happy to announce that Biz Connelly – Lizard Breath – has agreed to marry me." I didn't know he was going to do this tonight. We didn't even discuss it. I'm a little overwhelmed, but not angry. I feel my eyes open wide as both my hands come up to cover my mouth as a little squeal of delight and surprise pops out. I hear even bigger squeals, from Jules and PJ. Davis scoops me up in his arms and with one hand uncovers my mouth and kisses me soundly. He pulls back slightly and whispers at my lips, "I said I'd wait, but I couldn't wait any longer. I am so in love with you. This was the perfect opportunity."

I whisper back to him, not wanting to share him for a few moments, "*I am so in love with you.*"

We are nothing short of attacked in the next few minutes. I see my dad's face appear next to us, as he hugs us both. Then my mother appears from the other side. She is crying and laughing and giggling, all at once. Once we are finally released, Davis and I kiss each other one more time and turn away from each other to receive best wishes and congratulations from the rest of the gang. I have heard Jules' distinctive squeal the entire time. She nearly crushes me when she gets to me, "OMG! Biz, we are going to have a wedding... a real one!"

That was odd. What does she mean by that? A real one? I blow it off and say, "I know."

PJ joins the girly squealing and jumping up and down, telling me that I "absolutely MUST let him make the veil." Who am I to argue with the offer of a custom veil?

"PJ, I think it's a ways away. This is all very new. We don't have a date yet. I don't even have a ring. I don't even know if I want a ring." I tell him.

"WhatEVER!" PJ groans sarcastically, "His family is loaded... you're getting a ring."

We stay at the party much longer than I intended. After the announcement everyone wants to talk to us, ask our plans. Of course, we have none yet. We haven't even talked much about this except for the day it came up – back in January. And Davis sprung this announcement on me. I … we have many catch-up steps to make. It really is time to leave. We manage to pull my mother away from PJ. That is an unholy match. The two of them could have my wedding planned and decorated in no time if I don't watch out. Actually, maybe that's a good thing.

My parents are staying with us at Davis' condo, in the guest room. Davis is going to make a show of sleeping on the sofa until my parents fall asleep. Then he'll come to bed. There are just so many agendas we can push tonight.

When we return to the condo, I am surprised that my parents want to stay up and chat some more. We discuss when Davis and I first knew we wanted to get married. I modify the story, leaving out the graphic details, but tell them it was very early in the relationship and we decided to give it some time. They don't seem surprised that it has only been four months. They may not have been this cool if I told them it was really only after five days. Davis excuses himself, saying he is going to get changed and get his stuff together for the couch.

My mother and father watch Davis leave the room and then move over next to me on my sofa. My mother starts, "What's the deal with Mrs. Brandon?"

I shake my head. "I don't know, Mom… I mean, she's been through a lot, but she seemed very…"

"Cold." My father finishes the sentence for me. "She is one cold fish. I never saw her smile all night. She looked slightly pleased when Davis hugged her, but man, she's cold."

"I… I really don't know, Dad."

My mother pipes up and says something so out of character, "Biz, she is sort of a… well, a bitch." I am surprised by my mother's candor. She is usually not so outspoken. She continues, "It will be challenging to have her for a mother-in-law. I'd be careful, sweetheart. She seems like she'll try to run your marriage." I smile at her supportiveness – even if it's not what I expected. "You just keep your eyes on her. I really like the Lt. Governor and I adore Davis, I just don't trust Mrs. Brandon yet. Something is off." Wow, this is quite a declaration from my peace-keeping, non-confrontational mother. It is right in line with her protective side, though. My mother stops talking when she sees Davis reenter the room.

"Well, it is very late," my dad announces, "and you have another show tomorrow, Princess Winifred. We are so proud of you …" He looks at Davis, too, "Both of you. For the show. And the engagement. So proud. Goodnight." My mom and dad kiss me goodnight. My mother hugs Davis. She looks small in his big embrace. Davis shakes hands with my dad. My dad takes one last look before he shuts the door to their room. He is checking to see that Davis is making up the couch. He is.

I make a big show of my next words, saying them loudly so my parents will hear me through the door, "Well, Goodnight Mavis…" I give him a big wet kiss. "… see you in the morning." Then I pad off to Davis' bedroom to get in bed and wait for him.

***

"Move over, baby. Lizard, move over." I roll slightly toward Davis' voice and just barely open my eyes. A fuzzy blob in front of me comes into focus. Davis whispers, "Hi, baby" and then pushing both of his arms under my shoulders and knees, moves me over like he is sliding a giant pizza into an oven with a paddle.

He climbs in bed and as I roll away from him I ask sleepily, "Time?" He spoons in behind me and pulls the duvet around us. I meant to say, 'What time is it?' but evidently lack the energy to get out a full sentence. Davis understands my meaning and with an audible smile tells me, "Late. I fell asleep on the couch waiting for your parents to fall asleep." I hear and feel him laugh into my shoulder saying, "Guess I wasn't the only one. Being engaged is hard work."

"Ha! Ha! Smarty boots," I slur with a yawn and push my bottom back into him. "Let's go back to sleep and I'll tell you all about 'hard work' in the morning."

Davis matches my contagious yawn with his own and says sexily, "Deal." We both fall asleep quickly because the next thing I know, its morning and he's frantically scrambling to get out of bed and back to the couch before my parents are up.

"G'morning!" I hear my dad say as Davis walks out of my door. Oh, no – busted!

"Uh, Um ...Hi, Mr. Connelly ..." Davis says sheepishly.

My dad teases, "Oh no, please call me Cal."

"Oh, okay... Cal. I. I was just waking Biz up. She...she should be out soon." I am giggling into the covers hearing this exchange. Davis is really tap dancing. The funniest part about all of this is we really didn't do anything but sleep.

"Uh, huh." Dad says. Then my dad gives Davis a bit of advice, "Davis, You might want to move away from the door or even get back on the couch before Diane comes out. I'm just saying."

"Thank you, sir."

"Cal, please."

"Cal" Davis repeats.

I enjoy listening to my dad give Davis a hard time. It's fun. Davis might be scared to death, but I know Dad is only messing with him. I don't know where Dad comes down on the whole "sleeping together before marriage" thing, but I know my mother is way against it. I think my dad might feel like he has to act that way. I get up, throw on my yoga pants and a hoodie, make a pit stop in the bathroom and then pad out into the next room. By the time I arrive, Davis is off the couch and entertaining my parents in the kitchen – making breakfast and being very solicitious.

Davis turns and greets me with an enthusiastic, "Hey, sleepy-headed Lizard!" and open arms. I walk right into them and cuddle into his chest as he kisses the top of my head. I turn my head slightly to peek at my parents, seated at the bar, and smile.

"Good morning, guys."

They say in unison, "Good Morning, sweetie" and "Good Morning, Biz kid."

I have to ask. "Did everyone sleep okay?" Davis and my parents all report they did. "'Cause I slept like a rock." I was about to say, "Right, Davis?" but bite my tongue just in time. Over the delicious breakfast of waffles, bacon and eggs that Davis has made, we discuss the show, how long it will run, the rest of the school year and what will happen after graduation. I'm not prepared to answer questions about the latter. I have some ideas. They just aren't firm yet.

I answer the best way I can. "Well, graduation is in what, six weeks? I'm mostly thinking of getting through the show and classes. There is a big Midwest audition/interview weekend coming up for theatres in the region to find actors and production staff, so maybe that will pan out. You think, Davis?"

"Yeah, I think we should both be able to find work for at least the summer. I go back to school in the fall. Still working on my Master's." Davis elaborates. He is walking in the graduation ceremony, but actually finished his Bachelor's in December. He has at least two years until his Master's is complete.

"So…" I interrupt, "everything is still pretty much up in the air about the summer and after that. I, of course, want to be near Davis, so … we'll see."

My mother can't stand it, she has to ask, "And wedding plans, right? You need to make those."

"Yes, Mom, but really I just need to take one thing at a time. When I, we, I guess I should say, have summer jobs and are ready to make wedding plans, we'll call. You'll be the first to know." She smiles, so I know I have appeased her a bit, for now.

I have a one o'clock call for a matinee of Mattress at 2 pm, and my parents need to get on the road to get back home. We all excuse ourselves and go to our respective rooms to get ready.

I don't know what my parents think of Davis following me into the bedroom, but they haven't said anything so far, so I am just going to act like it's no big deal and hope they do, too.

Once alone in his room, Davis grabs my hand and pulls me back to him, placing his hands on my ass and mashing me up against his pelvis. He questions, hot, naturally-guy-linered eyes burning. "Hey, you were pretty elusive with your parents out there. You *are* still moving in with me, right?"

I answer, "Of course, that's my plan." Okay, now Davis is kissing me and I am getting flushed and excited. When he moves on from my lips to my cheeks, ears and neck, I finally get out, "I...I...I just, I'm not ready to tell them yet. I don't have a job. And yes, we are engaged, but that's all new for them, too. I figured once we had jobs and some firm summer plans, I would tell them." His kissing intensifies. I really just want to push him on the bed and forget my parents are a room away.

"Mmmm....babbling...sexy."

"Davis." Oh, I don't want him to stop. But. My parents. "Davis ... Mavis, baby." I push him away slightly. He looks so sad. "My parents are Right. Next. Door."

"So. They are probably doing the same thing we are. I mean, come on, your Mom was pretty hot in her leopard PJs." Oh my God, he did not just say that. I open my mouth in genuine surprise.

"What? They were smoking,'" Davis jokingly protests, huge grin on his face and raised eyebrows.

I smack him on his arms and chest to get away. He doesn't let me loose. "You are a sick man, Mr. Davis Brandon. That's my mother and I don't even want to think about their – oh my God, sex life."

"No. What would have been sick was if I said your father looked hot in *his* leopard jammies. That's twisted." He is having a great time, chuckling to himself and teasing me. "I know when I look at your mom, how you got to be so adorable, that's all I'm saying."

I let him know he is forgiven with a big, passionate kiss, opening his mouth with my tongue and stroking under his top lip. Then I proceed to suck at his tongue suggestively, a promise of more. When I finish I pull away slightly and we both groan, "Mavis, I want you to hold that thought...the one you are thinking right now, and I am feeling down there." I point between us to our shared excitement – his quite obvious. "My parents are leaving in a little while, let's get them out the door and get my matinee over and I swear, I am all yours for the rest of the weekend."

Davis' eyebrows arch with anticipation, "All mine? Every bit?"

"Every bit. Yours." I turn out of his arms, step out of my yoga pants, pull off my hoodie and run naked to the bathroom. Looking over my shoulder at him at the last minute and smiling. He charges after me and I shut the door just in time.

Davis bangs on the door to the bathroom, "Do I really have to wait?"

"Yes. Now, go get dressed."

"I'm dirty."

"Tell me about it."

"No really, I need a shower."

"Okay, I'll be out in a minute."

Davis moans, "You really ARE going to make me wait, aren't you?"

I sigh softly to myself, leaning against the door, hugging myself around the waist and stroking my own skin lightly, wanting him as much as he sounds like he wants me. Then I tell him through the door, "It will be worth it."

***

Um, it was *totally* worth it.

I just arrive in my dressing room after curtain call when there is pounding the door. I have never had a private dressing room until I landed this role. It's not fancy, but it's so nice to have a place to prepare before and decompress after a show in private. The pounding, is, in all likelihood, one of the freshman dressers, there to collect my costume for cleaning.

I yell, "Come in."

It's not the dresser. It's Davis. His eyes are smoldering, dark forest green, pupils dilated. He shuts the door behind him and locks it, smirking, mischievously. He scoops me up with his strong arms and locks me to his chest, and announces, "Mine, every bit."

I still have my costume on. Before I can tell him anything – that I need to change, remove my make-up — his hands are deftly releasing the many, many hook and eye closures at back of my dress. He isn't kissing me – no distracting himself or me from his desired outcome – which is me, out of costume and "all his." I step out of my dress, pick it up and turn to hang it on the hanger on the back of my door. As I do this, Davis is behind me, unlacing my corset. Once removed, I place my corset in my dirty clothes bag, also hanging on the door.

Davis and I are not speaking, just moving. I am naked from the waist up. Davis turns me so we are facing the lighted mirror. I bend forward and put my palms flat on the dressing table. Davis leans down and removes my character shoes, placing them under my table. He moves back up and skates his hands around my waist, sending shivers through me. Our eyes make contact in the mirror and burn into each other. He's barely touched me and I'm already aching for more. All I have left on are my panties, tights and my hairpiece. Davis slides his thumbs under my tights and swiftly pulls them down my legs. Without taking his eyes off of me, he reaches back and sticks the tights in the dirty clothes bag. I watch all this in the mirror. He is very determined.

Now, just in my panties, he pulls me back against him. He is fully clothed, but I can feel him – every bit. We've been here before, me naked, him clothed – he seems to like this. I'll have to reciprocate sometime. Still watching him in the mirror, he takes my breasts into his hands, pinching and extending my already rigid nipples. He kisses my shoulders, never removing his gaze from mine in the mirror.

A loud knock comes on the door. I freeze. Davis doesn't.

"Yuh ...Yes?" I cry out, huskily.

"Miss Connelly?" It's one of the dressers. They are trained to address us formally, as they would in professional theatre. "Miss Connelly, I am here to collect your costume and laundry."

Davis must have known they were coming. In the mirror, I see him put one finger up to tell me to give him a second, then he puts it up to his lips, indicating that I should be quiet. He hands me my light robe off the back of my chair, drapes it over my breasts and wraps my arms over the cloth. He moves me off to the side, away from the door. I ache with need at the loss of his intense touch and stare. Davis takes my costume and dirty clothes bag off the back of the door and barely opening the door, holds it in the open space. His hand comes back empty. He shuts and re-locks the door.

"Uh, Thank you, Miss Connelly," the confused freshman says loud enough to be heard through the door.

I cock my head at Davis, who has turned back and is approaching me, and call out toward the door with a deep laugh, "Thank *you*."

Davis takes the robe out of my hands and throws it back on the chair. He reaches up, and I have no idea how he knows how to do this, begins removing bobby pins from my hair to take out my hairpiece. He is touching me nowhere else, only my hair and scalp, but standing there nude, being attended to, has me vibrating with anticipation. He removes the hairpiece and places it on the dressing table behind him, without even looking. He rakes his fingers through my hair, smoothing out where the hairpiece was, still touching nowhere else. I tip my head back and moan, as my hair tumbles down and tickles my shoulders. It feels so good. It feels so good all the way down to my panties. Panties that are in danger of becoming flammable, if he doesn't remove them soon.

Finally, Davis slides both his hands down to my cheeks and, holding my face like a gem, delivers a kiss that would have me on the floor, if he wasn't holding me up. I can't take it. If he isn't going to touch me. I am going to touch him. I tear at his crisp, white button up, unbuttoning as I melt into his kiss. I slide the shirt off his shoulders and arms and let it fall to the ground. My hands grab for his muscular chest and slide down to feel every hill and valley of his six-pack abs. If I wasn't so caught up in his kiss, I would get on my knees and kiss those abs – and more.

As if reading my mind, and still without speaking, Davis is on *his* knees. He has backed me up to the wall of the dressing room. Those nearly flammable panties? They are gone in a heartbeat, and he is delivering a million kisses on my lower abdomen. He lifts my right knee and puts it over his shoulder. I am completely exposed. I hold his head and shoulder to steady myself, as after one last look up at me –scorching me – he begins his careful accosting of my most sensitive area. Working his tongue with intermittently changing pressure and rapidity. Again, he is focusing all of his attentions on only one area, but this area was already about to combust. Still holding his head and shoulders, I tip my own head back. It hits the cement wall with a slight thud. The dull ache only seems to intensify my desire as I try to absorb the growing sensation below. I pull on Davis' hair as the build progresses. I am glad he is bearing part of my weight on his shoulder because the leg holding me up is starting to shake. I can hold on no longer and with a spasm of excitement, I pitch forward, grasping Davis' head in desperation and releasing in a crash.

As I come down from the pinnacle, I allow my head to fall back against the cement wall again, this time not as hard. Davis is panting at my waist, holding my buttocks and kissing me at the crease of my legs and up to my navel. He is almost worshipful. I reach down and cup my hands under his jaw, pulling his face up to look in his eyes. This gorgeous, gorgeous man is all mine. And I am his and I tell him, "All yours."

I want to make him feel as good as he has made me. I bend over to kiss and taste his soft lips. Slowly, he rises to his feet, our lips and tongue still entangled. I move him quickly backward until he practically falls into my dressing table chair. I bend down and reach for his belt buckle, but Davis grabs my hand.

In a deep, satisfied sounding voice he tells me, "We can't stay in the dressing room all night and I intend for this to go on and on. If we are going to get locked in a building, it will be in our building, in our bed. After all, you *are* mine for the rest of the weekend." He looks down at my hands on his belt buckle and then up at me, one eyebrow arched and intones, "To steal your words, Lizard … hold that thought."

He said OUR building and OUR bed. I've never heard him say that before.

Davis stands up, finds my street clothes and hands them to me. I am still in 'let's get naked' mode. He grins hotly down at my lack of clothing. "Get dressed, I want to get you home, so I can take them off again." Insatiable boy.

Davis practically carries me to the car. When we arrive at the condo, I realize it's been one of those car rides when you barely remember anything except leaving and arriving. We are both in a haze of excitement to be alone together.

Flying through the door to the condo, Davis and I leave a trail of apparel all the way to the master bathroom. I guess, I mentioned I needed a shower or something, I can't remember, I am in such a thrall. We have been in constant physical contact since getting out of the car and I can't even bare to stop touching him as he turns on the water and checks the temperature. I step in behind him, through the glass door of the shower. Davis backs me into the pounding stream of water, tipping my head back and wetting my hair. He turns me, so my back is to his front and carefully washes, rinses, conditions and re-rinses my hair. Davis then lathers up his hands with the apple scented body wash I have left there and washes every inch of me, taking great care. When I am completely covered in suds, I turn and wrap my arms around his neck. I kiss and slide my body over his, using it to wash him like a human loofa. I am rewarded with a large, intensely happy smile from his beautiful lips and eyes. We rinse each other off and I take a few moments to wash my face more thoroughly of my stage makeup. Davis has not taken his hands off of me the entire time. I am beyond turned on. I need more of him immediately.

Davis steps out, grabs a soft, fluffy white towel, turns back to me and wraps me up in it, tucking it in at my breasts. The brief touch of his fingers moving lightly over the top of them ignites something in me. I rip the towel off and in my now only slightly dryer state, I begin drying him off, while simultaneously moving him backward out of the bathroom and toward the bed. This time, he will not stop me. I know what I want. He has encouraged me in the past to ask for what I want. Now I think I will just take it.

The back of Davis' legs hit the edge of the bed, causing him to sit suddenly. I have him right where I want him. I am feeling a little giddy with power right now. I start at his shoulders and move the towel down and down and down with my hands until I am kneeling at his feet. I gaze at his long, proud erect cock in front of me and practically smack my lips. To use Davis' words, "All Mine," is all I can say, in a low, purposeful voice. I think I've surprised him, because when I look up, he seems in awe, eyebrows raised, head turned and tilted a bit, looking down at me, daring me with the sparkle in his eye. I accept the challenge. Not a stitch of clothing on, either of us, it all feels so charged, erotic. I push up into a taller kneel, with one hand firmly encircling the base, I lightly lick and then tease the notch at the crest of his hardness with my tongue. I feel him twitch beneath my lips and then sigh heavily, "Lizard, Oh God, yes..." I want to do this for him. Do it right. I begin to stroke firmly but slowly, giving a slight rotation on the upstroke. With the other hand I hold and weigh his balls and tease the area in between them. Davis' moans of pleasure increase. My tongue and mouth are in heaven. I plunge my lips down onto his silky hardness, practically gagging, spinning my tongue as I pull up to the tip, flattening my tongue and licking hard along his entire length. When I reach the tip, I suck with vigor and tease again at the notch on the underside. I continue repeatedly. With each plunge, Davis holds my head, grasping my hair and pulling ever so slightly. It spurs me to continue. I can feel myself becoming aroused and wet, as he grows ever harder. His groans are coming more rapidly now and he is pulling at my head and grasping at my shoulder, much as I was earlier in the evening. With an animalistic grunt, I feel his entire body and his erection spasm, as he comes in my mouth, spurting hotly. I swallow quickly. I didn't know what to expect, but it is not displeasing. Actually, it pushes me further in my excitement and I feel myself creeping closer to the edge. Keyed up, I move one of my hands to my clit and flick it only slightly with my index finger before I come myself, right after him. When I finally look up into Davis' eyes, I see pure love and satisfaction.

"Oh, Lizard baby…" His voice is so deep it reverberates. "That was so amazing, unexpected and amazing." Davis pulls me up off my knees and as he pushes backward onto the bed, pulls me on top of him. I feel a little shy. I hide my face in his chest and lick my lips. Mmmm…Davis. Then I kiss his chest and look up at him.

"So, it was okay, then?"

"Lizard, it was… I am speechless."

I'm pleased I could make him feel that way and I smile hugely and wink. I usually never wink. But I am doing *a lot* of things I never thought I would do before, now that I have some newfound confidence. It feels great to tease him.

Chapter 5-MAY

A year ago, life moved excruciatingly slowly. I was sad, scared and thought I'd never get through feeling that way. Neil had crushed me and thrown me away to Randall. And Randall ... I still fear the day when I really remember what happened. It seems forever ago. The hard parts of life drag.

Then there are sections, segments of life when things are good – golden. It's these times you'd like to remember perfectly, frame by frame, forever. And coincidentally, these are the same moments that whoosh by the fastest. I've worked hard to try and keep a mental film of all the times with Davis since the beginning, but true to form – the better the event, and the more hopeful I am about retaining the memory, the faster it flys by.

Time has moved at warp speed since the closing of Once Upon A Mattress. Davis attended every single performance, even when we extended the run, adding a second show on the last Wednesday, Saturday and Sunday. He admitted to me that he would leave his seat right after the part where "the mouse devours the hawk," and Prince Dauntless tells off his mother, the Queen. I had a guess about why, but I must have given him a strange look because he told me it was because he knew Rob (the actor playing Dauntless), was about to kiss me. Davis said he sat through it once and barely kept it together. I had no idea. Honestly, I thought he didn't like that part because the prince confronted his mother (and maybe that was a little "too close" to real life for his liking).

I felt a bit bad because I giggled when he confessed his jealousy, "Mavis, it's only a play. Rob is gay. You know that, right? I mean, I actually think he has a thing for PJ."

Davis huffed a little and then told me, "I didn't say it was rational. I just said I couldn't stand watching somebody else kiss you. Fake or not." Davis – he's a heartbreaker.

I'm trying to remember all of those exchanges, but it's difficult to keep up with how fast change is occurring.

Immediately after the close of the show, I mean immediately, like the next day, the Midwest Theatre Auditions and Interviews occurred at a large convention hotel in town. Theatre companies from around the region come to one central location to cast and staff their companies for summer theatre. Davis and I got very, very lucky. At least I feel that way. We both scored jobs in town at The Forest Park Theatre. I got a job as a production assistant and Davis as an electrician. I think he would have preferred a lighting design position, but at this theatre, design jobs go to people with established names in the business. It's a large outdoor theatre. They run seven shows over the course of the summer, seven days a week with little turnover time between shows. They generally bring in one or two B-list celebrities or rising Broadway actors for the main roles of each show and cast the remainder of the cast regionally. I didn't even audition at Midwest. I just interviewed for production jobs. I'm still trying to figure out what I want to do when I grow up and I'm not sure it's acting.

My classes are winding down and I am beginning the parade of "lasts" of my college career.

The closing night party for Mattress was my last closing night party at Weldon. Happy and bittersweet, all at once. I went to my last Springfest as a college student. I know I'll be around all next year, since Davis will still be going to Weldon, but I don't think it will be the same. I had my last voice lesson with Dee. We prepared for my final – my voice jury, in front of three of the music professors. Yikes! I have finals in acting and dance, but I'm not too worried about those.

Production class. That's the class I am most excited about since ending Mattress. We've moved from talking about theatre and film production to television. Weldon University is focused on fine arts, so television may seem a bit pedestrian to some. I have actually, through the course of the class, come to appreciate television more. The immediacy, the fast production schedules. It seems exciting and challenging. A speaker came in from one of the local affiliates, a producer of local programming, Gail Patton. She talked for quite a while to the class, explaining the different levels of producers. She said that most people start out as production assistants, doing their time, paying their dues until an on-air or assistant producer job comes up. It intrigued me. I had little production experience, but enjoyed the bigger picture. After the class, I introduced myself to Ms. Patton. She gave me her card and told me to give her a call if I wanted to speak further or pursue television in the future. I thanked her and then literally, put the card and the idea "in my back pocket."

***

We graduate tomorrow. I catch myself doing the reverse of what I did nine months ago. I am sweating. Lugging boxes and sweating. It hasn't changed. I still hate sweating. This time down the stairs from my dorm room to Davis' Escalade. Again, no help from the Disco elevator. Just in time for move-out days, it banged to a halt, maybe for the last time ever. Little Jan is fretting over fixing or replacing it. If it goes, it will be missed. A bit of Weldon history and tradition gone. Lots of important memories happened in that elevator. Probably for more than just me. I am one of the last people out of Lawrence Hall. Anyone that is staying for the summer has moved to Merton. I've already checked that my floor is clear. A few more things and I can turn in my key to Little Jan.

I'm moving in with Davis. Not just talking about it. Really doing it. Almost all of my stuff is in his car. We spent last night in the dorms – my last night as an RA and student. I haven't told my parents yet about moving in with Davis. I have e-mailed them about graduation but avoided phone calls, claiming to be too busy. It's not a complete lie. I have been busy. I have my last box in hand, mostly filled with dirty clothes and my sheets and blankets from last night to be washed, as I approach Davis' car and him.

"Why haven't you been answering me?" Davis scolds.

I frown, "What are you talking about, you never called."

"I did, I have been. I have been down here packing the car and I called up to you like four times. You never answered your cell."

I put the box down by the car and pat the pockets of my jeans. Key, check ... andddd – no cell phone. "I must have left it upstairs, but I never heard it ring. Did you try the landline?"

Davis sighs and replies, "Yes, it was already cut off. You better go back in and look for it."

I agree. "I'll go look. Good thing I didn't turn my key in yet."

I drag myself one more time up the stairs and unlock the door. I see my cell phone bouncing slightly and buzzing silently on the floor behind one of the legs of my bed. My former bed. I pick it up and see, yes, there are four calls from Davis, a couple from my parents and one from Jules. It's strange the ringer was off. I thought I had turned it back on this morning. I shrug, probably knocked it to mute while packing. I look around my empty room one more time and as I walk out into the hallway, up and down the hall. It's hard to believe I won't be back to this place I've lived in most of the time for four years. Wonderful things have happened here. Mostly wonderful things. And a few really terrible ones. I sigh to myself, the good really has outweighed the bad overall.

After a final stop at Little Jan's to return the key and a really unexpected hug and "keep in touch" (I never thought she'd say that, I figured she thought I was a pain in the ass,) I return outside to Davis. I hold the phone up as I approach and say, "Found it!"

He shakes his head at me and gives me his smirk smile, "I swear, I am going to staple that cell phone to your forehead."

I shoot him a look, bug my eyes and tell him, "Funny."

Once we are seated in the car, Davis turns to me, leans over slowly toward me, trapping me in his green eyes and says, "Let's go home." His smirk increases and his eyes are full of the devil.

I kiss him soundly and repeat the last word he said.

Home.

***

Home. Davis' condo. Strike that – our condo. I'm going to contribute to the running of the household. I don't really know how. Davis won't tell me the rent or house payment or however he pays for living here. I am beginning to suspect it's completely paid for. Who has a paid-off home at age 25? No one I know. At least not until now. I'll do my part and give him money for utilities or buy the groceries or something. I have *never* had anyone take care of me, except for my parents, and I'm way beyond that now.

The place is trashed, primarily due to my boxes of stuff. We have slowly been bringing boxes over, but have unpacked nothing. It's all been just dropped into the entry hall, spilling into the family room. One look at it exhausts me. I know I need to tackle the pile and begin unpacking, but really I just want to sit on the couch like a lump and eat whatever we can order in. Davis' cell phone rings, he turns to me and mouths, "Be right back," holds up a finger and moves to the kitchen. I walk over to the pile of boxes. I am just about to open one on the top, when my cell phone rings. I pull it out of my pocket and see it is my dad's number. I have been avoiding him while packing. Time to face the music and tell my parents I am moving in with Davis. I hit the *ANSWER* button.

"Hi Daddy… Oh, you guys just got in? Good. Good. Where are you staying? Oh… wow, nice-The Chase Park Plaza." I am stalling with every word. "Yes, yes, I'm all packed. Ready for tomorrow. No, no I am good. Davis is helping. As a matter of fact …" I am just about to let the cat out of the bag and tell my dad about my new living arrangements, when Davis comes up behind me and snatches my cell phone out of my hand and takes over the conversation with my dad. He holds the phone up to one of his ears and wraps his other firm, muscular arm around my waist and squeezes me up against his chest.

"Hello, sir... Yes, right, Cal. Hello, Cal. I'm just helping Biz and was wondering could you and Diane meet us? Over at the condo... in say, an hour and a half for dinner? Yes, it will be nice to see you, too, Sir – I mean Cal." Davis ends the call and whispers in my ear, "Caught that call just in time."

I'm puzzled, "What do you mean? We have to tell them eventually... you know, that we are going to live together ... even before we are married. I know that sounds prudish, people live together all the time, but my parents are a little ... traditional."

"Just in time, because you know that phone call I got as we came in ...?"

"Yeah, what about it?"

"It was Dr. Longworth, with an offer to design this summer." Strangely, Davis looks happy and just a little worried.

I can't believe he is not more enthusiastic. This is what he wanted, designing, not hanging lights all summer at a hot, outdoor theatre. I question him, "That's great. Right? You're going to get to do what you love, not just some theatre job to pay the bills." Davis is still not smiling; in fact he looks pained, frowning almost. I sense something is off.

Davis pulls me firmly against him, holding my head to his chest. He runs his hands repeatedly through my hair. His breathing deepens, as if he's trying to soothe himself. I haven't had the glimmer of a panic attack in months, haven't used my mantra, have felt solid, but now I am teetering. What could be so bad, in the midst of this good news? I begin to shake.

Into the top of my head, accompanied with soft kisses, Davis finally speaks, "Lizard... Lizard, baby... I was offered the design job, and that's great, but there is a big disadvantage to it..." He continues to explain, all the while holding me tighter and tighter as I shake in his arms.

Davis is going to Chicago for the summer. Outside of Chicago, actually. To work at Chicagoland All-Summer Shakespeare Festival. He has connections up there that he's been in touch with all year. Dr. Longworth, a Weldon professor we have both worked with frequently, is directing one of the shows and has convinced the artistic director that Davis should do the lighting design. All the shows aren't decided yet – Romeo and Juliet, A Midsummer Night's Dream and one more, probably another tragedy.

I can hear Davis' excitement about the job growing in his voice as he continues to explain the offer. The Shakespeare festival does three shows in rotating rep and even though Davis is a designer and still has to do some of the labor, he will get lots of creative control. I can't tell him not to go. That would be so selfish of me, but being six hours away from each other feels too far. We just found each other.

"Well, that sort of solves the problem of telling my parents about living together" I hoarsely get out through unshed tears.

"I can turn it down, Lizard. I won't go if you don't want to me to. I'm torn about it, too," he says softly.

I don't like the idea, if I am being completely honest, but I can't let him pass up this opportunity because of my insecurities. I decide to "put on my big girl panties" and face it down. Before I look at him, I check my emotions, will myself not to shake or cry and then pull my face away from his chest to look up at him. All I see in his face are questions.

I give him an answer. One I don't really want to say, but the rational, grown-up side of me knows I should. "No, you should go. You should do it." Davis frowns a bit. "I mean it. I can't tell you I love the idea, but it is a huge deal for you. Better than being just a technician all summer. We'll work it out." A slight smile returns to his face.

"Really? Lizard? You aren't just saying that? I mean, I am excited about the prospect of designing, too, but being away from you …the thought it sort of, well, kills me."

"We'll work it out." I answer a bit flatly. Feigning a bit of cheerfulness I redirect the conversation, "It's all good. Hey, you invited my parents over in a little bit, umm … perhaps we should get ready. Why don't you order some Chinese or something? I need to go clean up a bit. I feel grimy from all that moving." I give him a forced smile and a quick peck and excuse myself to the master bathroom. It's all a deflection. I need to be alone to process this change of course.

Once I get to the bathroom, I lock the door behind me, turn on the water and well, turn on the waterworks. I can't stop the tears. I held them back with Davis, but now small droplets are appearing in my eyes. A few roll down my cheeks before I look in the mirror. I don't quite know if I am sad or panicking, but I use my mantra, "I can do this, I can do this," reassure myself it will all be fine and then wash my hands and splash water on my dirty, streaky face. I've ruined my mascara with the water, so after a few deep breaths and patting my face dry, I reapply my make-up. Okay, a little better. It will be fine. Davis and I will work it out. We did not get this far for nothing.

The time before my parents arrive is a little awkward. Davis and I are setting the table and waiting for the food to arrive, in relative quiet. Occasionally, Davis drops some information about his new job, like the fact that he has to leave for Chicago on Monday. Two days after graduation. I busy myself with finding placemats and napkins.

I'm downright relieved when the doorbell rings. It's my parents. I am so very pleased to see them. I give each of them a big hug, pouring a bit of my new sadness into it. They are pretty intuitive and each ask, "Hey, Bizzy girl/Biz, everything okay?"

I reassure, them, "Yes, I'm fine, just tired from the moving and anxious about graduation." It's then when their eyes lock onto the boxes of my stuff strewn about.

"Something you need to tell us, Bizzy?" Dad inquires.

This is going to be easier than I originally thought given Davis' recent employment bombshell. "Well, yeah, Dad ... Mom, I'm moving in." Both of their mouths open and then shut in a frown.

Davis interrupts as he enters quickly from the kitchen, "It's not exactly what you think, Cal, Diane. Biz is moving in, but I'm not going to be here this summer, so we sort of ARE and AREN'T living together." Davis ushers us all into the family room and just as we are being seated so that Davis and I can elaborate, the doorbell rings once more. Davis excuses himself and opens the door to retrieve our dinner from the Yin Cheng delivery guy. He pays and tips him and then takes the food over to the island. My parents and I just watch the proceedings with the food, not re-engaging in the "living together" conversation.

Davis returns, "Maybe we could talk over dinner? I would hate for it to get cold."

I think this is Davis' way of trying to decrease any additional intensity a conversation like this might have. My parents both agree. Soon, we are seated and passing around cartons of Chinese yumminess.

Once everyone's plate is full, Davis bravely gets back on topic. "We want to be honest, we originally were going to be living together this summer. We're engaged and will eventually be married, so we saw no point in waiting. BUT, circumstances have changed. I just received an offer to design at a summer stock near my hometown. Biz and I have only had a chance to talk briefly, so there's lots to figure out, but I won't be here for most of the summer. I was thinking that perhaps that would give you, Diane and Cal, a chance to be more comfortable with us living together?" I am impressed with how well he presented all of this.

My dad pokes at his food with his chopsticks a couple of times and then clears his throat. Okay, here it comes. He looks up at my mom, frowns and then smiles. He looks at me and says, "Are you okay with all of this, Biz kid?" Wow, not at all what I expected.

I ask, "What part?"

"Well, first the living together, but not living together part and, I guess, the being alone all summer part, too."

"Dad, I was always okay with living with Davis. I've never really had a roommate since freshman year, and we *are* engaged." I glance over at Davis and wince a bit, "I'm not thrilled about NOT being together this summer, but the day was going to come eventually when we had to be apart for a while, given our careers. I don't know about the alone part. It's too soon. I haven't had much time to think about it."

Surprisingly, it's my mom that speaks next. "Biz, Davis, we were preparing ourselves for the fact you would live together before getting married. I don't know if I'm okay with it yet, but like you said, you're engaged and both adults. Not much we can do about that. I just want to offer a bit of advice – living together is different than being married. It just is. But you don't need me to tell you that, you'll figure it out."

The whole conversation is different than I imagined it would be. I thought there would be a lot more getting upset and refusal on my parents' part. Instead, they are cautiously supportive. I'm surprised but pleased.

"Thanks, Mom and Dad. You're right. We have a lot to figure out. I …" I look over at Davis and then reach out my hand to him. He takes it and brings it to his mouth to kiss my knuckles and smiles, "WE… really appreciate the support." Even with my parents sitting right at the table with us, Davis' kisses do something to me way down deep. I feel a flutter in my lower abdomen and only hope that I am not giving out signals that I'd like nothing more than to ignore everyone else and jump this man.

Davis' next statement comes completely out of left field, "I heard Kathleen is looking for a new place to live. Maybe she could move in for the summer?" What? Where did *that* come from?

My parents speak simultaneously. My dad saying what a great idea that would be. My mother asking, "Isn't that your former fiancée, Davis?" I just sit there looking between the three of them with my mouth hanging open.

"Oops." Davis says with a look of mock fear on his face, "Maybe I shouldn't have brought that up right now."

I'm still speechless. I turn my head slightly to look at Davis fully, "Um, yeah … I'm just wrapping my head around your leaving for the summer." Then I pause for a moment and tap my chopsticks on my fingers and then my lips. "But if Kathleen were here, I wouldn't be all alone. I would have someone to hang with and Smitty would probably be over. It might not be a bad idea, Mavis." Davis appears relieved and rubs my hand, the one he's been holding throughout this exchange, even when I pulled it back from him slightly in surprise, he held on. He knows me. Well. We have the details about this sudden change in plans to discuss and in a very short amount of time.

Davis and I continue to sneak looks at each other throughout the remainder of dinner, each, it seems, willing time to move slower so we have more time together and faster, so my parents will leave and we can be alone.

My parents get the hint. They leave immediately after finishing their dinner, wishing us good-night and confirming the times for the graduation ceremony tomorrow. Davis and I see them out the door and all the way into the hallway, saying good-bye again as they descend the stairs.

I turn to go back into the condo, when I am swooped up at the knees and tossed over Davis' shoulder, my butt in the air. "Oh my God, Mavis, what are you doing?"

"Carrying you over the threshold. Like I should have when we first got here this afternoon."

I protest lightly, "I believe that's for when we first come back to our home, married."

"Then we'll do it again then, too."

Davis carries me past the table, littered with empty Chinese take-out cartons and into the bedroom. I expect him to throw me on the bed and try to make me forget all that is changing. He doesn't. Instead, he slides me down his body, so I can feel all of him against all of me. Davis bends, his face in the crook of my neck, he slowly runs his nose up the side of my throat and stops just below my earlobe, giving me a soft kiss that leaves me tingly.

"I want nothing more than to strip you naked and make love to you, Lizard, but first we are going to figure all this stuff out. I want you thinking about *us* when we are together, not about us being apart." I can barely believe his control. I want him, too, but I know it would be bittersweet if we were just starting in on series of good-byes without talking.

We sit down in the middle of the bed fully clothed. Neither one of us says it, but we seem to have made an unspoken agreement not to touch, not to distract each other while we make a plan. We talk for what seems like hours. Davis will go to Chicago. I will stay here and work at The Forest Park Theatre as planned. Davis has to call and turn down his job there tomorrow, then pack on Sunday and leave early Monday morning.

We will be apart for almost three months, only a little less than we've been together. Davis says at least ten times – he doesn't have to go, he will stay with me. I refuse all ten times. I won't stand in the way of his career and I won't give him any reason to resent being with me. He assures me that would not be the case. I just don't want to risk it. It's killing me inside. What I really want to do is beg him not to go. That would be too selfish.

We reassure each other it will be fine. We'll talk daily. It's not like it's the 1900's. We can text and videochat. He'll be home in August. He could drive down on his day off. I could come up. It will all be fine. I think we both keep saying the word "fine," to try and convince or at least rationalize with ourselves. Once again, if I say it enough, it will be true. I'm not sure it will be.

I can feel a palpable lightening of Davis' mood, once we finally talk through the plan. He seems relieved. Relieved to be able to design all summer, relieved that the talk is over or relieved that I am okay with him going? I am unsure. I just know he, outwardly, seems happier than I do, inwardly.

During the conversation, we move from sitting up on the bed to lying down. Davis on his back, head against the headboard, me, on my stomach, clutching a pillow as if it were a life preserver and looking up at him. When we have come to the end, agreed on what happens moving forward, Davis finally touches me. He brings his hand up to the side of my face and strokes his thumb downward. He wipes away a tear that I didn't even realize escaped from my eye. Crying from sadness or just exhaustion? I don't know. It doesn't matter.

He says only four words, "Thank you for understanding," before bringing his other hand to my face and then pulling my whole body up to and on top of him, kissing me with tenderness and meaning. I'm shaking. We make love slowly and carefully, as if apologizing in advance for our upcoming time away. It feels different, but in a way even more powerful than some of our frantic passionate times together. Davis kisses every part of me and makes sure to leave me shuddering, long after he is out of me. The last thing I remember is kissing his chest and letting out a long cleansing sigh.

***

"Wake up, Biz … Lizard, wake up, baby. You don't want to be late to your own graduation, do you?" Davis is rubbing my arm, almost shaking me. I groan and pull the pillow up around my ears with both hands. I don't want to hear it. It's too early. He's persistent, scooping his arms around me, pulling me close. I eventually open my eyes and am rewarded with Davis' devilish smirk.

I inform him, "You snuggling me is not inspiring me to get up."

"What is it inspiring?" he asks with an arched eyebrow.

I giggle and smirk back, then shyly say, "Other stuff," while bumping my pelvis up against him.

Davis laughs aloud, "Sorry, sleepy-headed Lizard. Not enough time. Later." And he smacks me on the derriere. "UP!" is what he leaves me with as he pops out of the bed and strolls completely naked into the bathroom. I open my eyes wider to take in the view. He's got a nice ass. I think I'll follow that ass. As I get up to do so, I look at the alarm clock. Crap! I only have one hour to get ready and be in line at the arena for the graduation ceremony. Why did I sleep so late? That's right. It was a long night of talking and well, non-talking. Smile.

I have never prepared for something so important in such a short amount of time ever before in my life. Davis and I make it to Chandler Arena, park and get in line in our caps and gowns with about five minutes to spare. We are in alphabetical order so Davis is ahead of me in line. I can see the tops of his shoulders and his head. Every now and then, he looks back to smile and roll his eyes at me. We made it. Graduation.

We walk in to the traditional Pomp and Circumstance. Once we are seated, by some fluke, I am seated behind and only two seats down from Davis. We can see each other. I could lean up and talk to him if I wanted. I shouldn't be surprised, since our last names are close in the alphabet. Brandon and Connelly. Sounds like a law firm.

I try my best to focus during the ceremony, but am way internally distracted. I keep replaying last night, going over the details of how Davis and I are going to make our relationship work long distance for awhile. I think about last summer. How alone I was. How scared I was of my behavior after the Neil and Robyn incident. Then I skate into dangerous thought territory… a place I haven't been for a long time. Randall. I still didn't really have any awareness of what happened with him before I ran away back to my hometown last summer. I decide, sitting and paying half attention to the graduation speaker, a famous sports announcer from our town, (interesting choice, but a Weldon grad), that I will call Dr. Matt this summer and see what he thinks about delving into retrieving that memory. The pros and cons. Something to focus on other than work while Davis is gone. A little self-improvement project, of sorts.

A concussion of applause stirs me from my thoughts. As I come back to the present moment, I notice Davis looking back at me, his head cocked, a questioning, concerned look on his face. He's clapping with everyone else, but focused on me. Davis mouths the words "OKAY?" I nod my head yes and join in with the applause.

The conferring of degrees takes the longest part of the ceremony, with each of us taking the stage to accept our empty folder (the actual diploma will arrive later in the mail) and a congratulatory handshake from the Dean. I don't think I've felt that many camera flashes since the night the photographers snapped us going to HeartSmash. Davis, Smitty and I are the only ones graduating from our group of friends. Suzette is graduating, too. I no longer consider her part of the group. The rest have one or two semesters to go. I pay attention until Smitty's name is called during the S's, then I get antsy. I just want a little more time with Davis before he leaves.

After the last diploma is given out and hats fly up and then rain back down on us like a flock of flightless crows, the three of us, Davis, Smitty and I find each other in the fray and then our people. Beautiful Kathleen leads the crowd of our well-wishers, waiting outside the staging area, toward us. She has eyes for no one but Smitty and he for her. She practically jumps into his arms and smothers him with kisses. I have my hand in Davis' and give it a squeeze as we both look at them, so happy together. Davis reaches out and pats Smitty's back as we pass by. Smitty never looks up from Kathleen's face. He just answers Davis' silent congratulations with a "Thanks, man," and is right back to kissing Kath.

My mom and dad, the Lt. Governor and Mrs. Brandon, Jules, Charlie, Mel and Kris are all waiting there to greet us. I kiss and hug Mom and Dad. They hold me tight and tell me over and over how proud they are of me. For a moment, we are just our little family of three again. Jules interrupts, hugging my parents as much as I am. They are hugging her right back. I feel a hand on my elbow and turn to see who's touching me. It's Charlie. He pulls me out of the Mom-Dad-Jules huddle and takes me aside where nobody can hear us.

Wrapping me up in a big hug and lifting me off the ground, he finally says a bit hoarsely, "Hey."

I realize I am hugging him, in much the way I was in the picture taken by Smitty. Just not as fiercely. It's hard to wrap your legs around someone in a dress and remain appropriate, so I don't. I pull back a little to talk to him and smile, "Hey, Charlie."

"I just want you to know you'll always be a sister to me. I would do anything for you. I don't think I ever told you that before, but I thought you should know that's how I feel. You're my second favorite girl." With the last words he looks at Jules. "Congratulations, Bizzy."

"Thank you, Charlie Boxwood. You're my second favorite guy." I smile even bigger and for some weird reason start to feel choked up. "I love you, too." I say the words he didn't say and we both sob a bit.

Davis appears, along with Jules, and breaks up our impending cry fest.

"What's going on over here? Who loves who?" Davis sounds slightly irritated.

I break any tension with, "I love all of you," and then proceed to hug and kiss Davis, Jules and Charlie. "Let's get out of here and celebrate." I really have no idea where we will go. With all that has been going on, I hadn't thought to plan any sort of post-Graduation party or reception or anything.

Davis turns me slightly and I see his parents waiting a few feet away. No one is near them. My parents are talking to Mel and Kris and Smitty's parents. "I think they'd like to congratulate you," Davis bends slightly and whispers sideways into my ear. I shiver a little. It never ceases to amaze me that at the most average of times with the most average of words, Davis' voice, his breath on my face and ear can make be so excited, so hungry for more of him. I shake that thought off and go to the Brandons.

James Brandon, the former Lt. Governor, seated in his fancy motorized wheelchair, looks dashing in his dark suit and tie. He is beaming as I approach. When I get close enough, he reaches out his stronger hand. I take it and bend to give him a kiss on the cheek. "There she is, there's my future daughter-in-law. Congratulations, Biz. It's a big day, huh?" he says. I nod. "And more big days to come..." James winks at me. It makes me smile bigger. Honestly, my emotions are sort of all over the place. Practically crying with Charlie, now bursting with joy with Mr. Brandon. I straighten up and come face to face with Meredith Brandon, Davis' mother. Perfect Meredith Brandon. Perfectly groomed. Perfectly coiffed. She is smiling at me – a perfectly fake, practiced smile.

"Biz, congratulations." That's it. That's all she says, along with her fingertips-only handshake. No hug. It is perfectly awkward. Thank God Davis has arrived. He puts his arm around his mother's waist and then his other around me and pulls me next to him. Flash! Flash! And poof, I appear in my first Brandon family picture. I hope I don't look like a complete idiot. It's anyone's guess what expression has been captured. Smile, surprise, frown. I only hope I wasn't rolling my eyes at Meredith when it was taken!

Any concern I had about where we would all go after graduation was not needed. Davis, of course, planned everything. He conspired with Jules and they arranged to have the outdoor patio area at The American Bistro reserved. I don't know who is paying for all of this, but there is an open bar and passed hors d'ouevres when we arrive. Later a light buffet is served. It is so nice and such a treat. A beautiful closing to my college days.

***

It was another late night. This one much more celebratory than the somewhat tense night before. The party moved to our condo after The Bistro and got a lot more casual. Smitty and Kathleen wound up staying in the guest room. The decision for Kathleen to move in was finalized.

My parents are leaving early this morning, so I said good-bye to them last night. Davis is caravanning back to the Chicago area with his parents on Monday morning. We have one more day together. There was no discussion about it, I guess we just reached some sort of silent agreement that no plans were to be made for today, our last today together for twelve weeks. We spend the day doing ordinary, everyday things. In the morning – eating breakfast, lying in bed, watching the news. Once we finally extract ourselves from the bed sheets after some very sweet kissing and cuddling, Davis begins to pack. I help him find things or sit and watch the process that, will eventually end in him leaving. We don't say much, but are never out of each other's sight and are frequently touching or nudging one another. It feels like we are trying to catch each crumb of one another while we can. While Davis is packing, I drag a box or two into the bedroom and unpack my things.

There is something strange about settling in while at the same time, getting ready to let him go. I can't even pinpoint what is going on in my head and heart. It's on the verge of panic, but not really. I thought I had felt heartbreak before with Neil, but this is altogether tougher. I am not angry, I am not hurt, I'm proud and hopeful and sad all at the same time. I am excited for Davis' new adventure and starting my own in two days. I just wish we were doing it together. I've been so preoccupied with graduation and Davis leaving.

I haven't thought much about my new job at The Forest Park Theatre. I start on Tuesday. All I know right now is that I am to be there at 8 am, when all the production assistants will be assigned their areas. They asked a bunch of questions about interests and abilities at the interview and on a questionnaire I filled out and mailed in. Sounds like they are invested in getting the right person doing the right job.

I move to the large walk-in closet I now share with Davis and begin organizing my clothes. I have never had such a large place to keep my things. I won't need to put away clothes between seasons with all the room in here. I empty two boxes of clothes, always with Davis in sight, just outside the door. We keep looking at each other and giving small sad but reassuring smiles to one another. When I hang up the last shirt from the last box, I turn to the doorway to glance out at him again. I don't have to look far. Davis is standing in the doorway of the closet, leaning with his upper arm propped high up on the door jam and his ankles crossed. His fitted t-shirt is pulling up to reveal his rippled lower abs and his happy trail, leading down to the edge of his boxers peeking out of his low slung jeans. Bare feet. I did it. I, blatantly, took a quick "eye tour" of him, top to bottom.

He catches me with his shining green-eyed gaze, "You've been very quiet… too quiet."

I stand almost frozen, taking him in. I want to run into his arms, but if I do I'll miss capturing this picture of him in my mind. When I finally speak, I blather, the words just come out without thought, "My head and my heart are fighting. My internal referee was working really hard at keeping them quiet. I thought you wouldn't notice."

"Umm, the silence was deafening." Davis says with a smirk, "Now, put down that empty box and get over here, because even that little bit of chatter you just gave me has me turned on."

I walk to him, my head cocked slightly, "Mavis … really, just a little talk from me? That's all you need?" When I get to the closet door, I push him back slightly with two fingers and pin him against the door jam. He chuckles at my girly aggression.

"Not ALL I need…" he replies, as I run my hands up and down his chest and he holds my upper arms.

I look at his t-shirt. It's light brown and highlights his wide shoulders, biceps and pecs. Speaking of pecs – emblazoned on them, on the shirt, is a picture of a chicken and a cow. I look up at him in confusion. "What's up with the farm animal shirt?" Davis chuckles even louder.

"Tell me what you see on it."

"A chicken and a cow"

"Uh, huh," He is leans forward and kisses me on the forehead and temple, while tugging my hips towards his, "and what color are the chicken and the cow?"

My core is warming as he pulls me closer. I can actually *feel* him laugh. I look at the t-shirt again. "Brown. Brown chicken, brown cow ...so?"

Davis' arms are completely around me, his hands have taken purchase on my ass and he is grinding into me. He is completely hard. The friction against my jeans and underwear make me hold my breath and exhale suddenly.

"Say it faster"

I do. "Brown chicken, brown cow"

He nods for me to repeat it. "Brown chicken, brown cow." Oh my God, it sounds like, "Bow-chicka-bow-wow" – the porn movie guitar riff. I've never seen porn, but I've heard people sing that phrase before. I finally get the joke. I'm just about to laugh, but pause when a picture of Randall flashes in my mind. Where did that come from? I shake it off and push out a little laugh. It feels a little fake, strained. I check Davis' face to see if he noticed my hesitation. He didn't. He's laughing harder that I finally "got" the t-shirt and is working his way down my neck with kisses. It's helping me to push away the Randall memory blip as I give into the feeling of Davis holding and touching me.

In between kissing and working on unfastening Davis' jeans I ask, "*Where* do you get these shirts?"

"It's my secret hobby. Ever since you laughed at the first one, I'm on a mission to find more that make you smile," he reveals. I give him the big smile he's worked for.

"There's my girl," Davis tells me.

I push up on my toes and against him to kiss him more, make him mine. I do all this while unzipping and pushing his jeans to the floor. He steps out of them. We are still standing, using the door jamb for support. I'm burning with need and my nipples harden almost painfully. I grab the bottom of his t-shirt and rake it over his head, only removing my lips from his to let the shirt pass between us. Davis bites and licks at my mouth, eventually opening my lips, licking and biting my lower lip, pulling at it slightly. When I come up for air, I notice, for once, I am the one with more clothes on. I take another look at him. No shirt, and a pair of boxers shorts with … are those? Lizards? On them? Davis planned all this to make me laugh.

"Nice boxers," I quip.

"It's my way of having Lizard in my pants at all times." Davis looks very pleased with himself.

"Good boy," I praise him and then suggest huskily, "Let's take them off," bugging my eyes at him.

"In a second." We begin walking around the bedroom, hand in hand, Davis tugging me slightly behind him as he draws all the black-out curtains. I don't mind at all tagging a bit behind him, watching his tight lizard covered butt. "I'm glad I finally got you talking, I couldn't leave you so quiet." He turns to me on our journey around the room and pulls me up against him again, "I will miss that chatter. I wonder if it will have the same effect over the phone." What? Is he talking about phone sex? I slowly shake my head back and forth. I don't know the answer to that question.

Davis has closed all of the black-outs. There are only the dimmed bedside lamps on. It makes the bedroom into a darkened, secluded cave. Davis walks me over to the bed and slowly undresses me. He doesn't kiss me or touch me in any way other than to remove my clothes, but his eyes touch me everywhere. I am shuddering with anticipation. Aching for him to touch me anywhere.

"I turned off our phones. I locked the bedroom door. I am not letting you out of my bed or my arms until tomorrow morning."

I can't argue with his plan. I don't want to be anywhere else. I don't want to think anymore about him leaving. I don't want to feel sad or mixed up. I just want to be swept up in Davis.

Finally, once I am in only my black boyshorts, Davis starts at my jaw and with the backs of his hands runs them slowly down my neck, over my collarbone and over the top of my breasts. He turns his hands over to cup my breasts, massaging them luxuriously. His thumbs roughly isolate and stroke my already hardened and now aching nipples. One of his hands runs down my side, as he ducks his head to lick and then suck a nipple into his hot lips. Sucking hard and rotating his tongue on my sensitized nipple, I feel the sensation lower, a pulsing and releasing beginning to take hold. I have barely moved, except to push slightly into his hands and mouth.

I haven't touched him, but now I can wait no longer. I push one of my hands into his boxers and take ahold of his plush hardness. How can something feel so marble-like, but warm and velvety? Touching him heats me even more and I moan with every touch.

Davis has moved on. His mouth has left my breast and moved onto the other and then down my side. He kisses across my stomach, stopping to swirl his tongue in my belly button.

I am unable keep my hands in his boxers. Now on his knees in front of me, I run my fingers through his silky hair, giving it a bit of a tug. Davis groans in response and lifts his head to catch me with his guy-linered, and presently, heavy lidded eyes. Heat and desire shoot right into me from them.

Grabbing my hips, Davis seats me on the bed and then lifts each of my feet so my heels are on the bed. I am wide open to him. He positions me, all the while holding my visual attention. Coming up tall on his knees, his body between my knees, he plunges his mouth onto mine and kisses me dizzy. He finishes the kiss and then immediately ducks his head and continues the kiss – between my legs.

His tongue is masterful. Delicate strokes, followed by increasing rotation and deep suckles, repeated over and over. At first my hands are in his hair, but then it becomes so intense, I must lean back on my palms to absorb the building tide of sensation upon me. I hear unintelligible moaning and garbled vocalizations and only after I come up from the dizzy spin of my deep orgasm do I grasp that it was me making the noise. Davis crawls up my body to kiss my lips.

"Oh my God, even your orgasm chatter gets to me. I am a complete goner for you, Lizard. You are aware of that aren't you?"

"I think it's more like me that's the goner, "I answer, still panting from my climax.

Davis' erection is insistent and pushing into me as he settles between my legs. He slides it against my already slick neediness, starting my build again.

I beg with my body, pressing the soles of my feet against the mattress and elevating my hips to meet him. He rears back slightly and then plunges slowly and deeply into me. After holding fast for a few moments, Davis begins a stroking measured rhythm that escalates into a powerful pounding rocking. I contract around him again and again – clawing at his buttocks – urging him deeper. Davis hands are on the mattress on either side of my head. I feel them push down as his back arches and his eyes squeeze close and his mouth opens and he growls out, "Biiiizzzz," and he empties himself into me. I shudder around him, falling further into bliss.

I promise myself I will not sleep tonight. I will hold Davis and kiss him and touch him until the moment he leaves.

***

I broke my promise. I fell asleep. I have awoken, one of the rare times, *before* Davis. The room is still dark, except for the bedside lights, left on all night. I have no concept of what time it is. I take the time, the little time left, to admire my beautiful sleeping fiancé and take as many mental snapshots as I can.

Davis alerts suddenly, his eyelids flying open, his expression wild as he yells out, "No," and grabs at me and pulls me tight to him. He is squeezing me so hard, pulling me closer to his chest. His heart is racing in my ear. I can actually feel his pulse pounding.

I run my hand down across his shoulder and ask gently, slowly, to give him a moment to regroup from whatever caused his alarm, "Are…are you alright, Babe?" He doesn't answer but I can sense him checking his own breathing and then is slows. "Mavis?" We both pull back from the clutch to look at each other. I am concerned.

"I, uh, I had a bad dream," Davis explains. Then he removes one of his arms from around me, lays on his back and runs his hand repeatedly through his hair. It's an infrequent gesture. I've only seen it before when he is irritated or concentrating very hard on something. I get no more information from him. "What time is it?" he asks and then reaches for his phone.

"I don't know."

Davis turned our phones off last night. I hadn't thought to turn them back on or check the time.

"Oh, crap!" Davis says after his phone tunefully turns on. "I'm late. I have a bunch of messages from my folks. Crap. They are actually outside waiting." He turns quickly to me and says with deep sincerity, "I am so sorry, babe. God, I hate to leave this way, Lizard, but I have to go…Now." He is already up and out of bed, throwing on his Lizard boxers and farm animal shirt. I move to get up and he turns on me quickly, "No," he says, "I want to have the memory I take with me, be of you, lying there, cuddled in our bed, your hair all mussed up after being made love to all night."

I give him a small smile and roll my eyes up to the ceiling to try and stop myself from crying. He pulls on his jeans and then sits down next to me on the bed to put on his work boots. I think he knows I'm barely holding it together. A small tear runs down one of my cheeks and I swallow a few times, working hard not to release any more. I want to be brave. I do.

Davis moves closer, gathers me in his arms and kisses me deeply, fully. His lips leave me and I am instantly wanting. We sit there a few moments more, forehead to forehead, breathing each other in.

"Don't cry. I'll be right back. I'm never really away from you, ever." Davis sighs and points to my heart, "Here," then pulling away, brings a hand up to my forehead, points to my head, "or here." He slides his hand down to cup my cheek and I tilt my face into it.

I can barely get the words out, my voice choked by the pending crush of tears, "I LOVE YOU, Davis, You have no idea how much."

"I LOVE YOU, Lizard and I think I do know how much." Davis voice sounds shaky.

I push him away gently. "Go … you have to go,"I say quietly, feigning that I am okay and in charge. Davis gets up and walks to the bedroom door, then turns, strides back to me one more time and kisses me – a slow, deep, not to be forgotten kiss.

Upon standing up, he tells me, "Don't go anywhere. I swear I'll be right back. It will be like no time at all. I want you right there when I return."

He points to me, then the bed and then flashes me his panty-scorching smirk.

Then POOF! He is gone.

I sit in our bed, numb. I let the tears roll out. I do not sob. I just let them come and smile thinking of his last words and his smile as he left.

Chapter 6-JUNE

It doesn't feel like "no time at all" *at all*. Davis has only been gone for two weeks and they have been the longest two weeks I've experienced since last summer. A long two weeks, even with lots of transitions happening. The first change happened about 25 minutes after Davis left, when I suddenly realized … I had no transportation. Without Davis and his car, I had no ride to work. I, we, had gotten so used to being together that I just forgot about needing a way to get to my job at the theatre, since he was no longer going to be working there and taking me. About the time it hit me, my phone rang.

"Biz?" It was Davis. I already knew from the caller ID. The way he said my name was a bit frantic.

"Of course, Mavis, who else would it be?"

He chuckled at my mild snarkiness. "Hey, I'm turning around. I just realized you don't have a way to get to work. You're car-less." What? Turning around? What can he do about it now?

"I know." I giggled. I really had no idea why I was giggling. It *was* sort of a problem. "But I don't know what good it will do you to turn around. You can't give me your car. You'll need it up there." I had an idea. "Hey, how far is the theatre from the condo, do you think?"

"I don't know, a mile and a half, two?" Davis guessed.

I offered a solution. "You know what? I can just walk to work. It will be good for me. Or maybe I'll start running."

"Lizard, are you sure? Because I can come back now and we can figure something out. I don't mind."

I reassured him, although I'd love for him to come back, "Yes, it's fine. And if you come back now, I don't know if I could say good-bye again. I might just lock you in the condo and not let you leave."

"I'd let you," he whispered. "I was secretly wishing for something to make me turn around."

I toughened up. "No. You keep going. It's all going to be fine. It will all work out. Call me when you get in and get settled. I love you." Davis told me he loved me too. We both breathed out heavily and after about a half a minute of hanging on the line with each other, said, "Bye, baby," almost simultaneously.

***

So now I walk or run the two miles to the theatre in the middle of the park to go to work. I shower in the dressing rooms. At night I walk home. Sometimes my new boss gives me a ride.

My new boss is Evan Wright, co-producer at The Forest Park Theatre. He is the younger business partner of the producing team, Black &Wright (pun intended). Evan is only 30 years old. It's pretty impressive in the theatre world to be a successful producer at such a young age. Evan's partner is Paul Black, who's in his late fifties. Paul has been in the theatre business for a long time. I get the feeling he is a bit of a fast talker. Someone my mother would call a "schmoozer." Evan became Paul's assistant after leaving acting a few years ago and only recently did they form Black & Wright Productions. The way I see it, Paul has all the connections in show business, but Evan does most of the leg work.

The first day of work at FPT, all of the production assistants are brought into one of the rehearsal halls. We are each called by name to meet with the Production Manager, Joe, and given our assignment. I don't know why or how I got the position as Evan's assistant, but I am extremely grateful. Along with actually getting a little money, I am learning a ton. And my job is primarily indoors, which is a bonus on the sticky summer days that occur in this river city. I feel a little bad for the PAs that are assigned to the stage managers or with a build or run assignment outdoors, because it can get hot during the day. I think I got very lucky.

Evan is a pretty great boss. Unlike his partner, he doesn't expect me to call him Mr. Wright. He told me straight up to call him Evan and he calls me "B." When I introduced myself as Biz, he tried calling me "Busy Bee." Umm, I shut that down right away. It's one thing for Davis to call me Lizard Breath or Lizard. He's the love of my life, my future husband. Evan just met me and we're colleagues. In my most diplomatic and charming way, I negotiated him down to B instead of "Busy Bee." It's far more tolerable. I never feel subservient to Evan. I don't fetch coffee or pick up dry cleaning. Very often Evan will bring *me* lunch. He likes to say, "I'm not your boss. We are partners in crime." I have to say, it is really an enjoyable working environment and Evan is probably my first non-school friend.

My task as Evan's assistant is primarily keeping the production office running. I answer the phones, take messages, arrange meetings, manage some of the other production assistants when they help out and generally just try to make things run more smoothly.

I was only in the office a week when the phone rang.

I answer it in my usual fashion, "Black & Wright Productions at The Forest Park Theatre. This is Biz Connelly."

"Um, Hello … Biz, is it?" A familiar voice with a New York accent replies, but does not give a name.

"Yes, how may I help you?" I ask.

The familiar sounding voice continues, "I would like to talk with Paul." I giggle inaudibly at the way the voice says "tawk" and "Pawl" for talk and Paul. It's driving me crazy not being able to recognize this voice.

I have to ask. "May I say who is calling?"

The voice answers, "Billy." Huh? Billy who?

"Billy who?" I press for more information.

Now the voice on the other end sounds a bit put out. "Billy Joel."

OH MY GOD! It's Billy Joel. The Piano Man. Big Shot. *I* have been speaking to Billy Joel. After a silent freak out during which time I have put my hand over the receiver, jumped up and down and whispered to everyone it the office, "It's Billy-freaking-Joel," I count to five to thwart a panic attack and then ever so professionally walk into Paul Black's office and announce that Billy Joel is on the line. He seems unimpressed, picks up his phone and shoos me out with a wave of the back of his hand. I hear Paul say, "Billy, babe...," as I leave.

***

This job is the distraction I need. I am lonely without Davis. Kathleen has moved in and Smitty is there a lot, but the condo seems too quiet without Davis' presence. Kathleen and Smitty are very wrapped up in each other. They spend a lot of time making out on the sofa when they are at the condo. It only makes me miss Davis more to see them so happy. I spend longer and longer days at work. Evan tends to work late, too. He's married. His wife, Guiliana, is currently in a production of A Chorus Line on Broadway. I get the feeling he's lonely, too. We eat dinner together in the little theatre café a few times a week.

I haven't seen Jules in a long time, even though we talk every day. Boxwood is out doing gigs and festivals around the region for the summer, and Jules is traveling with them. I read about how well Boxwood is doing in the local arts paper.

Whenever someone asks me, "How are you?" I say fine. I am not fine.

Fine.

I hate the word fine. It is descriptive of nothing. Socially acceptable filler with no true meaning. It's what you say when you are checking your feelings, unwilling or unable to let yourself be too happy or too sad. Fine. It's an emotional bookmark. A pause until you can continue the story.

In that way, I guess I *am* fine. Living in the pause. The pause in my story with Davis.

I keep busy while at work, distracting myself. I miss Davis. I talk to him every night, but the talks are getting shorter and shorter. His shows are going up soon and he spends hours in technical rehearsals, only able to call me during his 10 or 15 minute breaks. He calls it "guerrilla theatre." The hours are bad, but he sounds exhilarated by his work. I can't admit to Davis how much I wish he were here with me. I make a conscious effort to be upbeat during our phone conversations. I am proud of him and never want him to feel badly about being away from me. In between tales of the theatre and excitement about his show, Davis never fails to tell me how much he loves and misses me – how he misses sleeping with me and making love to me. A few times I fall asleep in bed listening to him talk. When I do, Davis always calls in the morning to wake me up and tell me he loves me. Sometimes when I hear his voice, my body actually aches for him.

Suzette. This is another aspect of my summer that is less than terrific. Suzette, my ex-RA colleague from Weldon and "ho" that slept with my boyfriend, Jake, was hired as the assistant to the design team at the FPT. She runs the design office on the opposite end of the building. Fortunately, I don't have to go to that end of the hall very often. When I do, she always has a shitty smile on her face and a dig to fire my way. I went for a few days before discovering she worked down the hall from me. That was sort of a 'cherry on top of the sundae' moment for me. As I walked by the design office, I found Jake leaning over the desk and kissing Suzette on the forehead. I froze and stared. When they saw me staring, Suzette grinned and ran her hand across Jake's chest. Jake turned to me and blurted out, "Biz!" sort of apologetically. I saw him move to come toward me, but Suzette tugged at his shirt and pulled him back. Was he going to come talk to me? Really what was the point? Seeing them together was just another reminder that they were together and I was alone. I was having quite the pity party for myself.

***

I'm not altogether sure when the shift occurred, but at some point I decided enough was enough. I was not going to be with Davis for many more weeks, so I threw myself into my work. I surprised even myself, when doing so helped me to be less sad and the time move more quickly.

A few highlights of my summer at Forest Park Theatre:

Number 1: Not only did I talk to Billy Joel, I hung out and had dinner with him, and Evan and Paul, when he came in town for the opening of our production of his show, Movin' Out.

Number 2: I was assigned to pick up a certain very talented starlet from the TV show Nashville from the airport. We went back to the bar at the hotel, had a drink and then went shopping. She was a hoot! The day was an unexpected gem.

And Number 3: Evan told me I was invaluable to the team and began dropping hints about hiring me full-time, to work with them even after Black & Wright went back to their home base in New York. I can't tell if he is serious or if it's just one of those things people say to make another person feel better. It's working either way. My self-esteem is pretty high right now. I can almost forget for a few moments at a time that Davis isn't here in town with me.

Chapter 7-JULY

Tonight, I'm going to get all dolled up and cut loose. Why? Because it is late in July and the last show of the summer is opening at Forest Park Theatre. There is an opening night party for every show, but since the shows are in back-to-back rep with only one day off a week during rehearsals, once the first show opens it's like a runaway train. Rehearsals for the next show happen during the day and the current show runs at night. If anyone in the company parties too hard, it is not good the next day or for that night's performance. But the last opening night party is different. There is no rehearsal the next day. Nobody needs to be at the theatre until right before show time the next evening. Everyone looks forward to finally getting to sleep in and having their days free, to shop or hang out or pack. The entire season closes in seven days. It's a bittersweet time.

I am attending the show and party with Evan. I asked Davis to come home for it, but he couldn't get away. The show schedule at his theatre did not allow for it. Davis and I haven't seen each other all summer. We've videochatted on our laptops and I am always happy to see him and hear his voice, but it's not the same as having him with me. Honestly, the videochats and phone calls have become a bit strained. We are truly living two different lives. He tells me about his shows and challenges. I relate stories about the cast and crew at The Forest Park Theatre. I even told him about having to endure seeing Suzette and Jake on a regular basis. He got a bit growly about that, telling me to steer clear of both of them… like I hadn't already planned on that. Some days all Davis and I get to do is text each other "Good Morning," "Goodnight," and "I Love You." I didn't think our schedules would be so different, since we are both working at theatres, but mine is in an office and Davis' is more technical. Only two more weeks and he'll be home. Then school starts for him and I'll be unemployed – again. But at least we'll back in the same city, the same house, and most importantly, the same bed.

Evan is picking me up at the condo after I run home to change for the show and party. It's nice of him. It means I can wear heels tonight. I have a really fun summer dress, too. It's a 50s vintage halter dress. A rich chocolate brown color, which looks great with my red hair and pale skin. It may be summer, but I am not a tanner, at all. Five minutes in the sun and I am as red as a lobster. SPF-Indoors for me. The dress has ruffles on the bust of the fitted bodice, a matching belt and a full skirt. I pair it with tall brown and pink polka dot ankle strap stilettos. If it were daytime, I could add a hat and be perfect for a garden party. I feel prettier than I have in a long time. I haven't really paid extra attention to my clothes or grooming since Davis has been gone. I haven't been a slob or anything, always professional. I just haven't felt the need to go all out. I look in the mirror to see how the outfit looks and decide to add a pair of swingy silver hoop earrings. Evaluating myself, I decide to take a selfie and send it to Davis. Weird, it's not something I'd normally do, but I want him to see how nice I look and maybe miss me a little more.

After I snap a few shots, I pick two to send to Davis – one showing the whole outfit and another, a close-up with me blowing him a kiss. Just as I hit the send button, the doorbell to the condo rings. I put my phone down and go to answer the door. It must be Evan.

Evan enters the condo, looking very handsome in a beige summer weight suit with a pink shirt and no tie. It almost looks like we called each other to match. As he comes through the door, after I open it wider and invite him in, he puts a hand on my hip and leans down to kiss me on the cheek.

"You look amazing, tonight, B." Evan says while pulling away from the kiss.

I automatically thank him. Strange. Evan has never been so familiar with me. I don't think he's ever even touched me before other than to shake my hand. The other strange thing is that I kind of like it and it makes me anxious and a little panicky that I do. I never really thought about Evan in that way before now. He *is* handsome, there is no denying it. Tall, lean, a dancer's body, as that is what he did before he became a producer. He met his wife while working as a performer on a cruise ship. I try to act cool about the kiss and turn away quickly, inviting Evan to make himself at home while I go to get my purse. I catch myself putting my hand up to my face where he kissed me and picturing his face as I walk into the bedroom. Then I stop and mentally scold myself. Why am I thinking about Evan? Why am I thinking about his brown hair that is not quite as dark as Davis'? Shorter and wavier. His warm brown eyes, so different from the green ones I adore and miss so terribly. That's it. I'm lonely. I miss Davis. I'm not excited about Evan. I just haven't been touched intimately in weeks and weeks. I haven't even had the energy or desire to touch myself. I take a deep breath, repeat my hardly used mantra, "I can do this. I can do this," and remind myself that in five minutes any panic will be over. As I reach for my small brown wicker basket purse, I glimpse my phone out of the corner of my eye. Davis' face and his words, "I swear, I am going to staple that cell phone to your forehead," run through my mind. It makes me smirk to myself. I check to see if Davis has responded to my selfie and then throw the phone in my purse. He hasn't. A little bit of disappointment washes over me. I wanted it to be Davis that told me I look pretty.

Evan calls to me from the other room, "Hey, B, I just got a call. There is a little trouble with something backstage. I told them we'd be right over. Are you ready?"

"Coming." I call out to him. Then I take one last cleansing breath and join him to leave the condo. Again, Evan touches me. Ushering me out of the door with his hand on my lower back. I don't know how to tell him not to do it. And, really, I don't know if I want him to stop. It's harmless, right? A flutter of panic shoots straight to my chest.

***

Arriving at the theatre, Evan rushes off to put out whatever fire caused the phone call. I hang out by the backstage gate waiting for him to finish so we can go into the show together. I check my watch a couple of times. They won't let you in the theatre after the first number starts. It's getting close to curtain time. Evan appears as I look up from my watch for the fourth time. He smiles a huge smile while rolling his eyes and head at the same time.

"What was the emergency?" I laugh, knowing this will be good.

"Some emergency." Evan bites out sarcastically, "Our darling leading lady was flipping out because her newest sugar daddy did not have seats directly in front of the stage."

I have to know, "How did you fix it?"

"Don't be mad, but I gave them our seats," he tells me, raising his eyebrows and wincing a bit.

I tell him it's fine and I mean it. I take his arm, locking my hand around his elbow and say, "Let's go." We take our seats just as the announcement about no flash photography and turning off cell phones echoes across the large outdoor auditorium. I quickly pull out my cell phone, check one more time to see if Davis has responded, and when I see there isn't a message from him, I shut off my phone and slip it back in my purse.

***

The show is, of course, wonderful. Black & Wright Productions chose to end the season with a hometown favorite, Meet Me In St. Louis. It is especially poignant since Forest Park Theatre is right in the middle of what was the fairground of the 1904 World's Fair described in the play. The show ends with a rousing audience sing along of the title song.

The closing night party is different from other cast parties. It is sponsored by several local businesses, so the food and drink are a little more upscale and there is a real DJ, not just the sound crew with an iPod. There is even a red carpet to walk. It feels a bit over the top, but I just go with it and link arms with Evan again to enter the party. We stop for a couple of photos as we walk the carpet. Wow, the business office went all out on this party. I think it is all an act until I see Smitty taking some of the pictures. Kathleen is standing next to him. She must be on assignment for Arch Scene magazine. I shoot them both a look like, "Can you believe this?" They both just smile and then Smitty snaps a couple of pictures of me with Evan. Again, I feel Evan's hand on my back and wish it was Davis'.

I have a couple of drinks. I know it's not the best idea given my current mood, missing Davis but pretending to be fine, but I just want to have some fun. I have been working so hard all summer – long days, late nights. I deserve a bit of fun. I am nothing if not good at rationalizing. After I dance with practically every male cast member, and some of the females too, Evan asks me to dance to a slow song. I didn't think he would. He's been spending the whole night networking. I noticed him chatting up Gail, the TV producer I met last semester in class. Evan really is a very good dancer. I don't even have to think about where I'm going or what I'm doing, I just follow his lead. Evan brings up the subject of me coming to work for Black & Wright again. I tell him I'd like to discuss it more, but not tonight. We agree to meet for breakfast in the morning, but not too early, to go over what the job would mean. Just as I am about to tell him I'd like to go home, Evan bends down, breathes out a sigh and attempts to kiss me. I am about to go with it and then, *I stop him*, gently putting three fingers up to his lips before he goes any further. "Evan, you are very good to me and very attractive …"

Evan interjects, "But?"

"But you don't really want to kiss me. You're lonely. I've heard you talking to Guiliana in your office. You're crazy about her. And I'm lonely, too, BUT we can't go there. We can't kiss each other because we miss *them* – Davis and Guiliana. It's not right or fair to any of us."

Still holding me in mid-dance, his head on my forehead, Evan agrees, "I know, I know. You're right. I just miss Guiliana so freaking much."

I continue gently. "Ev, I don't want anything spoiling our friendship. I really like you. You are the first real-life grown-up friend I've ever had. My partner in crime." My last line makes us both laugh. Later, when I think about it, I get it. I do love Evan, not love like the way I love Davis, not a sibling-like love like I have with Charlie. It's sort of a professional friendship/respect kind of love. We stop our "non-dancing" dancing, settle on the details of meeting for breakfast and, since its after one o'clock in the morning, Evan takes me home. By the time he drops me off any residual awkwardness from our nearly intimate moment is gone. No goodnight kisses, just a friendly handshake.

I take off my pretty dress and my cool stilettos, pull on Davis' HOT SPOT t-shirt, sniff it to inhale any remaining Davis scent, wash my face and get in bed. Right before I put my tired self to sleep, I check my phone. I realize it's been off since the start of the show. Shoot, I wonder if I've missed a message from Davis. As it cheeps on, I see I have one message — from Davis.

> It says, **You look so pretty. I wish I was there to show you off.**
> I text back quickly, **I am so sorry, my phone was off for the show. I'm glad you liked my outfit. When you're home, I'll let you take me out in it (and take me out of it ;) Soon. Goodnight, Mavis. I LOVE YOU. (and yes, I am shouting that.)**

I wait a few minutes, no return message. I put my phone on the charger, roll over and let sleep take me. Tomorrow, I'll meet with Evan and maybe, get a new job.

***

There is no message from Davis when I wake up. It's not like him to go so long without even a short text back. I am starting to get a bit worried. I send one more text to him before changing into my running tank, short and shoes and leaving the condo.

> **Are you okay? I haven't heard from you. I am beginning to worry. Please text me back.**

Kathleen and Smitty's shoes are in the front hall, so I know they haven't gotten up for the morning. It's only 7:30. I really didn't expect them to be awake. I don't know why I am up, except I told Evan I'd have breakfast with him and I might as well run over and get my work out done at the same time.

Evan's rental apartment is only about a mile and a half away. That's fine with me, I am really not in the mood to run any further than that. It's already 85 degrees and muggy outside. I'm starting to get more than worried about Davis' lack of texting. I'm starting to get mad. So much so that as I run I decide to call him. No answer. By the time I reach Evan's, I am in a bad mood and sweaty. Oh yeah, did I say I hate sweating?

I'm huffing and red-faced with exertion and emotion as Evan opens the door. I don't even say hello, I just gruff out, "Ugh, I am so gross. I didn't think this through, running over here to meet."

Evan chuckles at me as he opens the door wider and gestures me in. "B, you are fine, but if it would make you feel better, I don't have breakfast finished, so go take a shower and then we can eat and talk."

"I'll just have to get into my gross stuff again." I say, putting off the idea.

"Borrow some of my shorts and a t-shirt. Just grab anything. Bedroom and bathroom are right through there." He points through an archway into what I can see is his bedroom.

A shower sounds like a great idea. I am seriously hot, sticky and smelly. I search around Evan's room and find a black t-shirt and a pair of shorts. He doesn't really have many clothes to choose from. I take them into the bathroom with me. I lock the door and check that it's secure – twice. I take off my clothes and pile them on the floor. I'll ask Evan for a bag to put them in to take home. The shower feels delicious. It is such a good feeling to get clean after being such a mess. I'm naturally nosy, so I check out Evan's toiletries in the shower. He has very expensive shampoo, conditioner and body wash. I wash myself thoroughly and rinse off smelling like amber and sandalwood. Manly. I'm drying myself with a fluffy dark gray towel, thinking about how wonderfully soft it is, when I hear loud voices through the bathroom door. I recognize Evan's voice, but it takes me a moment before it registers that the louder voice is Davis'. Davis? What is he doing here? I finish drying myself, grab the t-shirt and shorts, rake them onto my body and wrap my hair with the towel. After scooping up my dirty running clothes, I hold them in a ball against my chest and open the bathroom door with my other hand. Davis' voice is louder.

"Where is she? Where is Biz?" He sounds really angry.

"She's fine, Davis… It is Davis, right? Hey, B, Davis is here!" Evan yells to me matter of factly.

I move through the arch just in time to see Davis lock eyes with Evan and then shove his shoulder and say even louder, "B? You call her B? YES, IT *IS* DAVIS. HER FIANCÉ. DAVIS. NOW, WHERE THE FU—"

"Fuck is she?" I say evenly, but loud enough to be heard, since it looks like a fight is about to begin. Davis and Evan disengage. Both of their heads turn to find me in the archway and they slowly stand down. "Right here," I add. There is a long, incredibly painful pause as Davis and I regard each other. It is impossible to correctly describe the emotions flying through me right now. He's here! Davis is here! He's okay. He looks… terrible. His hair has gotten longer and it's disheveled, like he's been running his hands through it repeatedly. Not a good thing. His eyes are red with dark circles under them. He looks exhausted. Oh, I've missed him. I want to run to him. But he's mad. Why is he mad? *I* should be mad. He hasn't been in contact.

"Liz-ard?" Davis says with a hitch in his voice, "What? What's going on?"

"Nothing. I came over here to have breakfast with Evan and talk about a job." I spit out.

"Why are you in his clothes? Why is your hair wet?" Oh my God. He thinks I'm cheating on him. He thinks I've been with Evan. Doesn't he trust me? I have to tell him plainly he is wrong.

I sigh and explain slowly so he can't miss what I am saying, "I ran over." I hold up the ball of dirty running clothes to make my point. "I took a shower. End of story. What are you doing here?"

Davis pushes past Evan to come toward me. I can't bring myself to move toward him, even though I want nothing more than to hold him and reassure him, but his palpable anger is not allowing me. I catch Evan watch the scene unfolding in his apartment and shrug at me. He puts up a hand to tell me it's okay and backs away into the kitchen.

As Davis comes toward me, he is manipulating his cell phone, pulling up something on the screen to show me. When he gets close enough he holds it up. It's a photograph of me. With Evan. On the Red Carpet. Evan's arm is around me. We are looking at each other and smiling.

"What …" he says and then pulls the phone away from me and swipes his finger across it's front, "the hell is…" swipe, swipe, "THIS?" He holds the phone up to me again. It's a picture of Evan and me, slow dancing, at the moment right before I stopped him from kissing me.

I drop my head, in a move I quickly realize looks incredibly guilty. "Where did you get that picture? Who sent you that?" But I already know. It was Suzette. I saw her at the party. I saw Jake there, too. And nobody else would send Davis those kind of pictures of me. They were sent to cause trouble.

"What does that matter?" he yells, then says softly, "You kissed him."

I quickly pick my head up and engage him visually. "Davis, I DID NOT kiss him." I tell him the truth, as emphatically as I can without screaming.

Davis puts his head down and shakes it back and forth. I take a step toward him, but he puts up both his palms to stop me. "Don't. Don't lie to me. I didn't stay. I told you I would and I didn't and now you've moved on."

Moved on? What is he thinking? I suck in a loud breath and steady myself. I am so focused on Davis, his anger and pain that I don't hear Evan enter the room and say in a very calm voice, "She didn't kiss me, man… I tried to kiss her and she stopped it."

Davis head flies up, his beautiful, currently bloodshot eyes wet and burning with rage. I nod to acknowledge that what Evan is saying is true. Davis turns and moves to attack Evan, I can sense it, so I run between them and push my front into Davis, securing his gaze. "Davis, baby … don't, don't go after him. Just…" I don't know what to say, so I tell him to go home. "Just go home." Davis' face drops, his expression moving from fierce anger to supreme hurt and confusion.

"You want me to leave? You want to be with him?"

I elaborate on my direction and stroke his chest to try and calm him. "No. I want you to leave and go home before you do something you'll regret. I need to gather my stuff and my thoughts. Evan will drive me home." I also need a minute to calm myself down.

Davis makes a grunt of protest.

I insist. "Mavis, I need to talk to Evan." I turn my head away from Davis briefly to catch Evan's eye, "We can do that while you drive me back to the condo, right, Ev?" Evan indicates that yes we can do that. Turning back, I hold Davis' attention again and firmly tell him, "You and I can talk when I get home. I'll be right there."

Davis goes reluctantly. It kills me to watch him walk out the door of Evan's apartment. I don't hug him or kiss him. I send him home. I only hope he'll be at the condo when I get there.

***

Evan drops me at the front door to the condo and asks, "Are you okay to go in there and talk to him alone? He's pretty mad."

I nod and press my lips together to keep from making any noise. I am barely holding it together. "Yeah, I'm good," I gasp out, "It would only make it worse if you went in with me. I'll call you later."

"You better."

"I will."

Evan makes me promise. "B, swear you'll call if you need me, okay? I am always here for my 'partner in crime.'"

Evan's joke name for our relationship takes on a whole new meaning at the moment, so I tell him, "I just hope Davis doesn't think we were partners in anything else."

Evan reassures me, "You've done nothing wrong, B. Nothing. Hey, we'll talk about the job on Monday at work, okay?"

I nod and press my lips together harder and get out of the car, still holding the ball of dirty running clothes. I never did get a bag.

Opening the door to the condo, I only have to look up from taking the key out of the lock to be immediately struck down by a pair of green eyes. My favorite green eyes, shining with tears and rimmed with red, boring into me. Davis is leaning against the back of the sofa that is about six feet away from the front door. He appears to have taken a shower, because his hair is wet. He is wearing his WARNING t-shirt, the one he had on the first day I met him. Some moisture from his skin is seeping through, making wet spots on it. He's got on gray lounge pants. His feet are bare, crossed at the ankles. His arms are crossed, too. His whole posture tells me he is closed off, but his eyes look like they are searching.

I stand just inside the condo after absentmindedly closing the door. Finally, in a thick voice and almost forcing the words out between inhalations, Davis says, "You didn't stay where I left you. I wanted to find you at home in our bed when I came back. Not coming out of some other guy's shower." He finishes the statement with a half sob/sigh, like he's relieved to have said it, but barely holding back.

"No, I wasn't where you left me. I gladly would have been right there waiting for you..." I attempt to raise my voice and succeed a bit, but my anger is being tempered by my own impending tears, "IF YOU HAD TOLD ME YOU WERE COMING! Why didn't you tell me you were coming? Why did you rush down here? Why didn't you just call me? Call Kathleen? Have her get a hold of me? What were you thinking?" I am shaking in my spot a few feet away from him. Why can I not go to him? I am so confused, angry and sad and excited to see him. It's all mixed up in my head and heart.

Davis is shaking too. He explains his actions. He got my selfie pictures and it made him ache to see me. I inhale and sob more when he says that. He couldn't reach me and, then he received the OTHER pictures, the ones of Evan and me. He didn't think, he just got in the car and drove all night.

He got to the condo this morning, apparently right after I left to go to Evan's. He woke Kathleen and she told him where I was. I don't know how he knew where Evan's apartment was exactly and I don't bother to ask. Davis still seems tentative, uncertain, and neither of us makes a move toward one another. It feels like some force is pushing me away and pulling me toward him at the same time. Like the feeling when you try to force the poles of magnets together.

I take a deep breath. My mantra has been playing in my mind for minutes now. I am actively panicking, trying to hold it together. I exhale and say, "Davis, I'm sorry. I didn't do anything. Evan and I are friends. He's my boss. That's all. Do you believe me?"

Davis swallows hard and answers, "Yes, I believe you. I'm just a jealous asshole. We've been apart for too long. I never should have gone. I should have stayed. We are not doing this again, ever."

I still don't move toward him, but I want to relieve some of the hurt, "No, I don't think we should ever do this again either. I think we are better when we are together. I mean, I learned a lot this summer. I learned I can function on my own, be independent. I also learned I don't like it very much. I was pretty miserable if you get right down to it, but I survived. I'm sorry. I was only trying to have a little fun last night. I'm sorry you saw those pictures. You can get so much from pictures, but in this case the pictures aren't telling the whole story. I was just acting. Acting happy, forcing fun to forget I wasn't there with you. Believe me, I was missing you, thinking of you the whole night. GOD DAMMIT! I am SO pissed at Suzette. It has to be her that texted you that crap! Who else would do that? I want to strangle her." I sob and totally shift gears, "Mavis, I love you so much... I... I am so happy to see you. I am so happy you are back." Then I laugh like a maniac, because for someone who is so happy, I am crying uncontrollably.

Davis smiles, his big beautiful smile that goes right up to his eyes. His shoulders visibly relax and he uncrosses his ankles and arms. Warmly, invitingly he asks me, "Then what are you doing way over there? Please let me hold you. I can't believe we are in the same room and you are so far away. If you are so happy to see me, come over here and let me hold you, Lizard Breath."

I'm crying and laughing at the same time. Laughing so hard my shoulders shake. Davis, still propped against the sofa, opens his arms wide and spreads his feet apart and invites me to him. I walk right into the space between his legs and into his arms. Nothing has felt better in a long, long time than his firm, encompassing embrace and being pulled right into his chest. I slide my hands up his arms and loop them around his neck, immediately tangling my fingers in his, now much longer, silky dark brown hair. I dip my head to the space between his neck and shoulder and take a big inhalation of him. The t-shirt I've been sniffing all summer has been a sad substitute for his amazing smell in real life. I can't stop telling him I love him.

Holding me tighter, bringing one of his hands to my hair and stroking it back repeatedly, he tells me slowly and sincerely, "I have missed your breath on me. I have missed you telling me you love me. I have missed your chatter. REALLY missed your chatter. Lizard, I ADORE YOU. I FUCKING LOVE YOU. And obviously, by my actions, I CAN'T LIVE WITHOUT YOU."

I can wait no longer. My lips are on his, biting and sucking. I am practically trying to consume him, it seems. He slows me down by placing both hands on the side of my face and then he kisses me slower and deeper than ever before. His tongue opens my lips wider and I give in to all the sensations, letting it ignite me everywhere. His hands move from my face. One of his arms reaches around, grabs my backside and pulls me even closer into him. I am completely straddled by his legs and I feel his growing hardness. I want him so badly. I pull away from our kiss with the intention of leading him to the bedroom, when his other hand appears between us, palm up, with a small red leather Cartier box in it. I look down, confused. Is that what I think it is? Now? After a huge fight? In the middle of making up?

I shift my eyes up to him and then down to the box and, while pointing at it, say just what I thinking, "Is that what I think it is?"

Davis chuckles deeply and finally, happily, "Depends on what you think it is, but probably, yes, it is what you think it is." He moves me back slightly and then just like every girl dreams of all her life, he gets down on his knees and asks, yet again, "Lizard, I am so in love with you and I never want us to be apart again. Please marry me. Soon. Please wear this always, so everyone knows you are mine." Then he opens the box and the most gorgeous diamond ring I have ever seen sparkles before me. It is so *my* style. A large, to me it looks *really* large, cushion-cut diamond, set almost invisibly in a silver-colored diamond pavé setting. Davis tells me it's platinum. There are no prongs. The diamond looks like it is just floating in the setting. Wow!

I am crying again. This time with the most overwhelming joy. "Of course, I'll marry you. I already told you, Mav."

Davis beams, jumps to his feet and scoops me up in his arms. "Good. When?"

"I don't know. Let's talk about it in bed."

"After we take everything off?" He asks with a tilt of his head and a smirk.

"Everything but this." I hold up my beautiful new engagement ring. Our promise to never be apart again. "I am NEVER taking this off…if I do you will know something is really wrong…" Then I add, and I don't know why, "and you need to come and find me."

With that Davis picks me up off my feet and carries me to the bedroom, kissing my neck the entire way, as I hold my hand out and away from me to admire my ring. My ring from him. The love of my life.

***

When we get in the bedroom and after a bit more thigh burning kissing, I have an idea. I push Davis away, but immediately reach for his hand.

"Davis, I want you to give me a minute…"

"No, Lizard, no more minutes…"

As I tug him back toward the bedroom door, he is resisting and trying to yank me back into his arms. He succeeds as we approach the door and

I'm reaching for the knob to open it. He pulls me back toward him, my back to his front, his arms wrapped around my waist. I could easily give in and let things progress, but I think he will REALLY like what I have come up with, so I lean my head back on his shoulder and kiss him fully. Coming up for air I tell him, "I have something I want to do for you, so I need you to be a little patient. Go outside the bedroom for a minute.." Davis opens his mouth to protest, but I cut him off, "Just... a minute, then knock on the door, okay? Humor me."

Reluctantly he agrees, "Alright, just a minute, no more," as he walks through the door and shuts it.

I am out of all my clothes in seconds. Then I run and dive into the middle of our bed. I position myself prettily, sitting upright against a pile of pillows. Pulling the dark brown sheets up so they cover only the bottom half of my breasts, I hold the sheets to my chest with my left hand, my new ring facing out. KNOCK, KNOCK. He wasn't kidding about only giving me one minute.

"Come in." I say, almost not recognizing the deep hot voice I am using.

Davis steps through the door and follows the trail of clothes I've left like bread crumbs with his eyes to finally land his gaze on me. He looks so delicious to me right now, I could jump up and grab him. Hmm, my fiancé. "Look..." the throaty voice has not left me, "I'm right where you left me. But now with extra sparkliness...." I switch the hand I am holding the sheet up with and wiggle the fingers of my hand with my dazzling engagement ring on it, at him. The somewhat concerned look Davis has had on his face the majority of the time since his return is completely overtaken by a huge devilish grin and arched eyebrow.

He growls, "I like you in nothing but a big diamond."

"I thought you might."

He leaps, that's right, leaps onto me, landing with his head at my chest.

"Mmm. Perfect landing," he informs me, resting his head on me and lightly kissing the tops of my breasts. Lifting my chin to give him more access, I put my hand in his hair and run my fingers through it and pull him slightly closer. His hands come up to slowly remove the sheet and cup my breasts. He takes a moment to regard them and then inhales deeply.

"Seems I've missed these too." As I look down at him, I see a half smirk on his lips, before they cover a nipple and draw it in. My heart is racing. I feel my breasts become full and my lower abdomen warm. I had not allowed myself to feel this while Davis and I were apart, but it only takes minutes for him to bring me to arousal.

We are in our usual state, Davis fully dressed and me completely naked, as things begin to heat up. I think he really does like it this way.

I question him about it. "You have too many clothes on. How come I am always naked first and you completely dressed?"

"You're the one that took all her clothes off first this time."

"True." I admit, cocking my head and gazing at him coyly.

"You could help me take mine off, but I have to warn you, once you do, I can't make love to you slowly, 'cause I'm not gonna make it much longer." Davis has already started removing his shirt and I join him to rip off his lounge pants and boxers. Still in the process of undressing, he crashes his lips to mine and begins to drive me crazy again. I can't keep track of where we are touching or what part of me is moving where. I can't touch him enough, everywhere. I know his hands go to my breasts again and then skate over my waist and hips. One finally arrives at the apex of my legs and I rock into it, my clit demanding friction, which Davis willingly and skillfully delivers. I slick up almost instantaneously, perhaps more from the intensity of our kisses than anything. Our moans give away our growing need. I reach down to feel Davis' hardness and run my fingers over his balls. A powerful shiver that I can appreciate travels through him and with a loud growl he pulls me swiftly down on the bed, his hands on my hips. Once there, he opens my thighs by running both hands firmly down my inner thighs and pins me at the knees. In moments, he is in me, hard, pulsing and wanting. We pause for a moment and I take in the full, stretched feeling I haven't felt in so long.

"God Damn, you feel tighter than I remember," Davis hisses into my ear before rocking with perfectly timed rhythm, causing my build up to escalate. We rock and rock into each other, eyes locked, until I can't continue and I close my eyes to absorb all the sensation.

We come together, frantic, loud and over-the-top.

There is a knock on the door.

"Welcome Home, Davis!" Kathleen shouts through the bedroom door, mischievously.

Oh my God, we were really loud.

Chapter 8-AUGUST

Davis went back to Chicagoland Shakespeare Festival for one more week, and worked out a deal to leave early. I went up on the Megabus the day after our last show closed at Forest Park Theatre to see his last show and drive back with him.

Now we are back home together, getting used to living together again. To be honest, it's a bit awkward. We are both unaccustomed to sharing space. Kathleen is still here, but moving out to live with Smitty soon. Davis will be back at Weldon in a few weeks, working on his Master's and teaching. My mother has been pestering me all summer about wedding details, but since Davis hasn't been around I haven't felt like I could make decisions. We have about three weeks until school starts up again. It's time to start planning.

Oh, and I am unemployed. Davis says not to worry about it, but I need to find a job. Evan offered me a great opportunity with Black & Wright Productions, but I am not willing to leave Davis, so I turned their New York offer down. Evan stays in touch and told me if an opportunity arises with Black & Wright here, it's mine. And by the way, I have a standing offer to come back as his "partner in crime" next year at Forest Park.

I try to push my concern about being unemployed to the side and enjoy the uninterrupted time I have with Davis right now. He's pretty enthusiastic about it. We spend time getting me completely unpacked, since I left some of that undone in his absence. It is starting to feel like "our" place instead of just his. Nothing right now is rushed – we are just focused on being together. It's been great to have this time to discuss wedding plans and we are very close to picking a date. Davis insists it MUST be before the end of the year. I have no idea how we could possibly pull it off that quickly. Thank goodness for my mother. The minute we decide on something, she runs with it and makes all the arrangements, but she is limited until we settle on a date. So, we have colors and flowers and the men's attire decided, in theory. I still need to find a dress. And a place to get married. And a date.

The "no-job" thing didn't start to bother me until Davis went back to school this past week. I spend all day every day while he is gone looking online for a job. It's Thursday and I think I may have to take out a loan and go to graduate school if I don't find something productive to do (that pays) pretty soon. Taking a break from my internet searching, my head in my hands and on the verge of screaming in frustration, my phone alerts. I push aside all the junk on the desk to retrieve it from its papery burial site. There is a text. From Evan.

> **Hey B. How is the job search going? Ready to come to NYC yet? :)**
>
> I text back. **Terrible. I can't believe how depressing this is. I swear I am going to apply to Law School or Hairdressing School or something.**
>
> Evan: **I think your talents would be wasted doing either of those things. My friend Gail is a producer at one of the TV stations there. She is looking for a production assistant.**
>
> Me: **Gail Patton?**
>
> Evan: **Yeah. You know her?**
>
> Me: **I met her in my Production class last semester. I think I have her card here somewhere. Is she really serious?**
>
> Evan: **Yeah. Find that card and give her a call**
>
> Me: **Should I?**
>
> Evan: **Yes, now**

Me: Okay. Thank you so much for thinking of me, Ev
Evan: Anything for my partner in crime
Me: Yes, we are a regular Frank and Jesse James!
Evan: More like a wimpy, platonic Bonnie and Clyde! But,
whatever. Stop texting me and CALL
Me: Okay. Bossy. Talk later

It takes me what feels like ages to find Gail Patton's business card. I remember that I put it in the back pocket of one of my pair of jeans when I got it, but couldn't recall which pair and if I'd worn them since I moved in with Davis. I've worn mostly shorts or cute little dresses this summer. I think I've only put on a pair of jeans a half dozen times.

After checking all the pockets of all my jeans, I recall that I shoved a bunch of business and rewards cards I'd collected over time into a small square box that I use to hold buttons, safety pins and other tiny objects. I saw it while we were unpacking the last of my stuff. My eyes fall upon it the instant I enter the walk-in closet in the master bedroom and flip on the light. Davis must have placed it next my jewelry box on the built-in dresser we share. I take it down and rummage through the pile of cards. The card is there, close to the top. I put everything back in the box and place it back on the dresser. Then I pace back and forth in the closet a few times, reading the card. I wonder to myself if I should e-mail her or just call. Evan said to call. I am so nervous. What if she doesn't remember me? Should I drop Evan's name? I take in a huge breath through my nose and blow it out my mouth, while silently and rapidly repeating my mantra, "You can do this, You can do this." Then I add, for extra positivity, "You got this!" I call. Gail Patton answers herself, no secretary. I tell her my name and how I know her. She remembers me and tells me that Evan Wright recommended me highly. Gail basically conducts an interview over the phone, telling me as we wrap up that after she receives my resume, there is no reason this job shouldn't be mine. It's all a matter of having Human Resources talk to me and having my references checked. I thank her profusely. If it all goes well, I should be working in a week or so.

By the time Davis walks through the front door of the condo, I have a job! That's right. Gail got right on it and by 5:00 p.m. I got a call from Human Resources at KTTA-Channel 5 offering me a position as a production assistant in the newsroom. I start the day after Labor Day. The minute I hear Davis' key in the lock of the door I launch myself from the barstool at the island, where I have just gotten off the phone. The poor guy barely has the door open, when I jump into his arms, ecstatic with my good news. He catches me in a loose embrace.

"I have a job!" I say with genuine glee.

"Really, where?" Davis asks chuckling at me. I haven't even given him time to put down his keys and computer bag. The bag is bouncing against my butt as I jump up and down wrapped in his arms.

I take his bag and keys from him and place them on the hall table. Then I lead him to one of the sofas. "Channel 5-KTTA. In the newsroom."

Davis pulls me in for a kiss and right before he does, whispers, "Congratulations." Davis kissing me is very distracting. I can get lost in the feeling very easily and I think he knows it. I am about to give in, when he sits me more upright, stops the kissing and with a playful smack on my thigh, questions me further, "So, how did all of this happen?"

I would love it if we would just go on kissing, but I am also excited to tell him the details of my employment. "I was here, looking online for jobs, moments from tearing my hair out and looking for a good cosmetology school to go to or something…"

Davis shakes his head, "Terrible idea."

"Whatever…anyway Evan texted me and told me to contact Gail Patton at KTTA. He knows her, and I met her in my Production class at Weldon at the end of the year. I even got her card. So, Oh my God, I was so nervous, but I did it. I called her and she interviewed me over the phone. I emailed her my resume; HR reviewed it and called with an offer. And now, you are looking at KTTA's newest production assistant!"

"RA, PA, You are all about assisting aren't you?" Davis teases me about only taking jobs with the word "assistant" in them. I roll my eyes at him. I don't see any problem with being an assistant. I need to pay my dues and I haven't been out of school for any time at all. I've been very fortunate so far. Davis doesn't disagree, he just tells me he thinks I am meant for more. Out of the blue, he brings up my therapist, Dr. Matt and the 'Don't hide your light" lecture he once gave me.

"You are going to be very big one day, Lizard, I just have a feeling. I don't know what it will be, but I just know you'll be successful." Wow! Where did that come from?

I slide up next to Davis and run my hand up his thigh from his knee, "Thank you, baby. I appreciate your confidence in me. Really, I am just relieved to have a job. I don't know about "making it big," I don't really think about stuff like that. I just want to be good at whatever I do."

"You are. You wouldn't have found this job so soon if you weren't. Now, before you 'assist me'…" Davis says with air quotes and a smirk, "can we set a wedding date? There are only four more months left in this year and if we are not married by December 31st we are flying to Vegas or some Caribbean Island and tying the knot and you, my little Lizard Breath, will be dealing with the wrath of your mom."

I inhale through clenched teeth and wince in mock horror, "*That* is a terrible idea!"

"I thought that might motivate you a little. That and I am not kissing you again until you get your calendar and we do this, now." I throw Davis a pout, which he shakes his head at to indicate it won't work. Then he points to my cell phone on the island in the kitchen. He wants me to get it to look at the calendar. I push myself up off the sofa, walk over and snatch up the phone. I'm trying to act annoyed, but I'm not, really. Returning, I plop onto the sofa with a faux huff.

"Okay, let's do this." I tease, adding an eye roll for effect. It does nothing. Davis is on a mission. He takes the phone from my hand and goes to the calendar app.

"Since September is next week, which won't give your mom any time, we are going to have to look at October or November. Personally, I want October – early October." He is so persistent.

"How about October 11th?" I suggest. "It's the day after my parent's anniversary."

Davis looks up from the phone suddenly, with a puzzled look on his face, "That's so weird, October 11th is *MY* parents anniversary."

It must be destined. October 11th it is. We both call our respective parents and then I call Jules. We agree to meet the next day for lunch in the Weldon cafeteria. Once I hang up with her, after squeeing, giggling and jumping up and down, I make my way back to Davis. He is just hanging up from talking to his parents. Leaning over the back of the couch I throw my arms around him from behind and kiss him on his neck below his ear. "Can we kiss now?" I ask.

Davis flips me over the back of the couch, so that I land, somehow, straddling his lap. I like this position. I can feel his growing excitement under me. "Definitely. Let the celebration begin," he growls in my ear, as he thrusts his hands into my hair and pulls me hard up against him. I put my hands on his wide, capable shoulders and then slowly slide them down his chest. I notice Davis suck in a breath between his teeth. Pleasure? I not too delicately rip open the snaps on his modern western-style shirt and quickly spy a large gauze bandage on the left side of his chest over the place where his COLE tattoo is.

"What's this?" I ask, a little more concerned now than turned on. "Are you okay?"

Davis bites both his lips between his teeth to try and suppress a smile. "I'm fine. It does sort of sting a bit if you touch it, but nothing is wrong." The full smile breaks through as he reaches up and pushes my hair behind my ears and holds my face in his hands. "Don't look so worried, Biz. I just had a little modification done to my tattoo. I hope you'll like it, 'cause I don't know what I'm going to do if you don't."

Davis runs his hands down my arms and continues to watch me for my reaction. I tilt my head, raise an eyebrow and ask, "Can I see it?"

"Sure. My tattoo guy said I have to keep the bandage on for 24 hours, but I think I can give you a peek. It is all shiny from the medicine they put on it." Davis slowly peels off the top edge of the bandage to reveal his old tattoo of his brother's name, COLE, now inside a red heart with an elaborately detailed and brightly colored lizard wrapped around it. The lizard's head is resting happily on one of the bumps of the heart and the tail is entwined around the point at the bottom. I examine it visually. It is unusual and beautiful in its meaning. At least, I think I know its meaning. Davis anxiously presses me, "What? Say something. What do you think?"

I keep my facial affect flat, I don't want to give anything away just yet. "So, the heart around COLE, that's Cole always in your heart, right?"

"Uh-huh."

"And I am hoping the lizard symbolizes me…"

"Yep."

"And I am wrapped around your heart?"

"Yes, you, my little Lizard, are wrapped around my heart, you have my heart… you protect it. You and Cole…You will always stay with my heart. So, what do you think?"

I have tears welling up behind my eyes and a huge lump in my throat. "I…I think it is the sweetest thing I have ever seen. I think you and I are the only ones that will understand it…"

"Nobody else needs to understand it."

I agree, "Exactly… It's strange and beautiful and perfect." I want to touch it, but I know it is still sore and the area needs to stay free from germs. There will be plenty of time to run my fingers over it – for the rest of our lives. The thought makes me smile.

Davis is watching me look at his tattoo and when I gaze up at him he asks, "Happy?"

"Really, really happy. You?"

"Yes, I'm happiest when I am with you. I find it amazing how I feel like I always will be… happy… like nothing can hurt us now," Davis muses.

I swallow a few times. Small, almost undetectable swallows. I have a nagging sensation of anxiety I haven't had in a while, but I push it down. Davis is right. Things are really good. I need to manage my panic. Own it. Don't let it own me. I don't know why that feeling just washed over me. Weird.

Davis reapplies the bandage over his newly modified tattoo and then places both hands flat on the sofa on either side of my thighs. "Well?" Davis queries, "aren't you going to continue? Was the tattoo that distracting?"

I laugh and sock him on the bicep, lightly. The right one. I don't want to get too close to the tattoo. "I remember where I was, thank you very much...I was just wondering how careful I should be about the bandage and the tattoo?"

"Let me worry about that," Davis chuckles and then slides his recently absent hands from my knees, up my thighs, to grasp me purposefully at my hips and then thrust himself against me.

"Okay...Deal." With that settled I move ahead with removing Davis' shirt and kissing every square inch of his muscular shoulders and strong chest (kissing around the bandage), every now and then coming up to bite and nip at his lips and chin. He is just letting me – letting me slowly devour him, humming with each touch. He is not kissing back, just running his hands up and down my haunches and pulling us closer together down there. Generally, his hands are all over me, so much so that I can't remember where they've been from moment to moment, but tonight we are going at a slow, steady, luxurious pace. I am on fire.

Davis grabs the back of my neck tightly with one hand and my hip with the other and in a smooth, sudden move has me on my back on the sofa. He is above me, his pelvis crushing into mine, rotating, pushing, stoking the growing burning in my panties. He leans over me, his forearms on either side of my head, his fingertips in my hair, rubbing the strands together. Davis bends his face down toward my ear and husks, "Mmmm, so soft." I think my entire face and scalp blush with anticipation, I feel so tingly.

I want him to feel the same, so I slide my hands down the back of his jeans, over his boxers and grasp his firm ass, pulling it even closer, "Mmmm, so hard," I tell him, mimicking his phrase. I slide my hands around to the front, still in between his jeans and boxers.

"And getting harder," Davis adds.

I quickly pull my hands out and then go after the button and zipper of his jeans. There is way too much fabric between us, even though I am enjoying the delicious friction it causes between my legs. I quickly peel the remainder of his clothes down his thighs. He lost his shoes and socks somewhere during our sofa wrestling, so he kicks his jeans and boxers off with relative ease. There he is above me, in nothing but a bandage and a smirk.

Evidently, it's my turn to be undressed, because as soon as his jeans hit the floor, Davis grasps the bottom of my dark red tank top and causes it to vanish up and over my head. I am lying there in just my bra, panties and white jean shorts one minute and the next minute my Houdini-fiancé has caused them to disappear too. After taking care of all of that, Davis slides himself up my body, using his hands to stretch my arms above my head. He takes both my wrists in one hand, so I am mildly restrained. I have to say, I enjoy it. I bring my legs up and around to wrap around his, rubbing against the backs of his calves.

My eyes widen suddenly and I stop moving. I just realize Kathleen has not moved out and could come home any time. I move to sit up, but am stuck. "Davis!" My voice changes, no longer are my words warm and gooey, but shrieky, "We can't do this here... We have got to move to the bedroom..." Davis is kissing my neck and shoulders, his hands are trying to pull my legs further up.

He tries to calm me, "We're fine…"

"But … She … They … Smitty could see …"

"We are fine, Lizard. Kathleen is staying at her new place with Smitty tonight."

I let out a huge sigh of relief and then almost immediately a groan, as Davis has succeeded in getting my legs open further, placing them up and around his lower back. His rigidity is sliding against my slickness. "I thought we were going to kiss some more," Davis says, raising one eyebrow and a corner of his mouth.

"Uh… okay." I raise an eyebrow right back and press my hands more insistently against his butt, urging him into me. And he does. He sinks into me with a low, deep growl that makes me shiver. I was completely ready for him. More than ready… the build up to getting here feels like it's taken forever. There is no waiting now, Davis is pounding into me, clutching at me, his arms encircling my head, holding tight. I am rotating my pelvis wildly, attempting to keep up. I feel myself get close to falling in and then moving away from release. Then, I feel it…it's so close. I bring one hand to the top of my head. Davis snatches it and pins it with his. My other hand stays on his lower back. He matches that move with his own hand, bringing it under my hip, lifting me, tilting me up, pushing himself into me further with a powerful thrust. Then all I perceive is our garbled, thick vocalizations of each other's names.

Davis stays inside me, rocking slowly and gently as I come back to earth. I'm vibrating from the inside out it seems. He stares down at me, leans down and just before kissing me again, whispers against my lips, "My Lizard."

Gently, I lay my palm against his bandaged chest. He winces slightly and then grins. I am still vibrating.

***

"Okay, Maid of Honor, you know the big news. We only have a few weeks to pull this wedding off. What first?" Jules and I are meeting in the Weldon University cafeteria to talk about the wedding plans and catch up. We chatted over the summer, but not had a chance for real "girl talk" in a while.

"Well, actually, first, you are going to have to stop calling me 'Maid of Honor.'" Jules scolds.

"What? No, you *are not* backing out on me, are you? 'Cause, Jules, I need you. I can't do this. I can't get married without you."

Jules has a huge crazy smile on her face and is shaking her head side to side. "I can't be your Maid of Honor – that would be deceitful. And I, like you, am not going to hide anything or be deceitful, if I can help it, ever again." That sort of gets to me. In my heart of hearts, I know I am still concealing a secret, but how can you be deceitful about something you're not sure even happened? I push the thought away and focus on Jules again to hear her announce, "I can be in your wedding, but only if I am your 'MATRON of HONOR.'"

"Matron of ... What? You're Married?"

Jules shakes her head rapidly, like a bobble head Gwen Stephani, curls once again bouncing. A giggle is welling up in her.

"To Charlie? ... Right?"

"Yes, of course to Charlie. Jeez, what are you thinking?"

"When? How come you didn't tell me?"

The truth comes out. Charlie and Jules have been married since the beginning of my senior year at Weldon – their junior year. Before I met Davis. Almost a year! After spending the summer before their junior year wrapped up in each other, they knew. Knew they wanted to be together always. Build their dreams together – his band, her ... I don't really know what Jules' career path is. She is highly organized. I can see her managing something or someone. So, after three months in summer school together, they ran away – to Vegas. Their first anniversary is on Labor Day. Sneaky kids. I congratulate her profusely and can't seem to stop hugging her. Everyone in the cafeteria must think I have lost my mind. Actually, since I just told her about the wedding date, I have a good cover story in case anyone asks what I was squeeling about. I make her tell me all the details about their wedding and how they have kept it a secret all this time.

"So *that's* what you meant about 'a real wedding' when Davis and I got engaged. Wait, you're still living with your parents. How do you deal with that?" I ask.

Jules opens her eyes wide, shakes her head and heaves a huge sigh, "It...is...killing me. Why do you think I asked you to sign me into the dorm so much? Why to you think I lied to them all the time and said I was with you when I was off with Charlie and Boxwood this summer. I just have to finish college. Then I can tell them. They won't understand and they will kill me, if they learn I got married before finishing school. They are still just barely accepting Charlie as my boyfriend."

"Okay, it's our secret," I reassure her. "So we'll both have to be deceitful a little while longer. You'll be listed in the program as Maid of Honor, I guess." Jules nods with a little resigned smile on her face. Trying to comfort her a bit, I say, "I wish you could tell them and everyone."

Jules sighs again and tells me a bit sadly, "Me, too. You can't tell anyone, not even Davis. Not yet. Soon, but not quite yet." Jules' tone and affect become more positive, "It will happen soon enough, but in the meantime, we have important things to do. We have to go find a dress for you!" And then smiling widely and goofily adds, "and more importantly ME! If I am going to be a Matron of Honor, at least I am going to be a hot one."

A pink flash appears in front of my eyes. PJ (and his hair) have joined us at the table.

He interrogates us as only PJ can. "Okay, ladies, what's going on? There's lots of giggling and shrieking going on over here. I need the dirt, and I need it now. Who's 'going to be a hot one'? Spill."

Jules and I shoot a surprised look at each other and then at PJ. I wasn't ready to have to fib just yet. Having been in practice for almost a full year, Jules covers beautifully, "I'm going to be the hot one. The hot BRIDESMAID, PJ. Davis and Biz have set a date – October 11th. We have to go find dresses today. Wanna come?"

PJ jumps up, comes around the table between us and with one arm around each of us, says, "Abso-fucking-lutely. I am going to ensure you both look amazing, and I'll need to see Biz's dress to make the veil. Come on, ladies. Let's shop!"

Chapter 9-SEPTEMBER

Four hours. I have been at KTTA for four hours and I already know. I love it. I love the energy, the excitement. I love my new job. Okay, I really don't know what my entire job entails and so far the PA I've been shadowing, Henry, has pretty much just delivered papers and gotten coffee for the staff in the newsroom, but this place is amazing. There is activity everywhere. Newsroom staff uncovering stories via the internet or on the phone with sources, guests for the morning news show being escorted to the green room and the live show broadcasting on monitors all around the station. I think this might be a great fit for me. My next stop is a quick lunch with Gail Patton, the producer to whom I will report. Henry walks me to Gail's office and knocks on the door for me.

"Come in!" I hear Gail command loudly from behind the door.

Henry opens the door and ushers me in with a wave and then shuts the door behind me. After taking a few steps in, I stop. Gail is on a phone call and looking out the window behind her. She turns in her chair, makes eye contact with me, gestures for me to come and sit in the chair in front of her desk and mouths "Come in, come in."

I sit quietly on the edge of the chair, my knees together, hands folded on top of them. I survey Gail's office, moving only my eyes to take everything in. I don't want her to think I am nosy. Gail has three, three! Emmy awards. I am not close enough to see what they're for. I can also spot a few photographs of her with celebrities.

"…Okay, okay, yes…yes we will look into covering it." Gail hangs up and switches her focus to me. I stop my visual exploration of her space to give her my full attention. "Biz, welcome to KTTA."

I reply, "Thank you for hiring me. I've only been here a few hours and I am so impressed."

"Well, Evan was very impressed with *your* work this summer at the theatre and I trust his judgment. When he told me you were looking for work, it didn't take me any time at all to remember meeting you in your Production class at Weldon. You immediately struck me as real and personable. Perfect for the kind of television I want to produce. Are you at all interested in being on-camera or are you thinking just production?"

"I have never really considered on-camera other than acting, I'm not trained for television journalism. I'm such a newbie, I guess I shouldn't rule anything out, but I probably should learn as much about the production end as I can before I jump into anything else." I just spit it out, without thought. A typical Biz babble.

Gail is nodding her head with her fingers steepled in front of her, touching her lips, taking in my words. "Hmm…very wise. I think you have the right idea there, Biz. I'm thinking I would like you to work in our Features area. With your arts background and knowledge, associations with photographers, rock singers… sons of politicians…" She *has* done her homework. "… you would do well working on the Happening in the STL show. It's my pet project. I'm very invested in it. I created it and now produce it. What do you think?"

"I, I'd be honored. I'd love to work with you. Thank you, Gail."

Gail, after a moment and a closed lip smile, states wryly, "Don't thank me yet, this production is a lot of work and it's not exactly glamorous at the beginning."

***

I get people coffee; a lot of coffee. All day long. Among other things. I also assist with making sure guests are prepped and ready for their segments, ensuring the green room is stocked, sending copy to wherever it needs to go – the hosts, the teleprompter operator, the producers – and pretty much anything else that is asked of me. Last week, in preparation for a segment about fall, Henry, the other PA on the show, and I drove across the river to an orchard and picked up apples, pumpkins and gourds. I never know what the day will hold and I think that's what I like best about being a production assistant. That, and learning about television production at a breakneck pace. We don't cover the hard news on Happening in the STL, so I'm not up on what goes on in the newsroom. We have a small news update segment created by the news production team and packaged for us to air during our broadcast.

About three weeks into my new job, I'm in the office doing advance prep for a Halloween segment when my phone rings. It's Green Eyes by Coldplay. Davis' ringtone. I've learned to keep my ringer on and answer when he calls. Since the incident with Evan, Davis has been sure to stay in communication with me. I don't mind. I actually feel calmer knowing where he is and when I will see him again.

"Hello, This is Biz" I answer. I know he knows who it is and that I know who is calling. I'm partially yanking his chain and partially trying to portray a professional attitude while at work, in case anyone is listening.

Davis chuckles down the line, "Yes, I know it's you. I, called you, Lizard Breath."

I smile and laugh back, "That's my 'I work at a very important job' voice. You like?"

"I love. And what, Little Lizard, very important thing are you doing right now?" he asks.

"Ummm…researching the best haunted houses in the Bi-State area AND the top ten Halloween costumes for the year on Pinterest." I reply, using my serious and important tone of voice.

Teasing me, Davis counters me, "Baby, that *is* very important. I was going to come and steal you for lunch, but I don't think I can pull you away from such important…"

I cut him off, "No, no. I have time. I do. Please come. I would love to show you where I work and have you meet some people. Um…how far away are you?"

"I'm about 10 minutes away."

I give Davis instructions to call me when he gets to the parking lot and I will make sure that he is let into the station. After I call down to the security desk in the lobby to let them know I'm expecting a guest, I shut down what I am working on, bookmarking what I have been researching before I do. I let Henry know I'm going out for lunch. I figure Davis and I can go eat and then I can bring him back to see the station and meet everyone on Happening in the STL. I gather my crossbody bag, grab my phone off the desk and head through the newsroom. It's just before the noon news, so the activity level is starting to gear up. The newsroom is always busier than our office. There is a bank of flat screen television monitors on one wall, broadcasting each of the local television stations, as well as a few cable news channels, on mute. The audio broadcasting in the room is ours, the feed from KTTA. There are more televisions scattered on the other walls showing the lead in graphics for KTTA News at Noon. Davis' ringtone alerts me and I answer, "Hello, Mavis," while still attending to the monitors. The anchors greet the television audience, telling them the time and date, then I see a familiar handsome face in a mugshot and hear:

> *Our top story this afternoon, local authorities have arrested this man,*
> *Neil Ireland, earlier today. Mr. Ireland, a teacher at a local Catholic*
> *All-Girls school, has been charged with multiple counts of sexual*
> *assault, transporting a minor over state lines for the purpose of sexual*
> *relations, and the production and distribution of pornography. He is*
> *currently being held awaiting a bail hearing. Police are also seeking*
> *information on the whereabouts of this man…*

A picture of Randall flashes on the screen.

Randall Ireland, brother of Neil Ireland, is being sought for questioning in his brother's arrest. At this time, he is not considered a suspect; police would simply like to question him.

Neil and Randall are... brothers? How did I not know that? My heart is pounding out of control. I am sweating and freezing cold at the same time. I look down at the phone in my hand, but can only focus on how much I am shaking – all over. I hear, "Biz? Biz? You there? Hey, I'm here. I'll check in and be up in a sec." I stare at the phone as if I don't know what it is and then realize Davis is talking. He's here. He's going to see the story about Neil. Oh my God, Neil? Sexual assault? And what's all the stuff about crossing state lines and porn? I feel very light-headed and nauseated. I can't breathe. I want to run, but I cannot move. Frozen.

Consciously, I know what is happening, but it doesn't matter, I am pretty sure I am about to die. Full-blown panic is setting in. There is no talking myself out of this, no mantra, no breathing. I am in it. Someone has taken my phone out of my hand, but I can't tell who, because everything in my visual field tilts severely and then becomes smaller and smaller until it goes completely black. I feel myself, still staring at the televisions, the continuing news story ringing, echoing in my ears, collapsing to the floor, my traitorous legs folding up underneath me. I can't see anything around me, but Neil's face appears before me and then morphs into Randall's. Randall is so close. He is grabbing me, kissing me violently, tearing at my clothes. I shake my head and he is gone, but everything is black again. My heart... is going to explode... I am sure of it. I need to make myself breathe, but I don't know how to control any of this.

I can hear voices in the distance moving toward me, but can't see anything. I think I hear someone say, "Yes...her phone. Something's wrong...She's on the floor. Yes, Yes, come up."

The blackness is fading. Dim, shimmery light is beginning to creep into the periphery of my awareness. I perceive that I am sitting up, my back against something hard, my legs bent into a star shape around me. I look down to see my hands flat on my thighs. I take a deep gulping breath and look up slowly. I'm still dizzy, everything around me spinning, except a face. I gasp out a cry. Thank God, a face I know. A face I love. Davis.

"Lizard...what's wrong?" I hear the face I love say. I can't respond verbally. I can only shake my head and pant and gulp for air. All I can see is Davis, moving in and out of my sight. I can hear him talking, I just can't catch everything he is saying. Then Davis yells for someone to find my purse. A sea of faces suddenly surround him. Some look familiar, like Henry. A voice asks him what's wrong. "She'll be fine. She just needs her medicine." Is he talking about my Xanax? How does he know it's in my purse? He's right. I need it. I begin reaching around blindly to help him find my purse. Then I notice that he already has it and is pulling a pill bottle out. I watch, mute, as Davis takes out a pill and asks me, "Is one enough, Lizard?" Somehow, I manage to understand and shake my head yes. He brings it to my lips and I open for Davis to place it on my tongue. Dr. Matt's words come to mind, "If you are in the middle of a bad attack, chew the Xanax, it will work faster." So I do, I chew it.

I can't tell you how long it takes, but soon, more quickly than I believe possible, I have regained perception of my environment. I'm sitting on the floor of the KTTA newsroom, leaning against a desk. My legs are now straight out in front of me. There is pressure against my right shoulder and as I look down at my hand, I see a thumb rubbing against my thumb. I follow the thumb upward to the arm it's attached to, and then the person. Again, Davis. Sitting right next to me, mimicking my position leaning against the desk, holding my hand, waiting for me to calm and return.

"Hey," is all I say.

Davis says it back, "Hey." And we sit there a little bit longer. The newsroom has returned to its previous busy state, with the exception of the occasional person stopping to ask Davis how I am.

"So, that was a panic attack?" Davis asks, quietly and soothingly.

"Yeah, that was a bad one." I finally squeak out a full sentence.

"What happened? One minute you were talking to me, and the next you were gone. Thank God you called down for me in advance and that someone grabbed your phone." Davis' expression is more concerned than I have ever seen before and his voice is low, like he is trying not to frighten a scared animal.

"Umm…let's go back to the office to talk." I am mortified. Here I am, new to this job and I experience a huge panic attack, one of the worst I've ever had – at work. People are surreptitiously looking at me as Davis helps me up and hands me my purse, and we make our way back to my office. I am going to have to ask Gail for help to spin this episode in a more positive direction.

When we reach the Happening offices, I pull Davis toward the cubby I share with Henry. Gail spots us and changes her current trajectory to intercept us.

"Biz? Are you okay? I just heard. You collapsed in the newsroom? What happened?" Gail looks at me intently, but then shoots a questioning glance at Davis.

Time to explain.

I introduce Davis and then motion them to follow me back to the cubby. Turning away from them, I slowly put my purse down on my desk, squeeze my hands together for a moment, let out a huge sigh and then turn quickly and… spill the whole story. I have a hard time looking either of them in the eye for very long. "That news story… about the Ireland brothers… that just broke on the noon news. I… I know him… them… both of them." I lay it all out. How I "dated" Neil in college and he used me and left me. That part is not so hard. Davis has heard it before. Then I move on to Randall, explaining how Neil moved me in with Randall and then ditched me. How creepy Randall was. And then, the big reveal…how before I moved out, ran away, really, from Randall, I think something happened. Something bad. I tell them how I woke up naked and alone in my rented room at Randall's. I suddenly recall, standing there telling them, that there was a video camera on a tripod in the room. How had I forgotten that detail all this time? Davis and Gail don't say a word. They just both come toward me and each one of them takes one of my hands. I'm surprised I'm not crying or panicking. Perhaps it's just the Xanax working.

I continue and as I do, something Suzette said to me while she was tormenting me last winter surfaces in my memory.

"I've known Neil for years … He and Randall are really 'good friends' – almost like brothers. Have a little 'business' going on."

I hear it all in my head. Even Suzette's snarky tone. Brothers. She knew they were brothers. And the "business." Their "business" was – porn?

It all makes sense, even though I don't have complete recall. The pieces come together for me, in my little cubby with Gail and Davis as witnesses.

"It's not entirely clear, but I'm pretty sure I was…sexually assaulted…" Now, I begin to weep softly. Davis sweeps his arms around me and says, "Oh God no, baby." He pulls me firmly into his chest. Gail keeps a hand on my back. I can feel Davis' shoulders and arms tense and release repeatedly. I continue, "I have a vague sense that Randall…umm…videotaped me…with him. I think that kind of might be what is being reported as 'production and distribution of pornography' and evidently I wasn't the only one. Suzette said they, Neil and Randall had a business. I think Neil might be a worse person than I already think he is. Davis, what do I do? Gail? How do I face the people in the newsroom? What do I do with what I know? Do I go to the police? I don't have any real evidence. It's just faulty recollections." I feel a bit frantic.

They sweep into action, my saviors, Gail and Davis. They sit me down in my desk chair and pull their own up close to me. I am never without someone holding my hand or patting my knee. They are making a safe zone for me. After deciding there is not enough information to go to the police with yet, we agree to tell everyone at the station that I became lightheaded from low sugar levels. It makes sense, I *was* on my way to lunch. Gail thinks I should go home and get in touch with Dr. Matt. Davis agrees. I do, too. I didn't have the opportunity to speak with Dr. Matt as much as I should have over the summer. After a bit more time to calm and regroup, we, all three of us, walk through the newsroom together. When people ask, Gail tells them emphatically that I had a bout of low blood sugar and that Davis gave me a sugar pill. Everyone seems to buy the story. When we reach the exit, she gives me a hug and tells me to take the rest of the week off, but to keep in touch. I argue that I can return to work, but both she and Davis shut it down. I have to admit, it is a relief to leave the station. I want to get away from the newsroom. I want to go home.

***

We engage in only the most minimal of conversation in the Escalade on the way home. I know what Davis is doing. He's just being there for me. Davis is amazing. I don't deserve him. He parks in the garage and we get out of the car and continue our slow journey to the condo.

Once inside I tell Davis I am going to the bedroom to call Dr. Matt. He pulls me in for a reassuring hug and a kiss on the forehead. I can sense he is being cautious with me. What must he be thinking, now, knowing that I was possibly sexually assaulted? He has been as quiet as I have, but I've seen him run his hands through his hair a couple of times and his jaw tense. Those are not good signs.

In the bedroom, I sit immediately on the edge of the bed and pull my cell phone from my bag. I search quickly for Dr. Matt's number in the contacts, because even though I probably know his number by heart, I just don't trust myself with anything at all right now. It rings twice and his secretary answers. She knows me well and tells me Dr. Matt is in session right now, but he will out a bit before the hour. She assures me she will let him know I called and that it is an emergency. I will need to wait about 15 minutes to talk to him. I spend the time sequestered in the bedroom. Not ready to talk to Davis about all of this yet, I go to the bathroom and wash my face with soap and water to clean off the tearstains and mascara smudges. Alternating between softly chanting my mantra and breathing with exaggerated exhalations, I feel calmer when my cell phone rings at me from the bed. I take the position I was in before, sitting on the edge of the bed, and answer.

"Hello? Dr. Matt?

Dr. Matt's familiar, soothing voice answers, "Hi, Biz. What's going on? What's the emergency?"

"You know how I've been trying to recall what happened early last summer, when I was living at that Randall guy's house and then woke up…" I'm finding it hard to continue.

Dr. Matt goes on for me, "…naked?"

"Yes…Umm… well, it turns out the guy I was with before him, Neil. Remember, I talked about him?"

"Uh…huh." He confirms that he recalls.

"Well… I have this new job at a TV station and a news story just broke. Neil's been arrested for sexual assault and creating and selling pornography. And they are looking for his brother, Randall."

I hear Dr. Matt inhale a bit and say, "Oh." He is as surprised as I was.

"Dr. Matt, I had a big panic attack when I heard the news. I also had some brief, fuzzy recollections. I think I may have been raped, but I can't remember anything concrete. Why can't I remember anything?" I am once again in tears by the time I say the word "raped." "It seems possible, but not entirely real. Could I possibly be making it up?"

There is the briefest of pauses and then Dr. Matt asks me, "Biz, where are you? Are you somewhere safe?"

I assure him that I am. "Yes, I'm at home with Davis. He's in the next room."

"Tell me about the panic attack. Are you recovered now?" It's so comforting to have someone ask me about the attack that knows about the disorder.

"It was bad. Sudden. I couldn't get my mantra or counting or anything going. I really felt like I was dying, even though I knew I wasn't. It was the strangest feeling. I collapsed, fainted I think. Then Davis found me and gave me a Xanax and I slowly settled down, but during it I had flashes – of Neil and Randall. It's irritating that I can't recall anything clearly." I know Dr. Matt can hear the frustration in my voice through the sobs.

"Hmmm," Dr. Matt hums for a moment into the phone, "Well, Biz, we have talked about the fact that possibly you are repressing the memory of being violated by Randall, but given your ability to recall some of the time before it possibly happened and afterward, when you 'woke up,' and the fact that these men have done this to others… is it possible you were drugged?"

It never occurred to me. I repeat Dr. Matt's last word like I've never heard it before, "Drugged." Before I can say another word or ask more questions, Davis comes flying through the bedroom door, grabs the TV remote off the bedside table and flicks on the television to KTTA.

"Look, Biz." Davis commands me, pointing to the screen with the remote. "Gail just called and said to turn on the TV."

I'm confused and move my gaze from Davis to the TV screen while telling Dr. Matt, "Davis just came rushing in and turned on the TV. Something must have happened." I push the speaker button on the phone.

It's one of the anchors from the station doing what looks like a promo for the five o'clock news. Neil's mugshot appears on the screen again.

> *Neil Ireland, arrested earlier today on charges of sexual assault, creating and distribution of pornography, and violations of the Mann Act, will go to court this evening for a bail hearing. He is expected to be granted bail as he is not considered to be a flight risk. Mr. Ireland is a teacher at a local private school and lives in town with his wife and two children.*

Two children? A video of Robyn, Neil's wife, holding what must be their twins, appears on the screen. She doesn't look as mean and vicious as she did when she confronted me in the cafeteria last year. She was angry and pregnant then, and now she looks like an exhausted mother of toddlers. She's surrounded by reporters. She's asking for her privacy and says the charges against Neil are false. She is still defending him and his behavior, but now she's also one of his victims.

The promo continues,

> *An unconfirmed report says that a 'date rape' drug, such as Rophynol or GHB, may have been used during these alleged sexual assaults. More on this case, as well as all the news, weather and sports at five o'clock.*

The anchor finishes and a commercial comes on. Davis mutes the television. I glance at him and then at the phone in my hand.

"Dr. Matt, did you hear that? Rophynol? GHB? Is that what you were talking about when you said I could have been drugged?" I question sadly.

Davis is pacing the length of the room, arms swinging, his face red, eyes blazing. I think I hear him muttering something about "effing roofies…"

"Yes, Biz. That's what I was proposing. Rophynol has a strong amnesic effect. And you seem to have all the symptoms of amnesia surrounding the time you can't recall. We'll never know for sure, but if those reports are confirmed, it would make perfect sense." Dr. Matt tells me his suspicions as sensitively as he can, while still being direct.

I am lost. I don't know what to do next, so I ask him, "What do I do now, Dr. Matt?" I look between the phone and Davis frantically pounding back and forth.

"Is Davis still there?"

Davis stops in his tracks and turns to look at the phone in my hand. "Yes, Hello Doctor, I'm here." he answers.

The doctor delineates a plan. "Davis, I want you to keep an eye on Biz. Biz, if you think you need to, I would like for you to take another Xanax in an hour. I'd like you to rest. Lay down. Try to sleep. Inviting more anxiety will not help with anything. It will only muddy any recollection or problem solving you have before you. Can you do that, both of you?"

We answer simultaneously, "Yes," and for the first time since the news story broke, we *really* look at each other. Davis comes over to sit next to me on the bed. He puts his arm around my waist, cupping his palm on my hip. I lean my head on his shoulder.

"Okay, Biz, I am going to go now." Dr. Matt is saying good-bye. I wish he didn't have to. "My next patient is here, but I want you to call at anytime, okay? You have my on-call number. You and Davis will have much to discuss tomorrow, but for now, please just rest."

I agree, "Okay, I will."

Davis interjects, "I'll make sure she does."

The three of us say our good-byes, I hit the END button on the phone and allow Davis to hold me a bit longer. We do as the doctor said. I get into a tank top and boxers and climb into bed. Davis puts my purse and a glass of water next to my bed, so I can take my medicine in a little while, then he closes the blackout shades. The room is dark, except for the dim glow of lamps we must have left on this morning.

Davis takes off his shirt and jeans, gets into bed next to me and pulls me close. I put my head on his chest. I have no idea why he is not running from me as fast as he can. I would be. But he isn't. He's here and he whispers warmly into my hair by my ear, "I am so sorry this is happening to you, Lizard."

To us, Mavis, it's happening to us.

***

Dr. Matt was right. Sleep was a good idea. I can tell it the minute I open my eyes and become aware of Davis spooned around me. I know he is awake because his fingers are running through my hair and then going back and smoothing it with his palm in a soothing pattern.

When my eyes are fully open, I spy my water glass on my night table. A flash of recollection hits me and I suck in a breath.

Davis leans over my shoulder and with his hand, turns my face toward his, "What is it? What happened, Lizard? Baby, what?" he rapidly questions.

I recount what I can. The glass triggered a vision of me…in Randall's kitchen, drinking. Drunk, really. Randall snatching the cup from my hand, taking a drink, swishing it around – splattering it over the sides. Could it be could he really have drugged me?

Davis sits up suddenly. His back is to me now. His head in his hands. Running his fingers repeatedly and violently through his hair, his muscles tense in his back and shoulders. I can't help but appreciate how physically compelling he is, even while we are in the middle of something so personally devastating.

"This is killing me, Biz." There is palpable rage in Davis' tone. Low. Dark. What is he saying? Is it too much for him? Is he leaving me? Breaking up? My mind is flying in all directions – many of them negative.

I sigh, resigned, "I know, I'm sorry… so, so, sorry."

Davis turns back to me slowly. His countenance is full of anger, eyes blazing. And there is something else there. Disbelief? "There is nothing. Not. One. Thing. For you to be sorry about, baby. It's those fucking assholes." There is venom in his voice. "Neil. Randall. They did this to you. To us. Don't you worry. They will pay. I WILL fix it for us!"

I stare at him and even though what sounds like a sob releases from my throat, no tears fall and I sense a smile break across my lips. The noise I made must have been all my pent up concern for how Davis was taking this, finally vocalized.

"Thank you." I say quietly. "For understanding, for loving me. I don't know how you think you are going to fix it, but I love that you want to."

I reach up and stroke his stubbly cheek – five o'clock shadow – and urge him to me. I deliver a soft, slow kiss, full of love and appreciation. He kisses me right back with the same intensity. We have a lot we need to discuss, but I relish this moment, because soon we need to get up and plan for how we will move forward.

***

The Ireland brothers story is still in the news but is no longer the top story. Gail texted me to turn on the morning news. The story has fallen to about number five in the line-up, with only a short blurb about Neil being released on bail last night. The story dominating the news this morning is about baseball. Evidently, the Cardinals, the hometown team, won a very important game last night. They have earned a wildcard slot for a shot at the Division Championship. I don't really follow baseball until the post-season, but I know this is a big deal in our town. There was footage of much celebrating around town last night and talk of how to obtain good seats for the home game on Friday night. Davis and I are drinking our coffee and eating bagels, seated close to each other on the couch as we watch.

"Looks like the thing with Neil is going to blow over in the news and I won't have to tell the police or anyone. I guess the only people it will affect are girls like me that got involved with him. I'm just relieved my parents don't know about him and that I was vague about Randall. Your parents don't know, do they?" I ask him.

Davis shakes his head and takes my hand. "No, I haven't talked to them about it. It's not my story to tell. So, nobody else knows the whole story? Only me?"

"And Dr. Matt…" then I remember, "And Jules. Well, she doesn't know the Randall part. Oh my God, I have to call Jules right now." I give Davis' hand a squeeze, pick up my breakfast dishes and put them in the sink. I'm just about to get up to go to the bedroom and call, when his phone rings.

Davis looks at the screen and then says, "It's my folks." He answers the call with, "Hi, Mom, Hi Dad…What?" Then he shoots a look at me, eyes wide. "You heard the news? What news?" A look of relief wipes away the shock and concern that was there. "Oh…the news…about THE CARDINALS." I heave a sigh of relief. The news about Neil and Randall didn't even register with them. Good. I clutch my chest and signal to Davis that I am going to the bedroom. I leave him to talk with his parents and go call Jules. Davis blows me a kiss.

***

Jules is frantic when she answers my call. "God, Oh Biz, I just saw. What the hell is going on? What's the deal with Neil? And did you even know that other guy was his brother? Tell me what's going on?"

I answer all her questions, giving her a re-cap. She already knows most of it. She just doesn't know what I suspect Randall did. I tell her that, evidently, if my experience is any indication, Neil's modus operandi was to find a girl and develop a "relationship" and then pass her off to Randall. Somehow, Randall would video himself or Neil with the girl at some point.

That was their "business." It's just a theory I am piecing together from the news stories and what happened to me.

I'm wrapping up with Jules when another call rings through on my phone. It's a 314 area code number. Local. It could be a call from the station. I don't know of any other person or place that would call me not listed in my contacts. I say good-bye to Jules, assuring her that, YES, I will call if I know more, or if I need her or if I just need to talk. "Yes, I will definitely call you, I need you right now. I need all my friends…Umm. I gotta go, Jules. I think the station is calling." I hit the switch calls button and say hello.

It is *NOT* KTTA calling.

"Biz Connelly," Neil says my name in the low, taunting voice that I used find seductive. "Hi, babe, long time no talk." I have said nothing since saying, "Hello," and seem to have lost my ability to speak.

Neil continues, "You still there?"

"Yeah," I barely eek out. Why is he calling me?

"Babe, you may have heard I've gotten myself in a bit of a bind." A bit of a bind? To say the least. Neil keeps talking in his cavalier manner. "So unless you want me to let everyone know about you, about you and my brother, Randall and the video you made, you're going to need to help me out."

I must be in shock. I can barely form the next words, "Help? You? You want me to help you? What?" Neil just confirmed it. There is a video.

"Are you alone?"

"No, my fiancé is in the next room."

"Aaaah, yes, the fine Davis Brandon. He figures in to all this, too. At least, his money does."

"I…"

Neil cuts me off, "Biz, just shut up and listen. I need money. Big money. Robyn was able to scrape enough together for bail, but I'll need more for lawyers. And you, Ms, Connelly…" he proceeds in an oily voice, "seem to have found yourself a cash cow. Davis Brandon is a rich boy."

I counter, "He's not rich, his parents have money but he doesn't. And why would I give you money, anyway?"

Neil groans into the phone, "Seriously, Biz. I just told you, or weren't you paying attention. I have the video of you and Randall, ummm, how to I put this … oh, I know, FUCKING. I'm sure your future rich in-laws will be thrilled to have you marry their only son, once they see it. And your parents, well, what will they think? So proud, I'm sure. So here is what you are going to do. You are going to get $10,000 and bring it to me…"

I gasp and say, "Neil, I don't have that kind of money. I only have about $3,000 in savings and that's for my college loans…"

"I don't fucking care WHERE YOU GET THE MONEY, Biz!" Neil yells, "You just need to bring it to me. Fuck, ask your fiancé, your in-laws. You're a fairly smart girl, figure it out. Oh, and now the price is $13,000, since I know you have more."

Desperate, I stall. "Neil, Neil, I need some time. I can't get the money right now"

"Of course, you can't get it right now. You have until Friday night. I'll call you with where and what time. And Biz, tell NO ONE. If I sense the police are on to this, I will post this video in an instant." And with that he hangs up.

Did that really just happen? What should I do? Should I tell? No. No, *I* am going to fix this. I don't need Davis to fix it for us. I need to do it. I just need a plan to get the money and then the whole Neil and Randall mess will go away.

A plan materializes for me when Davis walks into the bedroom and tells me about his phone call from his parents. They're coming to town for the game on Friday. They're staying with us, in the guest room. Davis rolls his eyes in a sort of apology when he tells me. Normally, I would be less than thrilled, but this might be the answer to getting the cash I need to pay off Neil. If I can talk to the Lt. Governor, ask him for a loan, I could make this all go away without Davis getting involved at all. I decide. That's what I'll do. I'll get Davis' dad's number from his phone and call him in the morning. This whole line of thought has me surprised. The call from Neil has placed me in a surreal state. I can't believe I am planning to meet him and pay him off, but what else can I do?

I must have a pensive look on my face. Davis comes to stand in front of me and asks, "Everything okay. Did you talk to Jules?" I almost forgot that's what I came in here to do.

"Yeah, yes, it was fine, she was great, very supportive." I reply automatically. I look up at him.

Davis, adorably, cocks his head and scrunches up his face while sucking in a breath through his closed teeth and 'sort-of' smile. "Are you okay with my parents coming? It's sort of weird timing."

I try to sound convincing when I respond, "It's fine. Uh … ummm…I'm going to get cleaned up…" I get up, taking my phone with me and walk toward the bathroom. "and then I need to go to the bank." Davis volunteers to take me and I agree to let him. If I protest about going alone it may make him suspicious. I wonder to myself what $3000.00 in cash will look like. Closing the bathroom door behind me, I lean against it and finally exhale. I hate lying to him.

***

Having obtained all of the money from my savings account, I now need to get Davis' dad's number from his phone. Rather than being sneaky and looking on his phone, I simply ask, giving a plausible reason for needing it. My mom needs it, of course. To give them information about the wedding. The wedding. It has been the last thing on my mind with all that has happened in the past 24 hours. Davis completely buys the reason and writes down both his parents' numbers for me.

I take the numbers and walk toward the bedroom. Over my shoulder, as nonchalantly as I can, I tell Davis, "I'm going to make some calls. My mom and then Dr. Matt, so I'll be back out in a while."

Davis is seated comfortably on one of the sofas, with his laptop open. He's not facing me. Turning his head slightly, but not fully giving me his attention, he says, "Okay, I've got some work to do. I'll give you your privacy to talk to Dr. Matt." I don't mind his inattention. It's easier to deceive him when I don't have to look at his eyes. "I'll knock when it's lunch time."

Lunch. I'm having a hard time considering everyday things right now. I just have to get this Neil debacle over with. I respond mildly, "K" and hurry up into the bedroom. Standing in the middle of the room, it still doesn't feel safe enough, private enough to make the call I need to make. The walk-in closet. Perfect. One more door to hide my lying to Davis behind. I move into it and lock the door behind me. I can't believe I am going to do this. Asking the Brandons for money, but what other choice do I have? None. None that don't expose me or embarrass the people I love. The person I love.

I sit on the floor of the closet, nestled in a pile of shoes, under Davis's hanging shirts, my back against the wall. I have made myself as small as I can, because that's how I feel. I'm in hiding because what I am doing *should* be hidden.

James Brandon, answers on the third ring. "Hello, James Brandon speaking."

I gulp quietly and reply, "Hello, Mr. Brandon...uh, James. It's Biz. Biz Connelly."

James Brandon's voice is upbeat, but curious, "Hi, Biz. How are you? Is everything okay? Davis alright?" I know why he's asking. I have never called the Brandons or spoken to them on the phone before, so this has to seem weird.

"I...uh...Davis is fine. I, I am so sorry to call like this, but I have a little problem and..." Oh my God. I can't believe I am going to ask. I don't know how to ask any other way, so I just blurt it out, "I was wondering if I could borrow some money for a little while. I don't want to ask Davis. It's sort of a surprise." Geez, that was lame. "And I need it by Friday. Friday night." I cringe so badly he can probably hear it in my voice.

I guess he doesn't, because James Brandon only says breezily back, "Sure, Biz How much?"

Here I go. "Ten thousand dollars."

"That's a lot of money." Now James sounds concerned. "And you need it by Friday night?"

God, I hate lying. I inhale, exhale, swallow twice and reply, "I know it's a lot of money, Mr. Brandon, James…and it's sort of a time – sensitive thing. I can't give you any details, and I don't want Davis to know. I'm sorry. I know you are coming down on Friday."

There is a long silence and finally James says, "I need to discuss it with Meredith, Biz. I will need her to get the money, if we decide to help you out. I have to say, I'm a little concerned about the need for secrecy. Whatever you are doing is legal, right?" No, blackmail is not legal, but I rationalize it by telling myself I am doing a favor for a friend. I barely know myself right now.

"Yes, yes sir, perfectly legal." Amazing how easily the lies are coming now.

James is going to talk to Mrs. Brandon and call me right back. I stay curled in ball in the closet, under the shirts that smell like Davis. I hope I'm doing the right thing. It feels like the only way I can go. I should do what I told Davis I was doing, call Dr. Matt and my mom, but I don't. Putting the phone on the floor in front of me, I put my head in my hands and rock back and forth. I am so screwed. I engage in my self-talk and work to slow my breathing. It seems as if hours have passed when my phone finally rings. It's only been 20 minutes. I answer immediately.

The Brandons are both on the line. They agree to give me the money and will bring it to me on Friday. They promise not to tell Davis, but are not happy about it. I begin to thank them profusely when Mrs. Brandon cuts me off, "Biz, we are giving you this money on ONE condition…"

I agree to it.

***

Friday. It's here.

The money my parents spent to send me to school to study acting? It has totally paid off this week. I have been needy, charming, and completely fraudulent with Davis. Reassuring myself that the end will justify the means is the only way I've succeeded. Now, I just have to get through this evening, pay Neil the money and we'll be free. At least free of Neil and Randall, if not the buried memories.

Davis has to go into Weldon today. He's missed quite a few classes babysitting me and he has a lighting design due at a production meeting. Sadly, I am relieved as I send him out the door with a kiss, telling him I am fine. A few hours alone, before the Brandons arrive. A few hours when I don't have to actively lie to anyone, but myself. A few hours to figure out an alibi to explain my absence tonight. I'm beginning to get edgy. It's 3 o'clock and the Brandons haven't arrived yet. I wish they'd get here. I'm meeting Neil sometime tonight. I wish Neil would call so I can settle on how I am going to pull this off without Davis knowing about it.

Neil finally calls at 3:30. He wants us to meet at 7:10 tonight under the Kingshighway viaduct bridge, at the recently closed skatepark. I know the place he's talking about. A group of skaters developed a skatepark under a vehicle bridge in the mostly Italian neighborhood known as The Hill. It was recently closed by the police for investigation after a skating accident. When I asked about the very specific meeting time, Neil clarified. 7:10 is when the baseball game begins. This is a baseball town. Everyone will either be at the game or in front of a screen somewhere to watch it. The spot is secluded. Only about two, two and a half miles away. I can easily walk to it from the condo.

Even before the Brandons arrive, I've got it all figured out. I'll have them tell Davis I went to see Jules and I'll meet up with them at the game after I give Neil the money. That should work.

James and Meredith Brandon arrive about an hour after I get off the phone with Neil. It is possibly the most awkward I have felt, ever, in my entire life. James is brought up by the nurse that assists him. James greets me kindly, but with obvious concern. Mrs. Brandon... Meredith... is frosty. I don't know why I expected anything else. After they are settled into the guest room, we meet in the family room.

"I want to say, straight out, I am not comfortable with this whole business, Biz. We're doing this because we trust you and you have agreed to the condition." Meredith Brandon says, her tone belying her words.

"I, I know this is un-unusual, Mrs. Brandon," I stutter, my mouth suddenly dry. "I wouldn't ask if it weren't very important. I wish I could tell you more. I promise I will pay you back, every cent."

Mrs. Brandon takes a large manila envelope, the kind used for interoffice mail, out of her black crocodile Birkin bag. I can't help thinking how ironic it is that her purse cost way more money than she's holding in her hand, and laugh a bit internally. She places the envelope on the coffee table. "There," is all she says.

Sheepishly, I look up at Mrs. Brandon and then over at James Brandon. He up-nods toward the envelope and tells me, "Open it up, Biz." I do as he says. "It's amazing how small $10,000 can be when it is in larger bills." He's right. It fit in Mrs. Brandon's purse. I'm relieved. Even with my $3,000 added to it, I won't look suspicious walking around with it. It strikes me, I have to walk, in the city, with $13,000 on me. This is becoming more and more unbearable. I just want to do it and get it over with. I check the time on my watch. It's a little after 5 o'clock. I want to be gone when Davis gets back and I need some time to get ready and get to the skatepark. I want to arrive before Neil.

Scrambling and popping up from the sofa, I sputter out, "I need to go get ready for the game. I was thinking I could go with Jules, take care of what I need to with the money and then meet all of you at Busch stadium. I can take the Metrolink down. Could you tell Davis when he gets home? I will be right there, probably after they throw out the first pitch."

They both nod their heads in agreement and Mr. Brandon says hesitantly, "Sure, Biz."

I clutch the envelope full of money to my chest and back away from the Brandons. I reach back for the French doors to the bedroom, turn the handle and quickly exit. I stop myself from thinking about what I am doing and just act. It takes me very little time to shove the money I got from Davis' parents, along with my $3000 into my black crossbody bag. It looks a little fuller than usual, but not full to a point where anyone would think it strange. Just a chick with lots of stuff in her purse. It's still warm for late September, so I throw on a pair of white capris, a red t-shirt and my cadet cap with the blinged out STL logo on it. It's perfect. I look like an enthusiastic baseball fan, not a scared blackmail victim. My own deceit is gnawing at me and I'm completely surprised I haven't had multiple panic attacks. I think the only thing keeping them at bay is my determination to get Neil out of my life. Putting some cash, my ATM card, driver's license and phone in my back pocket, I look at myself one last time in the mirror over the dresser. I shake my head and push my lips together in a line.

"You can do this." I say softly, sadly and with disappointment. It's not the way I'd usually say it to calm myself. It's in a resigned, last-resort sort of way.

With that, I push the French doors from the bedroom open and as cheerily as possible announce to James and Meredith, "I'm going. Jules is downstairs waiting. See you at the game." I have a fake smile plastered on and give only the briefest of eye contact. I'm almost certain I have broken the bedroom-to-door land speed record.

As I close the door, I hear Meredith Brandon ask, to no one, really, "What was that?"

I wonder myself.

***

Jules isn't downstairs waiting. Since I'm lying, I thought I'd go all out. The Brandons will never know the difference. I got away before Davis got home. If I can dodge his calls and texts for a bit longer, I can just show up at the game like nothing happened.

Walking the couple of miles to the skatepark is almost settling. I do have to walk along a major thoroughfare, over two viaducts, one over a highway and the other over railroad tracks, before I see the one with the skatepark beneath it. It's a strange configuration. The bridge used to go over a two-lane city street. When the city rerouted the street, it became a dead end, right under the bridge, and then the skatepark just sort of happened. A grassroots project resulted in a really nice venue for skaters that had been kicked out of other places. I know a bit about it because I had been thinking it would make for a good story on Happening in the STL.

As I approach, it seems deserted. There are no cars parked in the vicinity. Then I catch a "swooshing" and "clicking" pattern of noise, echoing off the concrete of the bridge as I move under it. Two skaters freeze, after stopping and flipping their boards up into their hands, and stare at me. We exchange no words. They simply turn away from me, throw their boards on the ground and leave the area, with more of the "swoosh" sound. I'm surprised. I always think of skaters as rebels, but they vacated the minute they saw me. The park *is* temporarily closed. Maybe they thought I'd call the police.

My phone vibrates in my pocket. I pull it out. It's Davis.

Where are you?

I ignore it and another text pops up.

I called Jules. You aren't with her. Where are you? I'm worried.

I ignore it, too and put the phone away.

A deep voice says "Hello, Biz". It echoes and sounds menacing, causing me to jump. I look up to see... Neil.

I don't know why I'm surprised. I am here to meet him. He just "appeared" while my attention was elsewhere, and so quietly. After I calm myself a bit, I look more closely. Being arrested hasn't seemed to cause him any distress. He looks like, well, Neil. Tall, dark, empirically handsome. Cool. Distant. No one could deny he appears to be everything a girl could want. But he isn't. He's bad, maybe even a sociopath, if everything being reported is true. My own experience with him would indicate that.

I do everything in my power to appear unfazed. "Hello, Neil." I sound... strong... not scared. I continue, "I have the money. 13 thousand, just like we talked about." I hold up the crossbody bag full of cash. I'm not giving it to him until I have the video. "So where is the video?"

Neil approaches me slowly. He shakes his head and chuckles, a phony, pushed laugh, "Oh, Biz, still so naïve. There is no video. I mean there *is*, but I don't have it. Randall is a complete freak about that video. He won't even show it to me. I have no idea where it is or what he did with you. God knows I'd love to." His cold, taunting words are tearing at me. I feel my throat trying to close, as I gulp and swallow frantically. Unable to move, I just stand there and take it. My vision is clouding with the tears welling up in my eyes. I'm dizzy. The ground beneath me seems to be spinning.

Then, in a flash, it all changes to intense anger and it's as if all the blood in my body is rushing to my head and heart. Rage and fire spew out of me as I scream at Neil, "What the fuck are you saying? You don't have the video? I did all this for nothing?"

Neil is directly in front of me now. His face, emotionless as he smoothly coos back at me, "Now, now, not for nothing, darlin'..." He snatches the bag off my body, ripping the strap and causing me to lurch up against him. "Mmm, this is familiar..." Neil is grabbing my shoulders and pulling me toward him. His face is so close. I twist my head from one side to the other trying to avoid his face, his lips. "Too bad, I can't stay around and 'enjoy' you..." he says, pulling me up roughly, kissing and then licking at my closed mouth with his tongue. I keep my lips closed as tightly, as I can, ineffective vocal protests behind them. "... but, I need to take this money and run. Three grand to get to Mexico and just enough more to not have to make a customs claim..." What? What's Neil saying? He's jumping bail? Oh, my God... I'm in so much trouble. I'm assisting a fugitive.

I open my mouth to say, "No," and make a grab for my purse, when Neil drops suddenly to his knees in front of me, screaming in pain. I back away and look down at him. He is now rocking on his hands and knees, a torrent of profanity filling the air around him. I look up to see what caused this.

Where Neil once stood is Randall, with his head cocked, sarcastically curling his lips at me. He's wearing a plaid shirt with the arms cut off, baggy cargo shorts and tan work boots. He looks in as need of a shower as I remember. He has a baseball bat slung over both shoulders, behind his neck. His arms draped over it. Randall smarmily intones, "Hey, Bizzy…hah! Bizzy, like 'busy,' like 'I love getting busy.' You sure *did* love getting … Biz-zy with me." Randall's insinuation makes me vomit into my mouth. I swallow the bilious taste.

Neil pushes off his hands into a kneel, rubbing the backs of legs. "Fuck! Randall, what the fuck are you doing?"

"Shut up, Neil!" Randall growls at his brother and without warning swings the bat off his shoulder and cracks Neil on the side of his head with it. All the air seems to empty from Neil's body with a "woof" and he crumples sideways in front of me. Waves of nausea brought on by fear, real fear, overtake me. The shaking begins. Randall snickers and steps over Neil's unconscious body. "Asshole. Mom always said he didn't know how to keep his mouth shut. He's gonna have one big ass headache when he finally wakes up."

Randall is circling me, twirling the bat in his hand in a threatening way. He stops, comes up behind me and sniffs at my hair by my ear. "You like the bat, Biz? I was going for a baseball theme. You get it? With the big game tonight and everything" he snickers. "You, Biz-zy, look as good as the last time I saw you. Mmmm. Maybe a few more clothes, but still, good."

I can't think of anything else to do, so I beg. I don't scream. I don't cry. I'm paralyzed on the spot, so I say hoarsely, "What do you want, Randall? The money? Take it."

Randall laughs again, "Oh, I fully intend to take the money, Biz," then he commands me, "Pick up the purse and hand it to me."

I bend to retrieve the purse, laying on the ground in front of Neil. Evidently, I don't move quickly enough for Randall, because he grabs my right arm from behind and wrenches me back toward him, pulling it out of my hand. I hear a *SNAP*! A white, hot pain shoots up my arm to my neck and then to the base of my skull. I scream louder than I ever have in my life as I'm thrust backward against Randall's chest. Surely, someone will hear me. I will my arm to move out of Randall's grip, but it is unresponsive and just hangs at my side. I reach up to support it with my left hand. Randall takes no notice, just continues to talk. "My asshole brother was going to jump bail and leave me to take the fall after he ratted me out. Well, when he wakes up won't he be surprised that I took the money and left town..." Randall, buries his nose between my neck and shoulder and inhales deeply, then completes his thought, "with YOU."

It is impossible to escape Randall's grasp, even though I twist as much as I can to endeavor to do so. It's futile.

"LET HER GO!" It's Davis. His voice is ferocious. I can hear him, but I can't see him. How did he find me? Painfully, moving my head side to side to try and look around Randall, I localize that Davis is behind us when he bellows, "NOW!"

Randall spins us both around in a single, rapid move. My arm flings out away from my body and I shriek. There is no stopping the cries now. I am engulfed in agonizing pain, fear and anger. My eyes meet Davis'. His face is stoic. Emotions masked, but I know – He. Is. LIVID.

Anger in his voice, Davis asks me, "Are you okay?" I don't hear any concern, only the anger.

"My... my arm," is all I get out between sobs.

Davis's looks away from me and focuses his fury on Randall. "Did you not hear me? Let. Her. Go!"

"Why, we were just leaving. Right, Bizzy baby?" Randall kisses me on the temple and replies, unaffected by Davis' tone. He's taunting Davis. I shake my head no and can see Davis rankle at Randall's words.

Looking down slightly, I notice Davis is holding something in his right hand, behind his back down by his thigh, and then I see it. Davis slowly brings up his right hand and points it at Randall and me, but it's not just his hand, it's a gun. Not a shiny cowboy-type gun, but a heavy looking squared-off flat black handgun, like a police officer would carry. What is Davis doing with a gun? He hates guns. I didn't know he had a gun.

I said, "LET HER GO. I won't tell you again." I have seen Davis angry before, but never like this. Never so intense and scary. He is scaring *me*.

Davis must be scaring Randall, too. I can feel Randall's heart rate increase and a drop of his sweat falls on my shoulder. Sirens begin to be audible and seem to be moving closer. Randall gulps in my ear and says to

Davis, "Okay, man, relax, you can have the bitch… I just want the money."

"You can have the money and, if you hurry, a head start," Davis tells him. "Now, walk over here and give her to me," Davis directs.

Randall pushes me forward, his hand still encircling my rag doll arm, his other hand holding the crossbody bag with the money, having dropped the bat to take it from me earlier. Davis lowers the gun ever so slightly. Randall roughly shoves me toward Davis, who catches me against his chest, wrapping his left arm around me. Davis whispers, "Got you, baby."

POP! POP! Loud gunshots ring out and I twist my head violently around to see blood running from the side of Randall's neck, near his earlobe. He screams, "FUCK!!"

A swash of black appears in my peripheral vision. Randall smashes the gun, which must have fired while he was wrestling it from Davis' hand, into the side of Davis' head. I collapse, with Davis, to the ground, trying and failing with my damaged arm to soften the impact. As we hit, there is a loud crack and an even more excruciating pain rips through my shoulder and neck. I'm pinned down. Davis is lying on top of my uninjured arm, his head on my chest. His green eyes are open, but glassy and without expression. He is not moving. Black and blue is forming on his swelling temple and face. One area looks like hamburger and there is blood everywhere, but I can't make out where it has come from.

With a earsplitting howl, I plead with Davis, "Nooo …wake up, baby, please, please, wake up." I can't move. I can't tell if Davis is breathing. I push the thought that he could be…dead…out of my reality.

Randall stands over us, Davis' gun pointed at me. I can now see that Randall's left earlobe is dangling below the rest of his ear, blood dripping off it, down his neck and onto Davis.

Randall rages, "He shot my fucking *ear* off."

The sirens are getting louder, closer.

Randall pins me with a glare and growls, "Get up, Biz. Get up, you're coming with me."

I don't even recognize the next voice I hear. "NO!" I roar, "I am NOT fucking coming with you, Randall. You have two choices. Shoot me. Shoot me right here. Right now. OR. Run... You hear those sirens, you sick bastard? They *were* coming for Neil, but they'll get *you*...so, shoot me now or RUN THE FUCK away! I'm good with either choice." I have never spoken to anyone ever with such hate and honesty. And I've never meant anything more in my life.

Randall backs up and looks away from us to consider the sirens. "We aren't done, Bizzy. I'll have you one day." Randall points at me with the gun and then he runs. I should have guessed he would. Slimy piece of shit.

I squirm under Davis' weight. I *think* he is breathing. God, I hope he is breathing and I'm not just wishing it. The sirens are really loud now. Exhausted, I place my head on the ground gingerly and look up to see the red and blue lights from the police cars dancing on the underside of the bridge above us. Turning my head away from Davis, I vomit spectacularly next to myself. I can see Neil lying motionless a few feet away. My vision tunnels and...

***

"One condition." Meredith Brandon howls at me upon storming into the ER treatment room in which I have been placed. "We gave you that money under one condition... that Davis not be hurt..." She pauses and holds her hand to her chest. There is a moment when I think she will sob, but it passes. Mrs. Brandon waves her hand in the air as if to dismiss the sadness and then continues in a low, threatening voice, "Biz, what were you thinking? No, I don't think I need to know. I don't *want* to know what you were doing with that man, Neil Ireland. The more I find out the sicker I feel. You didn't abide by the condition. You know what that means, right?"

I do. I know exactly what it means and I have been dreading this conversation ever since Davis fell to the ground.

"Mere – Mrs. Brandon, I can explain. Please don't. Please don't make me." I plead

"Give me the engagement ring, Biz"

I am sobbing relentlessly. I knew the risk and I took it. For Davis. To protect him and my family, his family from embarrassment. Now, I have to pay the price. I am unable to take my engagement ring off myself, because my right arm is in a sling from a bad shoulder dislocation and I have a brace stabilizing my broken collarbone. There is an IV in my left hand, delivering pain medication. This is all so surreal. I hold my left hand up to Mrs. Brandon and she takes my engagement ring.

As she yanks it off, through sobs, I ask, "How is he? How's Davis?"

Mrs. Brandon replies, her voice bitter, "I shouldn't even tell you." She grinds her teeth audibly. "He is alive, no thanks to you. He just got out of surgery and they are keeping him heavily sedated for now. They evacuated blood from his skull to release the pressure. Subdural hematoma. Repaired something in his ear. Cleaned up and sutured his face. His face, Biz! We'll know more later, but he's going to be okay." She gulps out the last few words between tearless sobs. Her anger takes hold again and she stiffly informs me, "We will give him the ring and tell him you've broken the engagement when he's well enough to hear it. You, Biz, have a day or two to come up with a good reason for the break-up. One he will believe. I'm sure Davis will insist on seeing you when he wakes up. Until then, STAY AWAY from my son."

"No, please don't do this, no, no, no, Mrs. Brandon, no." I would beg on my knees if I could get off this gurney.

Mrs. Brandon's next words drip with malice, "Stop it, Biz. Begging is pathetic. Now, I need you to tell me you will honor your promise."

Biting my tongue, an expression I've heard, but never done, I wince and shake my head no, then stop myself and say, "I…I will."

Without another word, Meredith Brandon turns on her heel and marches out of the sliding door of the treatment room, sliding it back into place hard.

After she leaves, I cry out in anguish. It reverberates off the walls of the too quiet room. She's right. I broke the condition. The condition was simple – If I used that money for something that hurt Davis at all, I would remove myself from his life. I thought I was going to save him from pain. I was trying to avoid hurting him and look what I did. Caused him real, physical injury. He could have been killed because of me and my poor decision making. I deserve this outcome. I can't stop the noises that are emanating from my mouth. Loud, pitiful moans and sobs. Like a wounded animal in a trap. A trap I set for myself.

A nurse rushes in, "Ms. Connelly, are you in pain?" She begins to adjust the syringes of medication infusing into my IV.

"YES!" I howl.

Yes, but not physical pain.

I answer, "Yes, more than you know."

I only calm when the pain medicine takes effect.

***

"Ms. Connelly? Are you awake?" It's a male voice I don't recognize.

I am awake. I'm just pretending to be asleep, because I don't want to talk to anyone. What can I say? I open my eyes a slit and stare at the privacy curtain next to the gurney. I half-heartedly try to make sense of the swirl of colors, what pattern they are forming. Anything to distract me from what I'm avoiding. Anything to stop the endless reel playing in my head of what happened last night in the skatepark. Anything to try to stop the worry about Davis.

My extremely kind and compassionate nurse, I can't seem to retain her name, tells the male voice, "Detective, Ms. Connelly has been through a lot. She has a non-displaced clavicle fracture and a dislocated shoulder. The doctors have everything back in place, but she's in quite a bit of pain and on lots of medication. I don't know if now is the right time to ask questions."

The male voice responds gently, "I understand, Carrie." Either he knows my nurse or he's reading her nametag.

There are footsteps and then a rugged looking man in his late 30s is in front of me, blocking my oh-so-important view of the curtain. He has short, cropped red hair, more red than mine, very fair skin and freckles across his nose. He smiles at me with his eyes only, but I can tell he smiles

174

often by the crinkles around them. The rest of his face appears serious, concerned. I can't make out what he is thinking. Then again, the medicine is making me sort of blurry. He's wearing a blue button down shirt, charcoal gray blazer and jeans. He raises a hand and flashes his badge.

"Hello, Ms. Connelly, I'm Detective Donovan Garrett, STL Metro Police. I'd like to talk to you about what happened last night, if that's okay," the face to which the voice belongs says.

I ask, voice slurred, "Am I in trouble? Am I under arrest?"

Detective Garrett answers my questions evenly, "Ms. Connelly, you and Mr. Brandon were found injured, alongside Mr. Ireland, a suspect on drug-facilitated sexual assault and pornography charges. There are three victims and no obvious perpetrator, as of now. You are the only victim that is conscious. You're not under arrest and you don't have to talk now. I just would like to get some more information about what occurred under that bridge."

I probably should have a lawyer, but I can't afford one. I just lost my entire savings to a sleazy, dirty pornographer and in all likelihood, rapist, and not the one I thought I'd lose it to. I start at the beginning and tell Detective Garrett everything. Meeting Neil, being handed off to Randall, my suspicions about being sexually assaulted, Dr. Matt's theories about possibly being drugged… Neil's arrest, his blackmail call to me after getting bail, procuring the money, and then all the events during the disastrous meeting under the bridge in the skatepark. I assure the detective that I knew nothing about Neil's plan to jump bail. I would never have agreed to give him the money, if I knew he was intending to do that. I was a moron and believed his story about needing the money for lawyer's fees. Detective Garrett is writing the entire time I am talking. As I tell the rest of the story – Randall arriving and attacking Neil with the bat, Randall's threats, Davis showing up and pulling the gun, I visualize it like I'm watching a movie. The gun? Where did Davis get a gun?

I even see myself in the movie, only I'm an observer watching the heinous events play out.

I shudder and ask again, "So, am I in trouble?"

Donovan Garrett is tapping his pen against his lips and swaying back and forth between the balls and heels of his feet. He seems to be thinking through everything I just spelled out for him. "I'll be honest, Ms. Connelly…may I call you Elizabeth?"

"Biz."

"Biz. Interesting name," the detective editorializes. "Biz, there is a risk you could be brought up on charges for assisting a suspect to flee, but since he didn't go anywhere thanks to his brother, that seems unlikely. I don't know what else the prosecutor might go after. This isn't an official statement you're making and you are currently on medication, which could alter your mental faculties. I was being straight when I said I just need to find out what went on. I'll be interviewing the other victims when they're able. If the prosecutor does have a beef, I think we can work a deal. You might have something I can use to bring the Ireland brothers to justice."

The medicine is really making me foggy. I can't really follow what the detective is getting at. The interview with him ends anyway when Charlie, Jules, Smitty and Kathleen all enter the treatment room at once. They all look questioningly at my present guest. Detective Garrett introduces himself.

Kathleen strolls up to Detective Garrett and asks flatly, "What's going on here? You aren't questioning her without an attorney present, are you?"

The detective doesn't flinch when Kathleen, beautiful, savvy journalist Kathleen questions him openly. He simply states, "Ms. Connelly is not under arrest. There are no charges against her that I know of. It appears that she and Mr. Brandon were victims."

Charlie interjects, "What about Neil Ireland?" Jules must have told Charlie what happened. I wound up telling her the whole story when I called her to come get me, after the nurse said I would need to be released in someone's care at discharge. I would have asked the nurse to call my ICE, Davis, but he is currently in the Intensive Care Unit, or so I believe.

"I'm not at liberty to discuss Mr. Ireland at this time." Detective Garrett informs Charlie. "I'll be in touch, Ms. Connelly." He leaves his card on the over-bed table next to me. "Feel better."

I watch four sets of eyes follow him until the detective is out of the room, sliding the door shut behind him. Then, I am surrounded on all sides. Charlie and Smitty each place a hand on my lower leg over the blanket and pat me. Kathleen leans over and kisses me carefully on the forehead.

Jules doesn't touch me. She looks puzzled and eventually asks, "Can I hug you without hurting you?"

I really don't know, so I tell her, "I think on my left side, if you're careful of my IV."

I have never been hugged so tentatively by Jules. It's not the same as her usual crushing squeeze, but it is extremely comforting.

Smitty and Kathleen don't ask me what happened. Jules must have brought them up to speed. No one says anything about my missing engagement ring. My discussion with the detective exhausted me. I apologize to my visitors, telling them I am about to fall asleep. My eyes are heavy and words are becoming hard to comprehend. Smitty, Kathleen and Charlie announce they are going to get coffee in the cafeteria and will be back. Jules sits in a chair by my side. She tells me she'll be here when I wake up and when it's time for me to be discharged, I'll go to Charlie's. They'll get my stuff from the condo in a few days. A tear runs down my cheek as I close my eyes and let myself drift. Sleep is my only solace right now.

✳✳✳

Kathleen has been tasked with getting me out to the car. Charlie and Smitty left to pull it around. Jules is going over the discharge information with my nurse – stuff about pain medicine and how much activity I can have. Kath helps me out of bed and into the wheelchair. It aches to move. I'm been given a set of scrubs to wear home. My clothes were ruined when they were cut off of me in the emergency room. Every article, thrown away. At least my driver's license, ATM card, cash and phone weren't. The nurse handed those four small things to me in a large personal belongings bag, when I signed my release papers.

I don't really care about the achiness or my clothes. All I want to do is see Davis. He's all I've been thinking about, wondering about how he is. The nurses won't give me any information. Mrs. Brandon hasn't reappeared since taking my engagement ring. I have a feeling Kathleen knows. I wait until she's pushing me out of the room, away from Jules and ask, "Hey, umm, Kathleen, do...do you know how Davis is doing?"

I can't see her since she is behind me, but I sense a knowing in her voice when she responds, "Yeah, I do. I was wondering how long it would take you to ask. You've been putting on a pretty brave front for all of us, or maybe it's the medication. If I were you, I'd be crying every minute."

"I brought this on myself," I explain. "I only hope I can get Davis to understand." I lied to Mrs. Brandon. I said I would think up a good break-up excuse to tell Davis. Actually, I'm trying to think of the lamest one I can, so he will never believe it. The only problem is, I may never get a chance to talk to him. Mrs. Brandon seems to have Davis under her thumb, even when he isn't injured. I know it is all a reaction to losing her other son, Cole, to a senseless suicide, but she is really controlling with Mr. Brandon and Davis.

"Biz, sweetie..." Kathleen stops pushing the wheelchair and comes around to stoop down in front of me – eye level. "Davis is going to be fine. He isn't awake yet, but only because the doctor's are keeping him sedated. They lift it every so often to check him, but he still has a bit of swelling on his face and head. He hasn't spoken. He's barely opened his eyes, really, but his vital signs are all good. He's breathing on his own without oxygen..."

Cutting her off, I command, "Take me to him."

Kathleen tilts her head and pleads with her eyes, "Really, Biz? Meredith was pretty clear. She doesn't want you near Davis. I don't think she'll let you in."

"He's unconscious. What can I possibly do or say to him that would cause a problem? I'm sure you can think of a way to sneak me in," I implore her.

Kathleen puts both her hands on her knees and pushes up to stand. I look up at her in an earnest appeal. She shakes her head, "I am going to get myself in a ton of hot water, but I really don't like the way Meredith and James are handling this. They have no idea how much Davis adores you. I'll call Meredith and tell her she needs to take a break, that she should meet me in the cafeteria for coffee. We'll hide around the corner from Davis' room. When I see her leave we'll slip in. James is probably there, but we can sweet talk him, no problem."

All I can do is thank Kathleen profusely over and over, while trying desperately not to tear up. I've cried so much lately, I can't believe I have any tears left, but I do. "You understand, don't you? I just need to see him. See that he's okay. Then I can go to Charlie's. I'll be miserable the entire time I'm away from Davis, but I'll be able to get through it if I can just see him. Even if he never wants to see me again once he wakes up, I just need to see him."

"Then let's do this." Kathleen cheers and pulls out her cell phone.

***

"No, absolutely not. Kathleen, you can't bring Biz in here. Meredith will kill me. Do you hear me, Kathleen?" James Brandon is driving toward us in his electric wheelchair, as Kathleen brings me to Davis. "I thought Meredith was meeting you for coffee."

I only glance briefly at James before all my attention lands on Davis. Kathleen wheels me right up to his side, leaves me there and goes over to appease James. I perceive an argument happening between James and Kathleen, but really it's all just background noise. Everything in me is focused on Davis. He looks like my Davis, but too still, too pale. There is a large bandage on the side of his face and his eye is swollen and black and blue. I reach up and take his hand. It's cold. Davis is never cold. I don't have much time, Meredith will be back soon. I can't get as close to him as I'd like, so I whisper up at him, "Davis, baby, it's me, Lizard Breath. I'm here, baby. I can't stay long. Your parents are pretty pissed at me. I just wanted to say…" There's no stopping the tears now and I sob on, "I am so, so sorry you were hurt. I was trying to keep the hurt from you, and you got hurt anyway. I'm so sorry. I wish you could hear me. I hope you can."

Kathleen comes over and puts a hand on my shoulder, "Biz, we gotta go. Meredith is on her way back up." Kathleen shows me the text on her phone saying so.

I only have a few more moments to tell Davis everything he means to me, even if he can't hear it. "I love you, Davis Brandon. I didn't know what love was until I saw myself in your eyes. I loved you almost immediately, on a cellular level, before my heart and head even caught on."

"We have to go Biz." Kathleen insists.

"Never forget – I LOVE YOU, Mavis."

Davis squeezes my hand. I look down at our hands and he does it again. It's weak, but there. He heard me! I know he did. I tell no one. Not Kathleen or Mr. Brandon. It's between Davis and me. That squeeze gives me hope. I hold Davis' hand as long as I can while Kathleen pulls my chair away from his bedside. As she rushes me out of the room, down the hall and onto the elevator, her phone alerts.

Kathleen answers it. "I know, I'm sorry," Kathleen says. She must be talking to Mrs. Brandon. "She wanted to say good-bye. Davis wasn't even awake. I know. Yes. Yes. I understand. I'll catch up with you and James later. Check in on Davis. I know, I know. Bye, Meredith." Kathleen sighs after hanging up, "Whoa, she was mad. Glad she didn't catch us." Then she laughs and pushes me even more quickly. Charlie, Smitty and Jules are waiting to take me home. No, not home – to Charlie's. Not my home with Davis.

***

I am living on pain medication, memories and updates from Kathleen. That's it. It's been two days since I was discharged from the hospital. I do pretty well if I take my medicine on schedule and don't forget a dose. It makes me pretty loopy. When I absolutely can't keep my eyes open, I let the sleep come and will myself to dream about Davis. It isn't hard, he is foremost in my consciousness. My phone is by my side at all times. Kathleen is being my spy and texting me information as often as she can about Davis' condition. The text I've been waiting for finally pops up in a little speech bubble:

HE'S AWAKE!!
And asking about you.

I text back:

Really? Do you think Meredith will let me see him?

Kathleen's response comes quickly:

I don't know. They kicked me out of the room. It got intense
pretty quickly after he woke up.
I'll text you as soon as I know something.

I get up and do a little dance around Charlie's living room. Davis is awake. He's better. Nobody is here to see me. Charlie is off at one of his new jobs. Since he's decided not to go back to Weldon to focus on taking Boxwood to the next level, he had to get day jobs. The first job is cool – a vintage guitar store. He sells and repairs guitars. I'm not supposed to tell anyone about the second job, but he's working at Hot Topic selling Twilight and My Little Pony merchandise. He does have a great look for the place. The sad part is he makes more money there than with the guitars. Charlie really doesn't care how he makes the money to live on, he just wants to make music. I hope he never stops feeling like that. Jules (his wife – ha!) is in class today. They only left me alone if I promised to stay in my pajamas and rest. I have kept the pajama part of the promise. I can only rest when I take the pain medicine. When I'm awake, I'm restless, thinking non-stop about Davis, wondering when Randall will appear again and concerned if I am going to get arrested or charged for the whole blackmail/money exchange thing.

I'm ecstatic that Davis is awake! I don't know what to do with myself. I'm going to break my promise. I'm going to get dressed, put on make-up, fix my hair. I'm hoping it will make me feel better *and* occupy my time until Kathleen texts me.

Clearly I didn't think this through. I got my pajamas off, my sling off, removed the figure eight brace stabilizing my collarbone, turned on the shower and got in. It's challenging washing my hair and body with one hand, but I manage to accomplish the feat. What I didn't plan on was afterward – after getting out. I also towel myself dry with one hand without much pain, but I can't put the brace back on without help and my arm is starting to hurt. So much for doing my make up and hair. I'm sitting on the toilet seat and squirming back into my pajama bottoms when I hear the front door open. I hold the towel up to my front to cover my breasts. My hair is still dripping wet down my shoulders and back. I call out, "Hey."

"Hey yourself." It's Charlie.

I need help, no denying it. I'm going to have to let Charlie assist. I yell out to him, "I'm so glad you're here. I got a little overzealous and decided to get cleaned up. It wasn't until after I got out of the shower that I couldn't do it without someone to help me."

Charlie asks, "Are you decent? And if not, can I come in?" Smart ass. "See what I did there?"

"You are hilarious." I fake laugh. "I'm decent, but you still need to come in."

Upon entering the bathroom, Charlie howls, "You are a mess, Biz. A hot mess." Charlie turns me, so I can look in the mirror. He's right. I look like a half drown crazy woman. Hair hanging in strings around my face. Old mascara ringing my eyes. Naked from the waist up, only covered by a towel, with my Hello Kitty PJ pants on. Charlie doesn't waste a second helping me pull myself together. He turns away and closes his eyes when I have to remove the towel. He puts my figure eight brace back on me without causing me any pain, assists me with my bra and t-shirt, all while essentially blind. He may have peeked a little to get the job done. I don't care. He is, for all practical purposes, my brother.

Jules holds her sides and squeels in amusement when she enters the bathroom to find Charlie blow-drying my hair. He's already assisted me with my make-up and actually did a good job at it. "OMG, it's like a slumber party in here. Where's my phone? I need to record this." Charlie and I both smile proudly and make silly faces at her in the mirror.

Charlie's phone chirps that a text message has been delivered. He stops drying my hair, pulls it from his pocket and flips it around to see who the call is from. Charlie looks at me in the mirror and with questioning eyes, like he's guessing at what my reaction will be, says, "It's Davis."

When I look at myself in the mirror, my expression is concerned. What does Davis have to say? Charlie's phone continues to alert several times before I tell him, "Read it."

Charlie taps on the message, but doesn't look at it or read it to me. He looks up at Jules and then me and says, "I'm not reading it to you if it will hurt you. Right now, I'm on the fence about Davis and his parents. I have been only just keeping myself from going down to that hospital, laying into them and shaking him awake."

"He's awake now." I tell them both. "Just read the message."

Charlie looks at the screen of his phone, "Weird…"

I can't stand it. If I could move better I'd grab the phone from his hand, "What. Does It. Say?"

Charlie makes a face at me and shoots back, "That's why I said, 'Weird.' Look." He holds up the phone for me to read the message. Which I do, out loud.

The mouse devoured the hawk-James Brandon

"It's not Davis." I say glumly. "It's his dad. And the message is a line from the musical I did last spring. 'The mouse devoured the hawk.' It's a metaphor for when the prince stands up to the queen and breaks the spell on the king. What's he talking about? Where's Davis?"

Jules laughs and I turn and stare at her. What's so funny? "Don't you get it, Biz? I think it means, Davis is the prince and…Mrs. Brandon…" Jules makes a sour face after saying Davis' mom's name. "is the hawk. Davis must have told his mother off."

Before Jules can say another word or I can text the Lt. Governor back, Charlie's doorbell rings. Charlie shrugs at both of us in the mirror and leaves to get the door, mumbling, "Now what?" Jules and I pad out after him and are stopped dead when he opens the door.

Meredith Brandon is standing in the threshold. Meredith Brandon, a woman I have never seen with an eyelash, let alone a hair out of place, is standing in front of me and is a complete mess. Her eyes are bloodshot and teary, mascara smeared and smudged. Her skin is blotchy, her breathing labored, and she is shivering. It appears she has the same habit as her son, because it looks like she's been raking her hands through her hair. Just as I notice, she does just that. Both hands fly to her face, she sobs and runs both hands back and through her now disheveled coif.

In a broken cry, Meredith steps forward and looks at me. Just me and pleads, "Biz, I was wrong…I…please, you have to come with me…" Now, she has me worried. Is something wrong with Davis? My concern and confusion are calmed with her next words. "Davis…he…he won't talk to me or let me be a part of his life, if…if I don't bring you back to the hospital right now. Please, I can't lose him. I've already lost one son." She doesn't say why he wants me back at the hospital. And Davis hasn't called me.

I ask, "He's okay? Right?"

Meredith chokes back her sobs, "Yes, just agitated. I'm sorry, Biz. Please will you come back with me?"

I'm scared. Scared to see Davis after what happened to him. What I caused to happen to him, but more scared not to see him. "Of course, Meredith, of course I'll come with you. You should know, I'm going to tell him the truth – all of it. Even the condition."

With a cleansing sigh, Meredith tells me, "He already knows that part."

***

Davis wants to see me alone. I don't know why I'm so nervous. It's Davis. I've never been closer or more intimate with anyone in my life. He's been moved out of the intensive care unit into a regular room. Charlie and Jules are standing behind me. I sense Jules come up beside me and stare at Davis' hospital room door with me. She rubs my back and not turning to look at me, whispers quietly, "Go ahead. He's waiting." I take a deep breath and knock lightly on the hospital room door.

"Come in." Davis says in an unusually weak voice for such a strong guy.

I suddenly miss him terribly. Everything about him. He's only feet away from me and I miss his voice, his touch, his smirky smile. Pushing the door open just enough with my good arm, I slide in. Seeing him in the same hospital bed I saw him in a couple of days ago – but now sitting upright with color and life in his face – causes my heart to practically jump out of my chest and tap dance on the floor.

I stand, just inside the door of Davis' room. I want to run to him. Mrs. Brandon said Davis wanted to see me, immediately. I'm hoping that's a good thing. Davis' face is impassive as he looks up and our eyes lock. I can feel him penetrating right into me and the pull, the buzz increases. Love on a cellular level.

Simultaneously, we each say, "I'm sorry." Only Davis' tone is deadly serious and mine is squeaky and apologetic.

Davis' voice is suddenly stronger, intimidating almost. He even seems to sit up taller in the bed, "No, Biz…I'm sorry. I am sorry my mother felt she needed to keep you away from me. I'm sorry you got hurt. I'm sorry I couldn't protect you…"

I interrupt, "You're sorry? But I, I put you in danger."

Davis bats my words out of the air, dismissing them, "No…you were…God, you were… you were trying to fix everything. I'm horrified when I think about what could have happened if I hadn't shown up."

Sadly, I interject, "You wouldn't be in the hospital."

Clearly frustrated, Davis shakes his head and rolls his eyes back, acknowledging my words, but continuing his thought, "And that degenerate would have taken you. Have you halfway to Mexico – Why are we talking about this… why aren't you here, in my hospital bed, kissing me?

I walk over and fall into his arms. Getting as close to him as I can without dislodging an IV or bumping his wounds or my shoulder. The electric buzz, the pull I feel whenever I'm anywhere near Davis, amps up. I was so worried I'd never feel it again. I survived all summer without it, but it's been worse since he was injured and we've been separated. Worse when I thought we'd never be together again.

Davis looks me over, moving his hands from my face to my arms and finally, gently wraps them around my waist. "Are you okay?" he asks, voice full of concern.

"I have a broken collarbone and my shoulder was dislocated a little, but that's actually feeling much better now." I say, trying to minimize my injuries. His are so much worse, but other than the bandage on the side of his head and face, he looks like my Davis. Heart stoppingly handsome, even in a hospital bed.

"Goddammit!" Davis barks out. There is palpable tension in his chest and arms. "I'm going to kill that guy." He sighs repeatedly, trying to self soothe. "I'm glad you feel better, but it never should have happened. You shouldn't have been injured or have to be in that sling contraption." He indicates the sling/brace I am wearing.

I pull away from his arms a bit to make eye contact, "I'm fine...I'm just worried about you...You, Davis... you had a gun?"

Davis bows his head and tells me that it was the gun Cole used to kill himself. Davis had it in his car. He didn't know what to do with it when the police returned it, so he hid it in his car and forgot about it. Repressed it. Something I understand. Davis remembered it was there on his way to find me, which he did, by the way, by installing a 'Find my Phone' app on my phone months ago, after I kept leaving it behind. Now Randall has the gun. I can't bear to think about him any longer and purposely move the conversation in a different direction. Davis looks tired. "How are you feeling?"

"Never mind about me." Davis is irritable, just like Mrs. Brandon said. He grips my shoulders, being careful with the injured one and pins me with his gaze. He's not happy. "Never. Ever. Do that again. Never leave me."

I shake my head no. Davis is wrong. I had no intention of leaving him. He has to know. "I won't. I wasn't. I mean, when I took the money to

Neil, I wasn't leaving you. I didn't leave you. I thought I was going to be forced to when your mother took my engagement ring…"

Davis heaves a huge sigh/growl noise from deep in his chest and runs a hand through the side of his hair that has been partially shaved off. "I knew it. I knew when she handed me the ring and said you'd broken the engagement… all I could hear was your voice, see your face, when I gave it to you. I remember you saying, 'I am NEVER taking this off…if I do you will know something is really wrong…and you need to come and find me.' I knew you'd never take it off without a good reason. I'm sorry I couldn't come and find you." Davis points to his IV and bed, "I was sort of tied up, and as you say, not in a good way." I almost laugh. "I tore into my mother. She had no right to do that to you, to us. And my dad, well, mom's been babying him and controlling him since the…since Cole died. We talked. She won't be controlling us anymore."

"She was only trying to protect you." I assure Davis. "I, sort of, understand."

"Biz, we've been letting mom get away with running things for too long. It was all to make losing Cole less difficult. In the meantime, my dad and I, well, I just have to say it, when it comes to her, we've been pussies. But no more, not when it comes to you."

"So?" I ask, "The mouse devoured the hawk, huh?"

"Uh huh." Davis says proudly. "How was that for irony?"

"Cute, Mr. Brandon, real cute." And with that, I FINALLY kiss him. It feels like a million years, even though it's only been a few days. I don't even recall feeling this relieved and content when he came home from his summer at the Shakespeare festival. My skin ignites and a vibration floods me with desire. I really have missed him. My heart has missed him. My body has missed him. Kissing, we come together like we are fused.

Davis stops kissing and commands out of the blue, "Lizard, baby, I need you to sit up."

I sit up suddenly. My arm and shoulder complain, but I ignore it. "Why, am I hurting you?" I look him up and down. He seems okay.

Then I see it. "No, I just need to put this…" My ring. He is holding it between his thumb and forefinger, wiggling it a bit so it catches the light. "…back where it belongs." Davis takes my left hand and places it back on my third finger. I think my finger missed the diamond as much as I did.

I look up, away from the ring; to see is a pair of clearly thrilled emerald eyes. What a girl wouldn't give to have those eyes and eyelashes. Then my gaze drops to see Davis smiling at me, but something is wrong. His smile is more smirky than before, as a matter of fact, he is only smiling on one side.

"Your smile…" My voice is thin and frightened sounding. "It's broken."

"I know," Davis says. I can't help notice the defeat pouring out of him in those two words. "Are you going to be okay with that?"

I'm stunned Davis even has to ask. I am, of course, surprised, but is it okay? "Davis, I am absolutely okay. I love your smile. It's a part of you, a part I am very fond of, among others …" I think I see Davis' one-sided smile grow. "…but I love the whole Davis more. I just…" I employ my trick of looking up at the lights to stop myself from welling up. "Randall broke your smile, and it's all my fault."

Davis pulls me toward him gently and whispers, "Stop it. It's not your fault, Lizard baby. It just happened. The doctors say it will get better. It'll just take time. And I'm not broken, not as long as I'm with you."

There are no words. Nothing comes to mind that can capture how I feel as well as Davis just has. Finally, I whisper, "That's it. We are broken without each other. We fix each other." As much as I wish I could show him right now, just how much, we are both exhausted and physically wiped out. Holding each other tentatively will have to be enough for now. I snuggle my good side back next to him and rest my head on his shoulder.

Davis leans down and kisses the top of my hair and inhales. When he exhales, I swear he says, "All better now." I'm so happy to fall asleep beside him again.

***

It flat out sucks, but I have to leave Davis – temporarily. I have to do two things. Go back to work. I'm fine with that. And talk to Detective Garrett again. I'm less fine with that.

Davis is going to be in the hospital for a few more days at least. Everything is looking good, but the doctors want to run some tests to make sure everything is working okay – in his brain. I didn't notice anything different about him except his damaged smile. Davis tells me his hearing feels off. Anything that's going on we will work through together. It's the newest promise we made to one another.

Returning to KTTA was not as difficult as I thought it might be. As a matter of fact, it was a relief. While I'd only been there a short time, everyone was pleased to see me, especially Henry, the other PA on Happening in the STL.

He greeting me with teasing. "Hey, you don't have to go and get sick or injure yourself to get time off, you know. You could just fill out a time off request."

I reply, "I know. I just don't like to do anything the easy way, obviously."

Gail, my boss and producer, must have heard our rambunctious banter and steps into the doorway of her office and says sternly, "Biz, can you come in for a moment?"

I grimace at Henry. My face turned away from Gail, I reply, "Be right there." I chuck my new purse at Henry. My old one, full of the Brandons' money and my meager savings, is long gone, God knows where with Randall – I silently lament.

I've barely crossed the threshold of her office, when Gail, still standing, looks up from her desk. I hope she's not going to fire me. I called in for a few days after the weekend, but I haven't missed that much time.

"Biz, sit down."

I do.

Gail goes on, "Biz, I am glad you're all right. I was worried about you. How is your fiancé?"

I tell her, "He's going to be okay. He has some residual nerve damage from the pistol whipping..." Wow, those are words I never in my lifetime thought would come from my mouth. "And he needs to be in the hospital a little longer, tests and stuff, but really he looks amazing, all things considered."

"Good, good..." Gail reaches for a remote control on her desk and clicks on the monitor to the left of me. "I want to show you how the incident under the bridge was initially reported." I open my mouth and then close and open it again. I hadn't even thought about checking the news coverage, I was so concerned about Davis. Nobody said anything. I wonder why not? Gail pulls me back from my reverie. "Biz, are you listening?"

I shake off my thoughts and respond, "Yes, I...I'm listening."

Gail cues up the footage. It's the news report from last Friday night's 10 p.m. news.

> *Last night, this man, Neil Ireland, recently released on bail for alleged sexual assault and pornography charges, was found assaulted, under the southernmost Kingshighway overpass. This area contains a skatepark that was recently closed by the police. Mr. Ireland was not the only victim. Two other, unnamed victims, a man and a woman both in their 20s, were injured, one of them seriously. The other has been treated and released from Barnes Hospital. Police are currently looking for Mr. Ireland's brother, Randall Ireland. Randall Ireland was being sought for questioning in his brother's case. Police report, with this assault, he has now become a person of interest.*

Gail pauses the footage, the picture of Randall hanging on the screen.

Gail places the remote back on the desk, comes around and sits in the chair next to me. "I'm sorry, Biz. We had to report something. We've been able to keep your name and Davis' out of it for now, but I don't know how much longer we can keep it contained. The police are helping. For some reason, they don't want it to get out that it was you or Davis there. We buried the story, only asking for tips about Randall. It has since fallen out of the news cycle."

With all sincerity, I say, "Thank you, Gail." I really hadn't thought through what could occur. It wasn't supposed to. I was supposed to pay off Neil and that would be that.

Gail smiles and shakes her head, then reaches over and pats my knee, "You are always so quick to thank me. Biz, here's how you can thank me..."

Gail thinks there is more to the story and, of course, she is right. I tell her everything from the beginning. I agree to give Gail and KTTA exclusive rights to broadcast the true story, if it looks like it's going to surface. Gail thinks the police are working on something and I'm beginning to agree. I received a call from Detective Garrett prior to coming back to work. He wants to speak with me... and Davis.

"What do I do in the meantime?" I ask Gail. All sorts of scenarios come into my head. People asking about the sling and brace. Why I've been out. Gail is a genius. She told everyone I had another low blood sugar attack, after the one here at the station, but it was while I was running, so I fell and injured myself. Nobody here knows Davis is hospitalized. The Brandons have dealt with the media for years and covered it on their end, stating Mr. Brandon was coming to Barnes Hospital for his spinal cord injury. I wondered why there weren't any paparazzi hanging around.

Gail has an immediate answer. "What you do in the meantime is live your life, as if none of this happened. Get Davis out of the hospital and back home. Get married..."

The wedding. I've been evasive in my conversations with my mother since the accident. She doesn't know anything about the incident with Neil and Randall. I didn't want my parents to worry. I caused enough of that *last* summer. The wedding is two weeks away. I wonder if Davis will be well enough by then. Should we postpone?

Tuning back in to Gail, I hear her finish with, "...and get back to work. As much as you can minimize this, make it look like you were nowhere near Neil Ireland or that skatepark, the better. Besides, I really need you back. Henry is losing his mind without you." Gail smiles and winks at me with her last words.

I happily leave Gail's office and go back to my desk, which is loaded with unfinished projects to keep my mind off of the convoluted swirl of a mess I seem to be in. Meeting with her provided some relief, but also brought up a whole raft of new worries. How can we keep this under wraps? What happens when Neil goes to trial? What if Randall returns? What if he doesn't? And my biggest question – What do the police want?

***

Going straight to Davis' hospital room after work, I sense the question that has been bouncing around in my head will soon be answered. Why? Because Detective Garrett and Davis are seated at the small table in Davis' private room – surely a perk of being Lt. Governor Brandon's son. Davis is not smiling. He doesn't appear angry either. There just seems to be this pinched concern between his eyebrows. When he catches sight of me, it disappears and happy surprise replaces it, cocked eyebrow, busted smile and all.

Detective Garrett's back is to me, but he turns after seeing Davis' expression change, immediately stands and greets me, "Hello, Ms. Connelly." Ms. Connelly, sheesh, I can't have him calling me that every time he sees me. I'll be twisting around looking for my mother constantly if he does.

"Biz, please." I say.

"As you wish, Biz, but then I'd like you to call me Donovan or Donnie." He replies. I'm suspicious why the detective has become so solicitous.

I ask, "Really…You want me to call you Donnie?"

"Donnie," he informs me, is what his wife calls him, and he thinks it might be easier than saying Donovan all the time. I have to agree. Davis has been strangely quiet through this whole name game. I peek over and give him a questioning look.

"What's going on?" I inquire.

Davis gave his statement alone yesterday. I was encouraged to go get coffee, so I did. Davis told me he felt like it went well when I returned. I was fine as long as Davis wasn't caught up in any of the potential legal fall-out from the incident. I had a feeling I would be called to the police station to talk with the detective more. I was dreading hearing what the prosecutor's office would come up with, but I didn't expect the police to come find me, especially in Davis' room. What was he doing here? Davis explains Detective Garrett – Donnie's, visit.

"Lizard." I notice Donnie's head swing back to look at Davis, perplexed. I forget how unusual Davis' nickname for me must sound to people that don't know us. Davis pays him no attention and proceeds, "Donnie is here to offer us…well you, really, a deal. I'm a bit concerned about it, but I want you to listen closely."

Donnie spells out the arrangement. I will have no charges placed against me, if I agree to assist the Metro Police with finding Randall Ireland. Specifics of what this means can't be determined at this time and that's the part that Davis doesn't like. The police will also not make our identities known to the public until Neil's hearing or if doing so will help bring Randall Ireland out of hiding. My head is spinning. How did I wind up in a situation like this? My first mistake was falling for a jerk like Neil. Seems my first bad decision has had a waterfall effect into my entire life. I sense the shaky, dizzy sweatiness of panic beginning to sprinkle over me. I silently repeat my mantra, while taking deep breaths. I think Davis is aware of what I'm doing, because he's vamping a conversation with Donnie to cover for my silence.

Finally, I blurt out, "I'll do it !"

Donnie and Davis stop talking. Donnie seems pleased. He stands, shakes my hand and gives me his card, saying, "You've made the right decision, Biz. Here's how to get in touch with me if Randall makes contact. I'll let you know if we need you on my end."

I'm not quite as convinced as the detective is and from the Davis' squinting and tight lips, I'm not sure he is either.

I shake on the deal with Donnie, telling him, "I just want this to be over. For the Ireland brothers to be a thing of the past and for my terrible judgment to stop coming back to haunt me."

Before leaving, Detective Donovan Garrett reassures me, "It will be, Biz. It will be over. I can't tell you when, but these guys are not going to get away with this…" Donnie shoots a look at Davis' bandaged head. "Any of this."

***

This looks nothing like a hospital room. There are round white lanterns of various sizes hanging from the ceiling, lit with dim pinkish lights. The lighting in the rest of the room has been lowered. What? There are waiters in black bow ties and vests passing appetizers and cocktails. A delicious looking cake with champagne colored icing is on Davis' over bed table. He is nowhere to be seen. I spin around to look at the door. Surely, I am in the wrong room, but then I realize there are people creeping out from behind the privacy curtain and…

SURPRISE!!!!!

Blinded by shock, I jump up and shriek, throwing my purse at the closest moving target, which happens to be Charlie. Jules and Smitty, howling with laughter, run over to calm me. I am flapping my hands in excitement and disbelief. Davis and I had agreed to just have a quiet dinner in his room for my birthday. I wasn't expecting all this. It's then I realize… almost everyone I know and love is here. Beside Jules and Smitty, there is everyone from school. Mel, Kris, Charlie, the other Boxwood guys, Simon, Ian and Colin and even PJ. Meredith Brandon wheels out James from his hiding place, along with Kathleen. Then, I see them… my parents.

"MOM, DADDY!!"

"Surprise, Bizzy girl!" my Dad's voice shouts. My parents race forward, steal me away from my friends and sweep me up in a big family embrace. "Happy Birthday!" They say in unison.

"Oh my God, you scared the crap out of me! All of you." The entire room breaks into laughter, "I mean, thank you, all of you…And mom, dad, you're here. You didn't call or give it away or anything."

"Trust me," my dad says, "That was no easy feat as often as your mother calls you about wedding details." My mom elbows my dad.

"Where's Davis?" I ask everyone and no one.

I perceive the other privacy curtain move, shifting my attention from all the party guests, to it.

The voice I love the most says, "Right here."

Davis is standing where the curtain once was. He is dressed in regular clothes. Jeans, a t-shirt, boots. Not the hospital scrubs he's been wearing as pajamas. There is no longer a bandage on the side of his head. From where I stand, I can just see the scar that starts about an inch from the side of his eye and terminates at the front of his ear. His hair has been cut, so the sides are even again. It's shorter than I've ever seen it before, but it makes him no less attractive to me. Davis cocks his head and lets loose his uneven smile that, while broken, still makes his eyes crinkle and my body shiver.

"Surprise, Lizard baby. Happy Birthday." Davis says sweetly. He has a big pink bow stuck on his chest over his heart. He strides toward me. Much as I love this surprise, now I really wish we alone. He looks just… yummy. When he gets close enough I can tell he smells just as good.

"Are you my present?" I ask so everyone can hear.

Davis, never taking his eyes from my face and ignoring everyone else in the room, slides his arm around my waist and pulls me close. Getting very close, he touches his forehead to mine and tells me, also loud enough for everyone to hear, "One of them…" and then he slides his cheek down to mine and with a deep, vibrating voice whispers, "We can talk about unwrapping me later…I have such mind-blowing memories of unwrapping *my* present on my birthday. Mmmm." I flash back to the condo and the lyrics to Cherry Pie ring in my ears, as well as the pictures of him "unwrapping" me in my head . OMG! My parents are in the room! I smack him lightly. He laughs a real deep down laugh. One I haven't heard in a while. Davis has his sense of humor back.

"Wait. Everyone." Davis says loudly and the room quiets. "Thank you for being here to celebrate my Lizard baby's birthday, but I have to give her the real present." What could be better than Davis feeling better and knowing we are getting married soon? I don't need anymore. I am about to open my mouth to tell him, when...

Davis steps back away from me and commands, "Read my t-shirt."

"What?" I make a crazy, question mark face at him. Then I realize he has on one of his trademark "Davis shirts." One I've never seen before. On the front it says:

I 👨 You

I read it aloud, "I mustache you..." Davis turns around and I see the rest of the message.

To Take Me Home

I continue reading, "...to take me..." and then I scream. "Home? I can take you home? Really?" Not thinking about his head or my injuries, I jump into his arms and begin searching his eyes for the answer. I hope this is not a joke. Davis smiling even harder, if that's possible, says nothing and slips a small stack of legal looking papers into one of my hands. I look down and see the word DISCHARGE on the top.

Still in disbelief, I ask again, "You? Can leave? We can go home?"

Davis runs his hands through my hair and then cups my face in his strong, capable hands, "Yes. Tonight. Right after your party."

I am still enfolded in Davis' arms. Everyone in the room is cheering or crying (in the case of my mother and Mrs. Brandon). I hear Charlie say, "I think this could be a really short party." He high fives Davis behind my back.

I push up on my toes to whisper to Davis, in his own words, "Best. Present. Ever."

He whispers back, "Not by a long shot, baby. We aren't alone, yet."

I wonder how fast we can have a drink, cut my cake, eat a small piece and leave without appearing rude. I am SO ready to be with Mavis. I have to get things going, so I announce to the room, "Let's cut the cake!"

Charlie leads the group in singing 'Happy Birthday.' The traditional version, followed by the Beatles' version. I make a wish and blow out the candles, thankful nobody asks me what I wished for. That would be completely embarrassing! For me at least. Davis would love it.

Davis and I spend a little time with everyone at the party, but focus on our parents. It doesn't take anything for him to charm my folks. They don't know the real story of how we were injured. I made up a story about being mugged. My father thanks Davis repeatedly for trying to protect me. It's a little painful lie to them, but Davis and I have agreed to reveal the truth to them *after* the wedding, to keep from upsetting them.

Meredith and James Brandon keep to the side during most of the party, joining in with toasts and applause. After speaking to my mom and dad, I indicate to Davis that we need to go talk to them. I make the first move toward them, taking Davis by the hand.

"Meredith." I greet Mrs. Brandon warmly. I've decided even though she's never asked me, that is what I am going to call her from now on. "I'm really glad you're here for my birthday." I surprise myself and her, I think, by stepping forward and hugging her fully. Over her shoulder, I look right into the Lt. Governors wet-looking eyes and tell him, "you too, James."

Mrs. Brandon speaks, and it's more than I've ever heard her say. And with more emotion. "We are very happy to be here, Biz. Thank you. Thank you, Davis. We...I...James just went along with the condition to appease me...I'm so very sorry. I don't know what I was thinking. Anyone can tell that you two belong together. I just...I can't deal with my family being hurt or sad. And Biz, that now includes you. Welcome to the family!"

I am shocked. Davis looks down at me, shrugs and then quickly pulls Meredith and me down with him to encircle James, in his wheelchair, in my second family hug of the night.

"Thank you," I tell them all, "I'm honored that I'll be a Brandon soon."

James clears his throat. "Okay, enough of this... emotional... stuff," he says, his pauses, ironically full of feeling. "Davis, take your girl home. Right now."

Davis laughs while saying, "Great, now Dad's the controlling one. Yes, sir. I'll be happy to take her home, right away."

I chime in, "I think I'm the one taking YOU home. I have the keys to the Escalade."

Davis doesn't argue, but I can tell he is not super happy about being coddled. He just purses his lips, nods his head and waves me toward the door. I catch him kissing his mom and dad goodnight and I stop and do the same to mine. I reassure my mother I'll call her tomorrow and we'll get together. Davis' bag is next to the door. I pick it up, turn, wave and thank everyone for coming. Davis' nurse appears with a wheelchair and tells him it is hospital policy – he has to be taken out of the building in it.

I hear him grumble something about being treated like a baby, so I lean down after he's in the chair and tell him, "Just let me baby you a little more tonight, okay."

That changes Davis' attitude. He tells the nurse, "Let's get out of here."

***

Home. Alone.

Davis and I both stand, holding hands, just inside the door and take it in. A few days ago, I feared it would never happen again. Us. Together. Here. Now, I feel we'll never be apart again. I squeeze his hand. He rubs his thumb over my knuckles, slowly. I wonder if he has any idea just how much that simple move gets me. I swing around to face him, reaching around to place my hand on his firm ass. Davis, while guarding my sling, pulls me right up against him, mimicking my movement but grabbing my ass with two hands. He dips his head to my neck and kisses me with slow draggy movements that cover lots of real estate. The little hairs all over my body are at attention. My nipples stiffen painfully. I want him to touch me. Take me. There is something swirling and molten overtaking my lower abdomen. A sensation I know well. My hands roam from Davis' backside to his chest. My legs are shaking from his kisses. I duck my head slightly and nudge at his cheek with my nose, eventually finding his lips, and then I crash into him. We've been careful with our kisses and touches while in the hospital, but I can't hold back any longer. I want to devour him. Davis receives my message instantly and our mouths open to each other, licking, biting and sucking powerfully. My core is tensing and relaxing in waves. Just kissing is pushing me toward excitement.

"This is okay, right?" I ask.

"Feels good to me." Davis groans into my mouth.

I laugh, "No, silly, I mean… sex… it's okay, right… with your doctor?"

Davis, still kissing me all over and bringing his hands to my breasts, holding them and skating his thumbs over my now at-attention nipples, chuckles, "Umm… yeah. His exact words were, "It's fine, if you don't get too rowdy."

I pull away, "Rowdy? What exactly does rowdy mean?"

Davis pulls my arms out of my t-shirt and over my head gently. He slowly removes my figure eight brace for my collarbone. And then my black push up bra.

"Rowdy… means nothing that could injure you…" He dips his head again and lightly kisses my collarbone. I am afraid it will hurt, but it doesn't. His kiss just elevates my need and I throw my head back slightly, pushing my breasts into him to take in the sensations running from everywhere he touches me. "Or me."

"So, slow-ly. Nothing too rough. No banging heads on headboards." I tease and lick at his ear.

Davis slides himself around me, so my back is to his front, and pulls my naked upper torso back toward him, caressing one breast in his hand and sliding his other down to unbutton my capris. He slides his hand down the front of them, cupping me over my panties. I know what he's doing. Davis is taking control. He hasn't had it for a while. I can feel Davis' erection digging at my lower back. I spin to face him. I know Davis wants control, but I can't wait any longer. Still kissing, ever more intensely, I wiggle out of my capris and then attack his jeans, ripping at the button and tearing down his fly with one hand. As he pushes them down his thighs and kicks them off, I pull his t-shirt up. Davis stops me when he sees me wince. Raising my arms is still a little painful. He finishes removing the t-shirt. We are practically naked and we haven't made it out of the foyer. I want him now. In my bed. I run my hands over his chest and slide them down his rippled abs until I am almost at his boxers. Suddenly, instead of touching the waistband, I move my hands to his and backing up with a tug, indicate with a tilt of my head that it's time to go to the bedroom.

Davis continues to back me into the bedroom, moving right up against me, pulling me up on my toes, practically carrying me there. Once the back of my legs touch the bed, I sit quickly and tear his boxers down. Davis is deftly relieving me of my bothersome panties. I lick at his abs, running my tongue over the taut, slightly salty skin. Davis reaches around and pulling my hips up, tilts me back on the bed, his mouth quickly on my wanting nipples. Each nip and suckle slick me up. My most sensitive area is convulsing. Davis seems to sense this and moves his thumb to my throbbing clit. I moan with the first flick.

He coos hotly, "Lizard… Baby… I want to do so many, many things to make you say my name, but right at this moment I can't stand not being as close to you as possible, being surrounded by you."

My only thought and word are, "Please." It is permission and pleading all in one. I reach down and stroke his hardness, thumbing the crested tip, while Davis kisses me into a frenzy.

When I let go, within moments, Davis plunges into me and I instantly feel whole again. I feel myself rippling and contracting around him and he hasn't even moved. And then we move, slide, rock and yes, pound into each other. Davis is so close I can tell. He is looking down at me very intently. My build-up is becoming unbearable, overwhelming. When his mouth begins to open into an "O" and I perceive the beginning of his spasm, my own shuddering, vibrating orgasm overtakes me and I can no longer keep eye contact. My chin points toward the ceiling, I scream out his name and slap his back repeatedly. Davis just pushes harder into me, his own head thrown back. A violent, almost painful, howl resonates from him.

We pant and grasp one another, rapidly and then slower as the crescendo resolves.

"Not too rowdy?" I ask, once I catch my breath and my scattered brain cells regroup.

Looking down at me while propped up with a forearm at either side of my head, Davis replies panting, "No. Well, I *am* a little dizzy, but…No." He pulls out of me and flops onto his back. Then he slides his arm across my stomach and hooks his hand on my hip bone.

"Good, because I'd like to explore all those ways you are going to make me scream 'Davis' once you get un-dizzy." I say.

"Um…yeah. I'm gonna need a minute. Or 800… to recover."

For a little while, I almost forgot we were both recently injured. I turn just my head to peruse his super handsome profile. "You take all the time you need, Mavis. Baby, I'm not going anywhere.'"

Davis' voice is slurred and slow, "Good, so good, baby…" His eyelids flutter. I think he's falling asleep. It has been a long, eventful day. "Hap.. Bir..Day, bab-." And he's out.

Chapter 10-OCTOBER

"Dad? Daddy? Are you crying?" I say, turning my face toward my dad, Calvin Connelly. He's a big tough guy, not girly or overly sentimental in the least. And he's struggling not to cry. We're outside the door to the Alumni House about to go in. Jules is standing in front of us ready to walk down the aisle as my maid, scratch that, MATRON of Honor. Except nobody knows that.

Davis and I selected the Alumni House at Weldon, also known as The Lum, for the wedding ceremony and reception, because neither of us is overly religious and quite frankly, it was the place we could get on short notice. Evidently, when booking a venue for a wedding any amount of time shorter than a year is "short notice."

My dad sniffles and tells me with faux gruffness, "No, I'm not crying. I think..." Sniffle. "I have something in my eye. Pollen from those damn flowers or something." I hand him the embroidered hankie I got from Meredith Brandon with the letter B on in it. It's my "something old." Her mother-in-law gave it to her on her wedding day. It's really quite beautiful. Hand tatted lace around the edge. My "something new" is my dress and my "custom PJ" veil. My dress is classic. European lace over silk. Very Grace Kelly. The "something borrowed" is a diamond bracelet, or rather my mother's diamond bracelet. And my "something blue" – a pair of dangly, diamond encircled, blue sapphire earrings, my birthstone. A wedding present from my husband-to-be.

My dad shakes his head, sniffles (in a manly way, of course) and hands the hankie back to me, "That's too pretty for me. And beside, these are tears… of happiness."

If it's possible to smile and frown at the same time, I do. "Oh, Dad. I love you. I'm glad they're happy tears, because I am happier than I have ever been in my whole life. Davis makes me very happy."

My dad pats my hand and kisses me on the forehead and then the nose, "I know he does, Bizzy Girl. I can tell how much he loves and adores you whenever he looks at you. As a matter of fact, I never understood the expression 'only have eyes for you,' until I saw you two together at your birthday party. It was like the rest of us disappeared off the face of the earth."

I lean into his kisses and say, "I feel exactly the same way, Daddy. I love and adore Davis, too."

I hear the second movement of Winter from Vivaldi's Four Seasons ending behind the doors. My parents insisted on a string quartet and trumpets for the wedding and I am so glad they did. The piece is gorgeous and reminds me of being with Davis when we first got together – in winter and the snow. It's almost time. Jules turns and waves her hand frantically that we need to move to go in. She bounces up and down a bit. It strikes me that she didn't have this kind of wedding, so it's a big deal for her, too. Our entrance music starts, The Prince of Denmark's March, a majestic trumpet voluntary. Jules goes first and I can hear the ooohs and aaahs. Her dress really is beautiful and … well, hot, just like she wanted. When Dad and I step into the doorway, every head turns toward us and the entire congregation all stands. I squeeze my dad's arm at the elbow. He pulls it toward his body. "Here we go," he mouths, looking down at me.

"Slowly. I want to see everyone." I whisper to my dad. He nods in agreement.

I purposely look back and forth to both sides on my way down the aisle. I want to see each and every person's face – smiling back at me. When we get closer to the end of the aisle, to where I know Davis is waiting for me, I allow myself to look straight ahead. Davis is looking down at his hands or his shoes or the floor, his head tilted to the side a bit. What's wrong? The second the thought crosses my mind, he looks up and I know why he was looking down. He was prolonging the anticipation of seeing me, or at least that's what I think he was doing. His face lights up and his green eyes twinkle with his smile.

When I finally get to Davis, I'm shaking, with excitement, sheer joy and a little fear... but not panic. Nothing like panic. My dad kisses my cheek and after shaking Davis' hand, places my hand in Davis'.

"Hi," I squeak, in the tiniest of voices, trying to control the swirl of emotions in my chest.

"Hi, Lizard." The catch in Davis' voice surprises me. "Oh my God, you are so beautiful. You are always beautiful, but today... you are just *stunning*. Thank you for marrying me."

Holding his hand tighter, I begin to tear up myself and say, "You're welcome, but we aren't married yet." And then I wink at him.

"Well, then, let's do this!" he says, in classic Davis style.

We step up to Justice of the Peace, together.

***

"You may kiss the bride," the Justice directs.

Davis takes my face in his hands, tilts his forehead and nose down to touch mine. He lightly kisses my upper lip and says, "I love you, Elizabeth Brandon. My Lizard Breath." Again, in a serious moment, he lightens my mood. I roll my eyes and shake my head slightly and with a laugh say, "Oh, Mavis." I tip my lips up and facilitate a real kiss. Our first married kiss. Being Davis' wife is going to be fun. Davis deepens the kiss and I begin to perceive some whoops and catcalls from the attendees. We pull away from each other a bit. I see that Davis looks like I feel, a little embarrassed at being so intimate in front of a crowd. We both bow our heads for a moment; look back up at each other, smile, and then Purcell's Trumpet Tune rings out. Davis and I, clutching at each other, march down the aisle of the Lum and out into the tented yard. We did it. Married. Man and Wife.

***

We've eaten dinner, cut the cake and had the toasts. It's time for the first dance. We've hired Boxwood to play. They've been working hard learning wedding dance songs that are out of their wheelhouse. 'Love Shack' and 'Unforgettable' aren't exactly Boxwood's style.

Charlie moves to the mic and says in rock star fashion, "Hello, Biz and Davis' Wedding! We are Boxwood! Is everyone ready to celebrate!?" His delivery, like he's in a huge arena, makes me, Jules and the rest of our crowd, howl. The more mature partygoers look at each other questioningly. Charlie shifts gears and with his next words, sounds like a typical wedding emcee. "It's time for Biz and Davis' first dance as a married couple. Ladies and Gentlemen, Mr. and Mrs. Davis Brandon."

Davis and I move to the floor as the first notes of "I Knew I Loved You Before I Met You," begin. That's when the idea hits me full force. Jules and Charlie deserve a first dance, don't they? I turn to Davis and say, "Give me a sec." Stepping up to Charlie's mic, I signal the band to stop. Maybe I've had too much champagne, but I think this is a brilliant idea.

"Umm…Hi…Everyone," I say, too loudly into the mic. Charlie moves me back from it a bit. Then I begin to chatter, "We'll get to the first dance in a moment. But there's something you should all know. Davis and I aren't the only couple about to have a first dance tonight…" I look up to see Jules frantically waving at me like an umpire repeatedly calling someone 'safe' and mouthing 'no.' I wink at her. Charlie touches my elbow. "… they've been keeping it a secret, but I can't stand it any longer…" They are going to kill me, but here goes! I look at Jules and then Charlie one more time. I wave a hand at each of them, in Vanna White fashion and say, "Ladies and Gentleman, Mr. and Mrs. Charlie Boxwood."

A huge gasp emits from the party. I see Jules' parents, Mr. and Mrs. Hagen's jaws drop. They look to Jules, who is now running over to them. I turn to look at Charlie, who, with a resigned smirk, only says, "Wow. That was an interesting choice, Biz. But, I guess it had to happen sometime." Charlie kisses me on the cheek, takes his guitar off and hands it to Simon, the bass player. "Time to talk to the in-laws."

Now Davis has reached my side, "Lizard, you know, that chatter of yours is going to get you in so much trouble."

I am feeling so sassy today, I wonder if that's what feeling secure and happy does. I put my arms around Davis' waist, kiss him from his jaw up to his ear and husk out, "Promise?"

Everything happened so fast, I just notice that the entire room is now in applause. And the very surprised Mr. and Mrs. Hagen? Are hugging their new son-in-law and daughter. Thank you very much! It was a good idea after all.

Boxwood starts up the first dance music again. Davis and I walk over to Charlie, Jules and her parents. "I'm sorry about the surprise." I say sheepishly to the Hagens.

"It *was* a surprise, Biz…but I think we knew it was coming," Mr. Hagen tells me kindly. Mrs. Hagen, a bit weepy, nods agreement and continues to hold both Charlie and Jules' hand. Then Mr. Hagen adds, "I think it's time for that first dance."

As we walk out to take our places on the dance floor, two married couples, Jules hisses at me, "You are so DEAD!" Then her tone changes and she giggles, "Thank you. I didn't know how I would tell them. You letting the cat out of the bag at your wedding turned out to be surprisingly perfect." Thank God. That could have really gone sideways. I scold myself that I really need to think things through before I talk. Then I shrug it off and tell myself, "Oh, well… how many people get to have their first dance with the love of their life, their best friend and their fake brother?"

The first dance song changes and Simon invites everyone to join us on the dance floor. I rarely take my eyes off Davis, but when I do, each time I am greeted by a smile and the eyes of another person that wishes me well and loves me. My parents, his parents, my friends. It's perfect.

Davis pulls me up close, our entwined hands clutched between us, his other hand holding me tightly at my waist, my hand on his shoulder. "You are something else, Lizard. Biz. I love you. So. Fucking. Much. This is going to be an adventure."

I gaze up into his eyes, his glittering, guy-linered, green eyes that are, now, mine to look into forever. "I love you, too. An adventure, huh?..." and then turning Davis' phrase back on him, I say, "HAVE FUN."

Bonus Chapters:
In the Hospital-Davis

I have the sensation of peeking through mini-blinds. The last few times it happened, I peeked and then, as if someone twisted the rod, the blinds slowed, tilted to a close and all the world disappeared behind it. This time, the "blinds" open a bit. I look out and can make out blurry figures hovering above me. Angels? Then the "blinds" flip open wide – the light and sound are almost too much. Overwhelmed, I squint and turn my head away. The "blinds" shut. It's then it becomes obvious.

There are no mini-blinds.

I've been out of it.

Unconscious, but for how long? A few minutes? Hours? Days? Peeking out of the "blinds" was how I percieved my brain waking up. The "blinds" slowly closing was my brain retreating. I, very purposefully, open my eyes and the figures come into focus. My mom and...someone else I don't know, are there. A man. He's really close. "Yes." He says, "I think he's coming around."

I hear my mom start crying. I feel her holding my hand carefully and then her other hand is on my cheek. "Davis, Oh my God, You're awake. You're going to be okay."

This is so confusing. I say, 'Mom?' to ask what's going on, but my voice sounds small and harsh, like a child that's been screaming. It's actually a little painful to talk. I swallow repeatedly trying to find any moisture in my mouth. That's painful, too. I try again, "Mom?" There, that sounds a little more like me.

My mother pats and strokes my face, saying, "Yes, darling. I'm here. Dad's here." She moves to the side. I can see my father in his wheelchair, smiling up at me, tentatively.

"Hi, Dad." It really is uncomfortable to speak.

My dad asks, "Davis? Son? How do you feel?"

I do a brief internal inventory and answer roughly, "I have a wicked headache and I'd kill for some water."

"Is it okay?" My mother asks the man I don't know, who I now realize from his white coat is a doctor. I'm in a hospital. How did I get here? I was just...

The doctor gives my mother permission. "Yes, just a small sip for now, though. I need to examine him before he drinks or eats much more, Mrs. Brandon.

My mother immediately leaves my line of sight and I hear water being poured, as she replies, "Yes, yes, of course."

Pictures fly in my mind. Skatepark. Bridge. Biz. As soon as her face appears, I bark out her name and sit up quickly in the bed. Hot pain shoots through the side of my head. I reach and leaning forward slightly, grasp my skull with both hands. The side of my head feels prickly. My hair? It's gone, but only on one side. Biz? Where is she? The last image I have of her is finally getting her away from that asshole, Randall and...the gun went off! I sit up even faster and stare at my parents. My head is killing me, but my physical pain is eclipsed by the pain of the thought that Biz is injured, or worse.

"Biz?" I ask both my parents. "Where is she? Is she okay? The gun...The gun went off."

My mother's back is to me. She's blocking my view of my dad. I see her shoulders go up and then down quickly, in what appears to be a sigh.

Something must be wrong. I'm so very confused when my mother turns back to me with the water in her hand, because her affect is breezy, upbeat. A contrast to what her body language was just telling me. She says in a high, strange voice, "Biz? Oh, she's fine, son. She injured her shoulder and broke a small bone. She was treated and released a few days ago." She hands me the water and I take a sip. The soreness in my throat calms a bit when the coolness of the liquid reaches it.

A few days ago. Weird. I vaguely remember hearing Biz's voice and thinking we were sitting, holding hands on the sofa in our condo, during one of the episodes when the "blinds" opened. I'm about to push the thought aside, when I realize – she was here! I want to see her. "Where is she? Is she here?" I ask. I want to see her now.

My mother, with no emotion, answers, "No, dear, she's not."

The doctor excuses himself by saying, "I'll give you a few moments, Davis. I'll be back soon." Then directing his attention to my mother, he continues, "I'll be back and then I must do an exam, Mrs. Brandon."

My mother waves the doctor off with a too cheerful, almost forced smile, and nod of agreement. Something is definitely wrong.

I keep up my questioning. "Is she in the cafeteria?" I don't understand. This makes no sense. Why isn't my fiancée here with me in the hospital? Where the hell is Biz?

"No." My mother sounds annoyed.

I hear myself getting louder and more agitated as I roar out, "Where is she, Mom? WHERE IS BIZ?"

My father is next to me in his wheelchair trying to placate me and saying, "Now, now, Davis, you can't get yourself worked up."

"I didn't want to have to do this yet, but..." My mother looks up at the ceiling, then reaches in her pocket, pulls out Biz's engagement ring and hands it to me. "She told me to give this to you. She said to tell you the engagement is off."

What? I shake my aching head and look down at the ring. A vision of putting it on Biz's finger comes into my mind and the words she said when

I did. She said she was never taking it off and if she did, something was wrong and I needed to find her.

Something *is* wrong! I knew it.

I lift my head slowly and pin my mother in my sight, "Mom, you need to call her and get her here."

"No, Davis. *She* broke up with you. She said she would talk to you when you were better. I really don't know why you want to see her after all she put you through." My mother appears to be purposely keeping us apart. What is wrong?

I am furious, "You don't know why I want to see her? I'm going to marry her. I LOVE HER. Get me my cell phone! Now!"

My mother has turned white, her lips are pressed together tightly. "No!" she snaps.

I have never spoken to my mother disrespectfully before, but I can't help myself. My fiancée is missing, I don't know where she is and frankly, I feel like I'm going to fucking hurl, my head hurts so much. "What have you done?" I ask, slowly articulating each word in a dark tone.

My mother speaks, quickly and firmly, "She made an agreement not to see you. We loaned her money to give to that maniac and the condition was, if you got hurt by it, she'd leave you. You got hurt. I made her live up to the condition. She's gone, Davis."

"NOOOOOOO!" I scream. I think my head is going to explode all over this room. I look at my father, pleading with my eyes.

"Meredith." He says, in his authoritative politician voice, that I haven't heard in a long, long time, "It's time to STOP this. I played along because, well, I didn't want Davis to get hurt, either. And frankly, I have been going along and trying to keep you from being unhappy since Cole died, but this…" My dad waves his hand in the direction of my mother and me and then Biz's ring. "This is just wrong." My dad reaches up to touch my arm and says, "Davis, Biz is fine. She was hurt, but she's going to be okay. I don't know where she is."

"Then I'll call her." I growl, as I glare at my mother.

She cowers and whimpers a bit, pleading, "Davis, honey…"

Frowning, my dad says, "Your mother made Biz agree not to see or talk to you until we called her."

I sit up even straighter. I don't care about the pain. I am two seconds from ripping the IV out of my arm and launching myself out of this bed to find her. "Mom, you need to go. Now! You need to go and find her. Find Biz and bring her back. I need to talk to her. If you want things to be right between us, you will bring her back to me."

The monitors I'm hooked up to begin to beep loudly. Not only does my head feel like it is going to explode, my heart, evidently, is joining along.

My mother looks at the monitor and then me.

"GO!" I bellow. My doctor, along with a nurse and a couple of other people come rushing in.

"Meredith, go now. Go to their condo. If she's not there, call her friend Jules…" my dad is shouting out directions as my mother grabs her purse and moves to exit.

My mother has a very concerned look on her face when she turns to look back at me. I could care less if she's concerned right now. The medical staff are trying to calm me and are checking my vital signs. They are saying things like "high BP" and "tacky." I could care less about them, too. I'm focused on getting Biz back, nothing else. I yell out, "Charlie! She'll be with Charlie!" The experience I am having physically must be like what Biz describes when she tells me about how a panic attack feels. It makes me empathize with her even more.

I turn to my Dad. "Get my cell phone. Find Charlie Boxwood's number and text him."

My dad asks, "What do I say?"

I have the perfect message. One I am sure Biz will figure out, if she's with Charlie. "Tell him, 'The mouse devoured the hawk.'"

Christmas...One year later

"Hey, whose genius idea was this? Because, I would like to thank them." I say jokingly to Davis. It's Christmas morning, almost two years after we fell in love, 14 months since we got married. We are cuddled in bed, warm, snug and safe. The world outside our condo is covered in snow, sending memories from our first days "together," flooding back to me. It's really quiet outside and in the condo.

Davis laughs, his amazing, warm laugh. I peek up at him from my position cuddled against his bare chest. "You mean about spending Christmas morning alone, with no parents? Uh, that...would be ... this guy." He points to himself with an elaborate and self-congratulatory flourish.

"Bragger." I tease. "I mean, Thank you, Genius Boy."

"Boy, I see no boy here. Man...Genius Man." Davis pounds his chest with his fist in a mock macho move.

"Okay, Genius Man," I concede. "What do you want to do first, eat breakfast or open presents?"

With one swooping movement, Davis pulls the duvet and blankets up over us and slides me down and under him. Now his head is nestled on my chest. Right between my breasts, actually. He takes a huge inhalation and then growls out, "Open presents. I'm already holding mine. It smells so good. I've unwrapped it before, but it's always a surprise." Ever since my gift of a birthday lap dance, anything involving gifts for Davis is about unwrapping me.

Attempting to be serious, which is difficult when Davis is being naughty, I tell him, "Well, I have another present for you, but I'd have to get out of bed to get it."

"Forget it, then. I'll open it later," he says. Davis has moved on to his task at hand – undressing me.

I want to talk to him before I give him his real present. I'm a little apprehensive. I don't know if he'll like it, so I start to chatter, "Davis, you know you're really hard to shop for, right? I don't really know if you'll like it. My present." Here goes. "I was wondering – did Charlie tell you what he got Jules? Because he told me. And…and…well, I thought it might be something you would like." Davis stops kissing my shoulders. His hand releases the grasp it has on my breast and his thumb, in mid-stroke, jumps off my nipple.

Davis speaks slowly from under the duvet. His words and breath on my skin and it feels so arousing. "Yeah. I know what Charlie got Jules." Davis flips the duvet up, slides off me a bit and props himself up on an elbow to look at me questioningly. "He got her pregnant."

I nod my head affirmatively.

"And you were wondering… if I would like…. something… like…? Davis, cool, collected Davis is visibly flustered. "Lizard, are *you pregnant*?

I shake my head negatively. Then I, quickly, roll away from Davis to the edge of the bed, reach under, come back up and roll over to him with a square gift wrapped box in my hand. I didn't look to see if he looked happy or disappointed when I said I wasn't pregnant. I hand the box to him and say, "Open it."

Davis takes the box and starts unwrapping, "Man, I am so confused right now."

"It will all make sense in a minute." I assure him.

Ever the 'Ripper' when it comes to gifts, Davis has the present open in nanoseconds. He lifts the lid and pulls out a plastic oval that looks like a compact. It's not a compact. It's a birth control pill pack. He tilts his head and asks, "What's this?" Then opening up the pill pack, a flash of understanding sweeps across his face. He looks up at me and speaks slowly, each sentence both a statement and a question. "You're not pregnant…but your pills are all gone…" He holds up the pill pack to show me what I already know – it's empty. "So…you'd like to try???"

"Yes." I reply confidently. Then I backpedal a bit, because I'm uncertain of how Davis will respond. I'm hoping he likes the idea. I fire off rapidly, "Only if you would. I mean we've never really talked about this, and I don't even know if you like kids, I like kids, I mean I think I like kids, I don't know, I didn't have any brothers and sisters, only, like, cousins, you know, but I think you'd be a great dad and I love you so much and…" God, I wish he would say something, because this is starting to make me feel panicky.

"LIZARD!" Davis raises his voice, but it's not angry, it's just to get my attention. "My God, that was the sexiest little chatter…Baby, I would love to try. I think getting you pregnant is the best gift you could have thought of." He encircles me and pulls me over, so I'm halfway on top of him. I can feel his excitement against my lower abdomen, so I have confirmation that my gift was a good one. "Plus it might take a while…so it's sort of an ongoing gift."

And then I see it.

Davis' smile.

It's huge and symmetrical. It's not broken anymore.

I tell him. "Baby, you're smiling…"

He replies, nonchalantly, "Hell Yeah, I'm smiling, the whole trying to get pregnant thing? It's a really *good* present."

"No, no, no … I mean… yes, it *is* a good present. I'm glad you like it. What I'm saying is …you are *really* smiling, like both sides. Your smile isn't broken anymore," I enthusiastically explain.

Davis says, "Really?" jumps out of bed and runs to the bathroom to look in the mirror. "It's really back. That's so weird." Davis is gone for a few moments, but then he comes out to the doorway of the bathroom, leans against the door jamb and crosses his bare feet at the ankles.

He's wearing nothing but his new and improved smile and his red Christmas boxers with candy canes on them. Davis flashes the biggest, sexiest, naughtiest grin I have ever seen and says, "Baby, this has been a great morning and I think the only thing that would make it better is if I could continue with my presents." The way he says the word 'presents' makes me want to rip his boxers off.

I flip back the covers and say, "Come on."

Davis runs and dives under the covers, returning to his previous spot, nuzzled against my breasts. I thread my fingers through his hair and kiss the top of his head, clutching him to me. Davis wastes no time unwrapping me, just like a real gift, ripping and tearing at my tank top and boyshorts. His hands moving over my body, gliding, grasping, kneading, and his tongue working my nipples to painful points, has me overwhelmed.

While he is claiming me, I manage to wiggle him out of his boxers, which I feel him kick off his feet to the end of the bed. I tilt my pelvis up to feel his hardness and slide my neediness against it. Over and over. I want him, so badly. Davis rears back a bit, removing himself from between my legs. With little warning, his tongue goes to work, stroking and licking my clit with precision. Circling and circling, causing my hips to circle in kind. The intense tingling vibration builds and descends, builds and descends with each circle and pause. So close, so very close and then it is upon me, like a thousand pounding, vibrating, massaging electrified pulses. I shudder, as Davis continues and I roll into another orgasm. Davis' tongue retreats and I pant out ragged breaths.

My head relaxes from its extended position and my eyes open to see Davis' face crawling up toward me. I reach blindly and pull him closer – into me. A look of peace passes over his face. We are both not moving, but I can feel myself spasming lightly around his erection. Davis thrusts gently a few times and then builds to a delicious rhythm. I let go again and when I do, Davis, his big beautiful smile lighting up his face, moans out my name and lets go too.

"Best. Present. Ever." I pant.

Davis laughs, a large hearty laugh, "I agree. Gift unwrapping and babymaking. Good job, Lizard baby."

"Well, yes, that too." I concede. "But I meant your smile. During it. Your Smile. BEST. PRESENT. EVER." And it is. Davis. Unbroken.

Acknowledgments:

Thank you:

Sharon Korn, my editor, for your enthusiasm for my writing. I can't trust this stuff with just anyone, ya know.

Sarah Hansen at Okay Creations. For the great idea for the covers of FIX IT FOR US and BETTER THAN ME. One word-Beautiful!

Dana Colcleasure for my author photograph. Best picture I've ever taken. Ever.

Jennifer Stevens-"The Blurb Whisperer"-Thank you, babe.

My Beta readers: Cathy A. (my "Alpha" Beta), Brian, Barb, Nikki, Kevin and Julie.

Jennifer Plaat: You really are my biggest fan. I appreciate that you haven't tied me to a bed and broken my ankles.

And again to the authors and bloggers/FB pagerunners I know well and some I don't know at all:

Jamie McGuire (again)-for your FAQs for Writers page on your website. It's sort of my publishing bible.

Isabelle Peterson/Izzy P. at Fictional Boyfriends Facebook page. Words are not enough. Thanks for believing in me (and Davis) and being a whiz at teasers and takeovers.

Liv Morris-MWAH!

Book Boyfriend Reviews-Sandie, Dee and Shannon.

Zoe at The Book Lover's Blog

Your Next Book Boyfriend

Maria's Book Blog

Give Me Books

Elle's Book Blog

Love Between The Sheets/Between The Sheets Promotions-Thanks for doing my cover reveal and release day promos.

Book Haven

Flirty and Dirty Book Blog

Reading Is Fashionable

And any of the other bloggers I've missed in these acknowledgements. I'm sorry if I didn't name you personally. Message me and yell at me. You'll be in the next one.

All the talented, wickedly funny, naughty authors in my Author Support Group. You've been a blessing. Thanks for including me.

To BC, The Connor Boys, and my monkey puppy – Sshhh! Mommy's writing (or taking over a Facebook page.) Love you tons.

About the Author

Emme Burton is the author of the new adult novels Better Than Me, and Fix It For Us. She lives in St. Louis, Missouri with her amazing husband, two teenage sons, and her "fur boy." Emme has never, ever been lost in a mall either as a child or an adult. Her mother, and now her family, have always known where to find her. At the bookstore.

Like Emme's Facebook Page: Author Emme Burton

And *Follow* her on Twitter: @EmmeBurton

Look for the third and final book in the Better Than Series, Still Into You, coming soon.